CURIOUS TUSKS

Anne Hendren

ISBN-13: 978-0692999110
ISBN-10: 0692999116

Curious Tusks

This is a work of fiction. Any similarity with real persons or events is purely coincidental. Persons, events, and locations are either the product of the author's imagination, or used fictitiously.

Cover images by R.A.R. de Bruijn Holding BV and Lukiyanova Natalia frenta. Cover design by Stephen Penner.

Acknowledgements

This book is dedicated to my father and grandfather, Robert Hendren, Jr. and Sr., respectively. "Senior," my grandfather, went on safari in the fifties, the "curious tusks" from his elephant were once balustrades on a curving stair case. The other "trophies" are scattered throughout our family. My father, "Junior," died before the book was finished but approved early drafts.

I hope our African guide, Omega will smile at his role in this novel and thank him and all our overseas tour guides who helped us understand the distinctive beauty of African culture.

I am forever grateful to my wise and generous editor, Leona Grieve, my publicist, Mark Sanchez, and the patient crew at Ring of Fire publishing.

My loving thanks to family and friends who supported this endeavor, especially John, Michael and Deborah and my mother, Merlyn.

PROLOGUE

Seattle Washington

George Atkinson's last visit to Seattle was for his son-in-law's funeral. The journalist, having spent most of his adult life in Africa, had learned the trivial reality of death. It was a goalpost that must be reached following a fine or poorly-executed run. The distance and quality were irrelevant; the result was the same. Silence. He arrived after the ceremony, refusing to attend western funerals. His only child, the sky blue pantsuit clad Madeleine, obvious in the crowd of strangers dressed in flowing fashions of all colors of the rainbow, had requested a cremation and short Christian service for her husband conducted at their Seattle home located on the Sound. His ashes were on the fireplace in a blue porcelain urn.

Born in Africa, married to a Northwest tribal historian, Madeleine was a criminal lawyer who enjoyed simple ceremonies performed within the family, but chose to receive their friends at a catered event because her husband enjoyed parties. Her only request was that no one wear black. Atkinson, who had spent hours trying to find an old Hawaiian shirt, had settled on a blue Ralph Lauren polo. White-haired and khaki-clad, he worked his way towards his daughter, a half-smile covering his deeply-tanned face. When he caught Madeleine's eye, her face brightened. The teenager Neissa at her side, who Madeleine had named after her childhood friend, Neissa from Arusha, Tanzania, looked down at the floorboards. From what George could see she was the same pale-haired child her mother had been at that age. Even though Madeleine was in her ninth month of pregnancy it was hard to miss the resemblance. Slender as he remembered his daughter, and fair, Neissa's eyes never moved from her feet. What color were her eyes? he wondered. Would the next child favor Madeleine or its father?

Neissa appeared unconnected—distinct—from her mother and her surroundings. Madeleine had told George she craved her daughter's friendship, but Neissa remained a loner. She told him she hoped the unborn child would be of a friendlier mien. In front of the pair at last, George Atkinson commented on Madeleine's health, kissed her lightly on the cheek and spoke to Neissa, who said nothing. The teenager shrugged and went upstairs to her room.

Madeleine frowned, looking at her father. "Neissa is at the anti-social age. Likes to be alone with her books."

Madeleine, whose criminal law practice had grown increasingly large and depressing, could doubtless use help with Neissa, George thought, with a faint twinge of self-recrimination. "Like her grandfather," he said, "With luck your next child will provide the companionship that neither I nor your daughter do."

Atkinson paused and thoughtfully regarded Madeleine. "I leave early tomorrow morning and will take my leave of you now that we've spoken."

He paused, slipped an arm around her waist and hugged her briefly. "Look after yourself. With regards to the unborn child, send it to me on its eighth birthday. I will tell it the story of your birthplace and my home."

Madeleine, eyes shielded by darkened eyeglasses, frowned. After several minutes of consideration, she said, "Fine, for several weeks in the summer. His Seattle education will not be compromised. Africa's a tantalizing place. I don't want to lose him."

"Not to worry," George said. "I do return every fourteen years when expats have to renew the blue passport so that I can enter places only Americans can go freely." He blushed. I just don't always phone you. Please do remember that Ian recalled me because my nationality permits him to assign me stories that only American reporters can access. Further, I was willing to work on airplanes and at airport hotels to meet excruciating deadlines."

Madeleine's brow wrinkled, remembering that the Atkinson family moved to Seattle against her father's wishes. When African nations sparked with war and freedom, numerous European Union nations' reporters installed themselves in-country. Ian had employed them at a low rate to write straight journalistic stories because they were on salary from other organizations. The investigative work that George specialized in writing was not as earth-shattering as the daily news on the continent and George Atkinson's long journalistic pieces became too expensive for the *Herald Tribune* and other journals to subsidize. George's African income declined.

Twenty years after Madeleine's birth, Atkinson and his wife had returned to Seattle where Madeleine was already in boarding school and where both had been born. They lived in an apartment near her school, George got a job at the *Post Intelligencer* writing overseas pieces from on-site. He used his vast collection of prize-winning photographs to weave stories about a mysterious continent, without requiring a foreign residence. Ian sent him the occasional U.S.-based story and he connected with "African themed" journals through U.S. reporters from the *Tribune*. They lived well and Madeleine continued at boarding school.

After his wife had died and his daughter married, George was relieved when Ian recalled him, saying the country was full of feature-length stories—not only straight journalism--and that he had a budget that could fund George's investigative skills and fearlessness. George and his wife had never sold the Arusha, Tanzania home and furnishings. He had only to return to a professional livelihood he had found more rewarding than straight journalistic work and whose results not only informed readers of social problems, but also were a catalyst to activate change.

Madeleine turned away from her father and began speaking to another guest. Watching her work the crowd, Atkinson thought what a different life his child had from his own simple life in Arusha. When he was not at home writing he was investigating or traveling to the location of stories Ian or other journal editors assigned to him. As he left his phone dinged—one such story awaited him.

After he'd gone, Neissa had returned to Madeleine's side and though neither moved, they watched the taxi take him away. Neissa slipped her hand into her mother's, squeezed it lightly and ran upstairs again.

The next day the fourteen-year-old Neissa was gone. Madeleine never saw her again.

Several weeks later, a baby boy was born. Madeleine was alone. When the nurse asked for a name she said, "Stuart Atkinson Lehrman." Not wanting to burden him with African friends' names or family names, she gave him an original name—one he could own.

Years later she would tell her son that Stuart was derived from steward. A steward was a person who kept order in a household.

CHAPTER ONE

Cambridge, Massachusetts

At 6:33 PM, Stuart Lehrman, principal of Erewhon Investments, picked up a lobster- stuffed mushroom at an Erewhon-sponsored celebration of its first major client, a physician-researcher pair who had just hit a milestone with their product. Stuart and his partner organized the cocktail party both to announce their clients' imminent product release and Erewhon's own successful collection of backers for the project. They had invited the researchers, representatives of the backing banks, corporations and all potential clients, entrepreneurs and business men in the Boston area to this event. The investment firm was still in the red and could barely afford the catering offered at this Harvard Medical School venue, which the clients and their own Harvard connections provided Erewhon. Picking up a cheesy-looking cracker, Stuart grinned, noticing that half the crowd was MIT and Harvard graduate students who were filling themselves with hors d'oeuvres for dinner. He remembered when his dinner was a fatty variety of foods over at the Business School. Let them eat, he thought. Tomorrow they'll start a company and need Erewhon's backing.

His phone buzzed as his business partner Rosalind Abel

approached him, her arm linked through one of the researcher's arms. The other researcher trailed behind them, her jet black hair curled softly on her bare shoulders.

He glanced down at the number on his silenced cell phone, grimaced, counted to three, then looked up, his face composed. "Doctors both and dearest Roz," he said, "thank you for this sweet success."

"And thank you, Raj and Ellen, for procuring Brigham and Woman's convention room," Roz added. "It gives us a chance to celebrate your first clinical milestone with the drug in a hospital and to celebrate Erewhon's first venture into the world of Big Pharma in an appropriate Harvard location."

Noticing the curious curl to Stuart's smile, she said, "What's up?"

"I need to step into the hall for a moment. Enjoy the mushrooms. They're wonderful. The cheesy crackers." He wiggled his hand from side to side, "Metza-metz."

All three watched the long-legged, rail thin Stuart as he strode to the glass hallway. He found a potted palm, leaned against it and dialed home. Stuart loved this hallway. He walked over when his apartment was too cramped to think because he liked the mirrored walls and the view. The one-way glass overlooked Boston Latin boarding school in Boston reminding him why he'd bothered to leave the west coast for the east in the first place. At the age of twelve, he had announced he wanted to go to boarding school far away from home. He was bored in public school in Seattle and anxious to escape from his mother's busy life and ever-present vigilance. Weeks later, his mother told him that his sister had run away because she was frustrated at home and not allowed to go away to school and she was unwilling to lose another child so he could go anywhere in the United States he chose.

He had researched Boston Latin learning, that it was one of the best schools in the country and was a gateway to the Ivy League, his Harvard-educated grandfather's best hope for him. Good teachers, good studies, difficult work. Companions that would challenge him. Entrenched in the environment, he had gone on to Harvard College in Cambridge, then crossed to Boston for his master's in Business Administration at the Harvard "B-school" where he'd specialized in startup venture capital funding, a roller coaster ride, always surprising and never dull. It was an ongoing game for the winning bid and the best collection of backers.

He dialed Seattle, grinning as a few more students entered the banquet room. He listened to the voice on the phone and shook his head.

"Why me?"

All of his mother's responses were specific enough that Stuart was finally convinced.

Rejoining Roz and another person she was interrogating about Parkinson's disease, Stuart murmured, "I need to go to Africa. My grandfather has sent for me. He has published several controversial articles in a series and there are more to be released. He fears for his life. While there are freedom of speech protections, my grandfather's editor was willing to place work that hadn't passed the censor."

Pulling Roz toward a table covered with hors d'oeuvres, Stuart whispered, "Are we now solvent?"

"We're not as broke as we were. We won't have to sell the building."

"Sweet," Stuart said, "did you notice we were mentioned in the Local section because of this deal?"

Roz nodded. 'We put together the winning package for the Virtual Safari gamers *and* you rescue your famous grandfather we'll make Front Page *Boston Globe* news for sure."

"Virtual Safari?"

"The safari proposal's on your desk. Its principal designer, Dalik Oweke, is from Nairobi. He's here somewhere. I'll text him to find us."

Within minutes a tall black man approached them. "Dalik, meet my business partner Stuart Atkinson. Stuart is going to Africa soon. Maybe you can show him around?"

The young black man smiled broadly. "Of course. Your needs?"

"My grandfather George Atkinson's needs, actually," Stuart responded. "He's a journalist and seems partial to writing controversial stories. I guess he has several of them coming out concerning illegal ivory trade, poaching and elephant conservation and other illicit trade. Seems these are not favored topics by the ivory traders involved. He's asked me to come rescue him. Once I have reviewed your proposal and I have accomplished my grandfather's tasks, perhaps we can meet regarding funds for your games. I have yet to study your proposal, but will have plenty of time on the flight."

"You're related to George Atkinson, eh? A favorite among Africans. Idealist with Africa's best interest as the focus in his controversial articles. My brother Omega works for him. I'll email him you're coming."

Roz grimaced. "Stuart and his family hail from the west coast where idealists are not passé and environmental issues, like disappearing breeds, become sacred, almost obsessive. We've lost a few jobs because his ideals crash into his business sense."

"Roz," Stuart interrupted, "the garment factory was filthy. Men and women were out of work because of illness contracted by working   there.   It   would   have   been   beyond   even   your entrepreneurial genius to get funding for such an operation."

"Yeah, yeah," Roz sighed and continued, "anyway if you have reason to be near Arusha, Dalik, contact Stuart and advise him how to find any African networks we should enter if your group decides to go with Erewhon."

"Glad you're coming over," Dalik said. "We need activists your age with money to invest in Africa. To be an activist and investor could be a total advantage for this project, intended to feed money back into our country. Though I live in Nairobi, teaching at both MIT and the University of Kenya, I'm often in Arusha," He turned to Stuart. "Do some homework before I catch up with you. We have several serious bidders in and out of country. Most of the hotel concierges know everything. Just ask. Omega and our family have a good finger on the pulse of African traders."

Stuart raised his glass to Roz and Dalik. "Thanks for the continental insight and sources. Here's to activism, rescue, virtual safaris and George Atkinson's flair for rooting out trouble. He raised his glass again looking directly at Dalik and said, "I look forward to catching up with you in Africa in Arusha or Nairobi and to meeting your brother Omega."

Stuart glanced at Roz. "And I look forward to persuading you that Erewhon is the best firm for capitalizing your videogame."

His phone buzzed again. He read the text and told Roz to go chat up their competitor Ralph Fieno, knowing she hated him. They'd invited him out of *schadenfreude* because his original backers switched to Erewhon and ultimately cinched the pharmaceutical contract for *Erewhon*.

"I need to pack," Stuart said, passing Roz on his way out. "The judge says now. I'll text you my flight."

The fog had thickened to light snow when a slightly tipsy Stuart reached for the low iron gate into his apartment complex.

Memories crystallized into frozen images in the mist—his mother's face, the Arusha house, a trailhead opening onto a green savannah, a laughing elephant on a bottle of beer. Hand at rest on the freezing latch, he studied them as they vanished. George Atkinson, his infallible grandfather, was in trouble. His happy-go-lucky grandfather, a photojournalist and poet who had listened to his Latin recitations one Christmas and told him to continue with mathematics and invited him to Africa when he was eight years old. George taught him to play soccer, to not worry about his bookishness. Came to Boston on his 21st birthday to celebrate with him.

Why Stuart's help? He was inquisitive and good at finding money, but would-be assassins? He couldn't even fire a gun. "He trusts no one anymore, except his newspaper editor Ian, and Ian is ten years older than he is," his mother had said. "Grandpa has written so many controversial stories," she had continued, "Anyone on the entire continent of Africa or Southeast Asia could be threatening him now. This group of five stories could be his undoing."

CHAPTER TWO

Arusha, Tanzania

Stuart watched the air flaps go down as the airplane skidded into Kilimanjaro Airport, missing the divots, the wandering gazelles and entering a heat he had not experienced anywhere else but here. Glad he had left his winter coat back in his snow-covered apartment in Boston, he had forgotten that equatorial February could be so hot. His nostrils filled with the unforgettable mix of dust and heat of the African air, heavy, almost impermeable, everywhere except in the open plains.

A tall black man clad in khakis and a safari shirt waved a sign furiously back and forth over his head, "Atkinson-Lehrman." When Stuart reached the unsmiling man, the African scrutinized Stuart from head to foot and murmured, "Stuart Lehrman?"

Stuart nodded and the man went on in a low whisper, "Your grandfather was murdered yesterday. You are too late."

Having slept very little on the eleven hour flight, the words jolted his jet lag into the beginnings of a headache. Dead, he thought, absently studying the neat folds on the man's elbow length shirt, which had transformed long sleeves into a t-shirt covering only his elbows. Stuart stepped away from the tall African, and rubbed his arms vigorously. He was shaking visibly, the hard information bringing on a nausea he not felt since he was first refused by a high school beauty for a prom date. Powerless, now as then, his guts wrenched. But death, not another dance, an end. He reached for the Maasai, his grandfather's driver's words echoing in his mind. "Your grandfather was murdered yesterday. You are too late."

George Atkinson was dead, his essence as meaningless as the words on the desperate note George Atkinson had sent his mother with an ebony elephant. "Send Stuart, Madeleine. At once." Would he ever know why he was chosen?

He must have been flying over Europe when his grandfather died. His favorite relative, out of reach, now out of sight forever, the seventy-year old journalist who had shaken government halls with his honest, gut-wrenching stories and his unforgettable photos.

"Any leads? An investigation? Who?" Stuart asked.

The native shrugged. "No one knows. No one investigates journalists. Everyone is waiting for you."

Stuart eyes glistened. "Take me to the Arusha Hotel. I need rest."

"That's an hour and 30,000 shillings."

Stuart shrugged, staring at the crazy traffic darting in and out of five lanes. The tiny cab was a three-wheeled vehicle, a motorcycle with a roof that could go anywhere in Arusha's curious streets, ranging from bike lanes to sidewalks to footpaths and narrow roads. The cab was on the sidewalk dodging pedestrians. A town built for animals and Africans walking single file was crowded with bulky over-sized American built Chryslers and Cadillacs. The small hand-crafted taxi fit perfectly in the narrow paths. The silence, wind and noise were broken by the soft buzz of his phone. It was his mother.

"Hello Mom, Stuart said, "I was too late. He's dead, mom. I was too late." *Harsh, he thought, but how else to say it?* He heard her gasp, her pleading voice ringing in his ears. "Me, mom? I'm sorry. I'm not an investigator. Yeah, I know he sent for me."

When her lawyerly sensibility took hold, Stuart's face relaxed. She cleared her throat and issued her instructions, one by one.

"The memorial in Nairobi? Why not here? His friends are here." Stuart sighed. "Ian, oh yeah him. I forgot the editor is older than dirt." Convenient, he thought, he could meet with Dalik, the head of the gaming group.

He reviewed his mother's words: "Go at once to Grandpa's house on Atkinson lane. I don't know what you will find there but it's worth a visit. Pay a visit to Farouk before you leave Arusha. He is an Indian who owns a camera store. Farouk may have been the last man to see your grandfather alive. And no, I don't know his family name. Everyone knows him by "Farouk." Third is Nairobi for the memorial in five days. Last stop is Dar Es Salaam where the former partner lives. I think you can book a flight from Dar to the States."

Stuart closed his eyes, savoring the air blowing across his face as the motorcycle taxi sped toward the hotel. Fatigue enveloped him. *His grandfather was dead. Murdered.* Tears crept slowly out of the corners of his half-open eyes. He felt a hollow pit in his stomach, the horrible airplane food moving up his esophagus. He coughed and swallowed, sending it back to his roiling stomach.

In the distance he saw the Hotel Arusha four-cornered clock tower, halfway between Cairo and Capetown, a remnant of the colonial past. The hotel had been one of his grandfather's favorite haunts.

He brushed away the tears and a smile spread over his face.

How he loved his childhood visit here—remembering everything from food to traffic to the infernal barbeque stench of Arusha and funny maize for sale up and down the street. How everything took four hours or four days longer here than in the U.S. because what was, after all, the hurry? And who, he thought smiling, was more fun than his grandfather? An adjacent cab driver grinned back at him, a white stripe across a black face glistening with February heat. In Africa again, he thought, frowning, but alone, his grandfather dead. "Stop," he said to the driver, "I'll take myself the rest of the way. I need some air."

The cab stopped abruptly. "Yes sir, I understand." He reached for Stuart's arm. "Name's Omega, here's my card if you need transport during your stay. Your grandfather was a favorite around here. Dalik's my brother. Said he saw you three days ago."

"Omega, that was the name. Was searching for it when I landed." He handed Omega 30,000 shillings and then some, thinking what a lot of money to pay for bad news and from the brother of a colleague. He settled his backpack on his shoulders. "Where's the body?"

"Downtown, police station morgue. I take you tomorrow. After you rest up," he sang in his British-accented English.

Stuart nodded, thinking he would call this guy. The red berets and khaki outfits of police guards in this country terrified him. They looked like the officers in some dictator's regime at the crossroads where they directed traffic. How much more terrible they must be at the police station, he thought. His eyes stung with heat and fatigue. Tomorrow. His Swahili was non-existent to terrible. Yes, he'd call Omega. "I'll phone tomorrow. Asante."

"Karibu," the driver screamed, moving toward his next fare.

Stuart walked into the lobby, checked into a room on the original side of the century old hotel and grabbed a copy of the

International Herald Tribune. A front page headline "Man dead outside Arusha home," Stuart scanned the article picking out the relevant material: "Antique Maasai spear pierced stomach. Police have no leads. No additional information. Family members have been notified." Inside the newspaper was one of his grandfather's "controversial stories," complete with byline. As though people in this tiny village didn't know who was dead, Stuart thought. Characteristic African—almost true to the Western rules, but a slip or slide, enough to retain their own open world.

He sat down in a chair on the terrace overlooking the pool and the extensive hotel gardens. His grandfather had loved this place, its gardens, unusual plants and cool evening breeze. The perfumed essence of the African night that George told him every Lanvin, Chanel and Armani had failed to capture. Only an obscure parfumerie in the Emirates got it right. George sent a bottle to Madeleine every Christmas. She wore no other fragrance. His mother. What must she be thinking? Untimely loss of mother, husband. Runaway daughter. Now father murdered in a land he loved.

When the waiter approached he ordered a sweet Tuskers lager, not because he liked it but because it was his grandfather's favorite and because they had a stash of it in Seattle for Atkinson's rare visits home. He smiled at the elephant. His mind blurred from fatigue, Stuart remembered that his grandfather had carried a Tuskers all the way to Boston from Tanzania so they could celebrate his 21st birthday. They'd gone to a local bar, George bought him a draft India Pale Ale (IPA) and winked at him, "Your first, eh? So congratulations on legality." When he brought out the Tuskers the barman shook his head, but laughed when he saw the elephant, "Anything you can't buy here you can bring in."

He pictured his grandfather on the bench at the Harvard

Square T stop, waiting for Stuart or someone to find him. George Atkinson was remarkable in his sixties. A thin, mustachioed five foot four inches, Stuart towered over him but the old man would pull himself to full height, challenging the younger man to hit him in the stomach. He did so once and remembered the pain in his hand as it bounced off the old man's rock hard belly. Grandpa's leathery face was eternally tan, colored from photo shoots in Africa, Israel, Southeast Asia—everywhere away from the rain of his childhood. Stuart sipped the lager, grinned at the elephant and started reading his grandfather's first so-called "controversial" story, "Knots on a Silk Road," published today, which noted two sequels, "Blood and Ivory" and "Elephants in the Wild," would be published soon. These were the stories, Stuart realized, that would finally bring him down.

...When you travel to Tanzania you are entranced by its endless skies, its bright colors and warm dirt underfoot. Untroubled parks—the Serengeti and Amboseli--sit silent in unutterable beauty, covered with acacia trees, rolling hills. Gazelles of the Thomsen and Grant variety, the former with slender white and brown stripes, the latter entirely sepia in color, chase each other gracefully through the clipped savannah grass as the herds migrate from field to field to dine. An occasional red buck is visible in the herd. The zebras are everywhere, because they remember the way. They know where the good grass is. The herd and other animals follow slowly behind them, even the foolish bearded animals, the wildebeest, move with them. The whole group is stalked by female lions, who study herd movement to decide which beast to kill for their lazy mates, who preen themselves on a hillside above the moving herd. An occasional elephant wanders by, males travel alone after fifty-five, tired of fighting the young bulls for control of their herd. The old tuskers, skin impervious to thorns, scratch their heads on acacia trees whose thorns can be deadly to humans

and other animals. The air is clean and clear, fouled only by the stench emanating from the hippo pools. I avoid those, sticking to the main road through the grassy clean savannah.

Circulation had sent me to a non-governmental agency (NGO), noting there was problematic news of exploited children. I pulled into the Red Cross center where a young English-speaking woman waited to talk to journalists. Her brother had sent her to the Red Cross surreptitiously, after abducting her from her pimp by buying her for a night. Child trafficking was just coming to international attention. Particularly in Africa, after the banning of ivory, no one watched the abuse or disappearance of women and children in Africa. Instead, activists counted the depressing reduction of elephants—income from the taboo breaking Chinese. Government officials paid the poachers to fill their warehouses so they could sell the ivory to the Asians, not to watch trafficking in women and children.

The UN indicates that nearly two-thirds of humans trafficked from Africa are women; children account for 1 in 5 of the victims sold to outside sources. I contacted a woman who recently adopted an African child. The child's parents were unknown. I asked her if she investigated the source that procured the children. She declined to comment and simply said, "We had been to many sources, many countries. None had children. We visited one child in Haiti we were promised. Then she was lost to the tsunami. I was losing patience and getting older. We wanted our child to have the best of our lives." While the elephants shrunk in number, African women, like brood mares continued to bear children to sell them abroad so their families could eat.

Stuart paused, wondering how people could have to make choices like this—feed my children or sell them. Slums were something he passed through, did not study. Did poor American fathers have to make choices like this? Would his mother know? Surely his grandfather had, but he chose to write of poverty and disease here, in Africa. Not in Seattle. He glanced through the rest of the article reading,

Before coming out to meet with the escaped woman, I had spent days in the library investigating Africa's children. I learned that in Northern Tanzania, the United Nations revealed that the number of Tanzanian children and women trafficked was not known. There were no laws against prostitution or trafficking. Judges I interviewed in Africa shrugged when I asked them about child prostitutes, indicating it was a métier, a way to earn money in a depressed economy. More than 800,000 persons are trafficked internationally, the UN estimates, whether to be prostitutes or stolen and sold to rogue intermediaries that get the children to couples willing to pay, no questions asked. While it is illegal in some African countries it is overlooked in many. The Red Cross camp had taken custody of the young woman I had been sent to interview. Beautiful, she had been sold as a teenager for a high price because she had not been battered at home. Handsome even in her torn chemise, this woman bore only a few marks where she had been hurt by clients.

She said she was in constant contact with her parents; she was a parent herself to several children whose whereabouts she did not know. She bore neither parent ill will, understanding why she had been sold, but hoped that by speaking this trafficking would stop. If the rogue sources were uncovered—several are known, but not revealed—perhaps people would go to families directly and ask them to adopt their children. Now they were being treated like dogs. The young woman begged for the world's respect for her people.

Stuart, like his grandfather in death, had dropped the paper.

Asleep, his chin on his chest, the waiter shook him gently asking him if he needed anything.

"My room, please."

The young man held out his arm and Stuart took the paper, leaving the unfinished beer on the table.

When Stuart woke the next day he noticed the rooms had not been refurbished for a number of years. Slightly unnerved by the absence of a shower curtain, he showered anyway and was clean and dry when his mother's phone call came through. "Yes, Mom, I'm going to get him. I'll have him cremated."

"I've made all the arrangements he requested," Madeleine said.

"Requested? So he knew he would die here?" Stuart said, his mouth gaping at the thought of a man so devoted to anyplace that he would fly there to die. He understood the bit about working at what you were best at in the place that had made you famous...but always knowing you were going to die? Stuart shuddered, amazed at how little he knew of George.

"Stuart, it was a just in case....and no he didn't fly there to die. No terminal illnesses, that one. Just a need to be at work he loved best among people who loved him for it."

"I get it. So where is the memorial and what do I do?"

"Nairobi? Sarova Stanley? One week, great. I've got to get his body, visit Farouk and check out the house, before I can travel to Nairobi. As planned, I'll do the Britzes last so I can fly out of Dar es Salaam."

He nodded and spoke into the phone, "Yes, mom, I'll be spending almost ten days in Africa to find out what I can. Did you read Grandpa's last story.....Shiiiit. Yeah, I know most of them are this revelatory. He was an investigative journalist, one who describes to readers unknown realities in their countries that they might not know or might not want revealed. His proof, based on personal interviews is not rock solid, but I guess the *Tribune* approved it. At least he offered both sides by not blaming the parents, rather explaining their predicament."

"And there are more stories next week. Least he's dead so it can't get worse."

Hearing his mother's silence, he added, "Let me go investigate his death. I'll ring again in a few days."

Wiping the sweat from his forehead, Stuart looked gratefully at the African breakfast buffet, then pulled out Omega's card. About an hour later, well-fed and alert, he stood in front of the hotel, waiting for the driver. When he stepped into the half taxi, Omega greeted him with a cheerful smile, a white stripe wide enough to reveal the spaces between his imperfect teeth. "Hello," Omega said. "Are you ready? All is good like brown sugar? Green like garden?"

Stuart's grim face brightened at Omega's light mood, marveling at the curious pair of similes that would greet him almost every morning for the rest of his stay. He frowned and said, "Of course. So let's go to the police station."

CHAPTER THREE

The Arusha police station, a white two-storied mansion, looked like a Mediterranean villa. The police walking back and forth in front of the door resembled palatial guards. Stuart's butterflies returned. No longer the friendly Africa of animals and natives, but the Africa of privilege and privacy. He sighed at his inner turmoil, remembering his grandfather had said that these evil looking men had provided him with some of his best human interest leads. In some cases their unwillingness to act on human behalf gave him fodder for a great story. His grandfather would go into the prisons, interview the inmates, find their families, research their crimes and develop stories that had appeared in most of the Western European major newspapers. *The New York Times* ran only his most sensational ones; doubtless they had the one he'd just published in the *Tribune*.

Stuart turned to Omega. "I have no patience with policemen. Will you be my guide and voice?" Noting the man's hesitation, he said, "I'll pay you 10,000 shillings for every hour you spend with me." Stuart pondered the five dollars an hour fee wondering if the invaluable Maasai was not worth more. He'd think about it and maybe give him ten dollars per hour or switch to a daily rate.

The African's bright eyes sparkled. "Yes sir, your guide,

your manservant, whatever. At your service. I not pick up other customer until I put you on plane." He smiled. "Besides, smart younger brother Dalik said I must do what you say and I not want to go against family wishes."

"Right now," Stuart said, "be my voice. Tell them we're looking for George Atkinson's body. Here's my passport. Atkinson is my middle name."

Omega walked to the sternest looking man and had him laughing within minutes. He took out Stuart's passport and muttered something in the song that was Swahili. Listening to the warbling men, Stuart was tempted to pick up his Swahili tape again but he grimaced, remembering how he failed speaking book-learned French in Paris, where even the waiters said he ruined their beautiful language. So, no, "Asante, Karibu and Jambo" (thank you, welcome/hello, hello/how are you)—that was enough Swahili for Stuart. He'd leave the talking to the natives.

Omega returned to his side. "You need to confirm the identity of Mr. Atkinson."

"Why?"

"Because strangers identified the body. The police would like a blood relative's confirmation."

"Do they want a blood sample also?" Stuart muttered.

Omega crossed a finger over his lips and mouthed, "Just do what they ask."

Stuart shuddered. "The body...or do they have photos?"

Omega turned to the officer, asked some more questions and turned to Stuart. "Body, I guess. Police provide photos of crime scene but you must identify face."

"Out here in the waiting room, sir, you can review the police photos behind those screens. These are not available to the public and are in our police file only. I will print some for you to review.

They must not leave this office unless the superintendent approves. Please wait in the carel and I will bring them to you." The officer pointed to a student-like carel on the side of the waiting room and Stuart and Omega sat there to wait.

Stuart blanched, shuffled through the crime scene photos, asked for copies and then looked up at the officer and Omega. "So let's go confirm the body is George." He followed them to the cold room, thinking how his grandfather's story "Fresh Kill" had described each detail of removing the skin from a trophy animal, the meticulous cutting up of the meat for a feast following the kill and began slow, even meditative breathing. Rangers gave hunters a card, allowing only one of each trophy. The game hunter would lose his license if he facilitated overkill. *Why was it no one intervened when his one-of-a-kind grandfather was gutted by a poorly thrown spear on the front porch of his own home?*

They arrived at a bank of metal drawers. Without commentary, the officer pulled open the drawer marked "Atkinson."

Unmarred, his grandfather's face looked settled in peaceful sleep, but drained of fluid his healthy cheeks had receded into the bone. Where his moustache had been a few hairs remained, only the high forehead and the set of his eyes and nose distinguished the sleeping man as his grandfather. Having seen the man only in the fullness of life, he observed how truly hollow he seemed in death. Picturing him kicking soccer balls to him and his friends, lecturing his mother from a seafood restaurant, Stuart screwed up his face, eyes glistening, emotions invisible. Atkinsons are brave and inquisitive, his mother and grandfather taught him. He moved the blanket to below his grandfather's gut, revealing a jagged puncture wound that entered his grandfather's stomach and opened onto the bones of his spine. Remembering that all good investigators took photos of everything, Stuart snapped two phone photos of the wound and the entire corpse, then covered his grandfather's corpse to his chin.

Stuart noticed a curious half circle shaped like an apostrophe behind each ear and snapped a photo of them also, uncertain if it had been part of his grandfather before his death. Might be a scratch from walking through the trees, might be a barbershop cut. Or, the marks might be important.

He turned to the officer and said, almost inaudibly, "That's George Atkinson." He idly wondered what he'd do with all these photos. Certainly not mail them to his mother. Closer to her in a curious way than anyone else, he could feel her pain. As George had been single parent to Madeleine through much of her life, George had been Stuart's only father figure. Madeleine's devotion to her father and the father of her children made her indifference to the rest of the world seem cold, hard, embittered. The burden of her love and his own love of the dead man oppressed him as he thought about the horrible gash in George's gut. What kind of person would want this gentle man dead?

"Thank you, you are done here." The policeman was speaking to Omega. Stuart had engaged the other policeman in English. "Do I have forms to sign to release Atkinson's body for cremation? Have you finished the copies of the crime scene?"

The policeman nodded. "I'll need forms filled out before his body leaves the premises. The copies I'll have ready when you leave."

"The cremation will cost 70,000 shillings."

Appalled at the outrageous sum of money to incinerate a slim gutted human, Stuart stared silently at the wall. Omega was at his side and overheard.

Omega shook his head. "Lower, perhaps. Maybe 50,000

shillings?"

"Fine," the policeman said.

"When will his ashes be back?" Stuart asked.

"He'll be ready next week. But I need the forms."

"My man Omega will help me out."

The forms were all in English with only a few "yes-no" boxes to check, so Stuart said, "I'll fill them out at once. Before I start, officer, do you have the murder weapon?"

"It's an open investigation and the weapon is locked up."

"Sir, few, if any people are looking into my grandfather's death. The newspaper has no money. Even your own people have stopped investigating the crime. I'm trying to find out what happened to my grandfather since no one else has the money or time. Wouldn't it be appropriate to show me the weapon?"

"Oh course," the policeman muttered, "follow me."

Stuart motioned to Omega who was chattering with the non-English speaking guy. "Omega and I will follow you."

They entered an ice cold room where the policeman put on lavender plastic gloves, and moved toward a tall broom closet. He reached into the closet and pulled out a plastic encased rod. The spear had a long wooden handle and a wide golden tip, empty of blood, that resembled a metallic peacock feather.

He laid the spear on the table. "Your grandfather was impaled on this."

"I hope you saved the blood." Stuart wondered if this was important, but what if it wasn't the murder weapon, or if his grandfather's blood wasn't on it? And was his grandfather killed by this or merely stabbed by it?

"What we could find is in the laboratory. The blade had been wiped clean, the officer said.

"Did you confirm the blood was his?" Stuart asked.

The officer shrugged. "I'll have to check the files."

"Kindly put a copy of the investigation report with the photos."

"I will ask my superior."

"My mother is a criminal judge and could have them subpoenaed and your facility charged with obstructing justice." Stuart smiled inwardly knowing as he spoke that what he proposed was impossible, that is mother had no jurisdiction here.

"Sure, I'll tell this to my superior. But," he winked, "I make you copy."

Stuart turned to Omega who responded, "Maasai spear, yes; but ancient, dysfunctional."

Stuart was silent. He had seen the spear at his grandfather's. It was, George had told him, an antique. *No wonder it ripped him to shreds. Hadn't been used to kill anything for decades. Must have been a huge person that pitched that heavy relic. Or maybe the spear was not pitched. Perhaps it was dragged through George after he was dead.* Stuart snapped a few photos and since they were bloodless he sent them to Madeleine for confirmation it had been in his grandfather's house. Again he was uncertain why it might matter, but "James Bond" types took photos of everything. And, if he were honest, the flat photos that would print out of his phone would help him deal with the drained and gutted form that had been his grandfather—the form now in an ice-cold drawer with only a name and a date.

"Thank you, officer," Omega said as he picked up the copies of the crime scene and ran to catch the nearly sprinting Stuart out the door. Stuart sat in the cab, his head in his hands and eyes closed.

Omega started the engine. Stuart looked up. "That sword was my grandfather's. Whoever murdered him knew him. I knew it wasn't random but I had hoped it wasn't someone who had been in the house."

"Let's get you back. Here are the photos and report." Omega smiled, "Loved your threat of justice obstruction, impossible but scary!"

Stuart nodded. "Thanks. I'll see you when I come back from my grandfather's. I've hired a car to go out to his place. I'll be safe there."

"Stuart, he was murdered there," Omega said quickly, his cracked voice betraying his fear.

"Not to worry. That's why I want to go alone. I'll phone if I need you."

"No Omega? No Omega come?" the African asked, with real concern.

"I need to be private detective for my grandfather's death and need to head out to his house in the hills...."

"Thank you. Wife is pregnant. Baby is due soon. Need Omega now."

Stuart laughed, then sighed, remembering. "Dalik told me." He thought of his grandfather's sensational story about children. "Omega, don't you sell that child. I'll pay you enough to keep it in Africa."

The black man laughed. "I read your grandfather's story. Omega's child will stay with Omega and wife, become good guide, good taxi driver. We want to commemorate his birth by our friendship with your grandfather. He will be namesake. He born girl, her name will be Georgina. No sell. You pay me big money when we go through Africa to find murderer. We not sell our memory child. Here's your hotel."

Stuart stepped out of the cab, cleansed his nostrils with the welcome scent of burning maize from the Africans on the street. Thankful to be among the living not the dead, Stuart said, "I'll call you when I need you. Maybe your baby will have arrived."

He nodded at the doorman and walked into the hotel and back to the terrace bar. When the waiter found him he ordered a Tusker's lager and an IPA. He lined them up, imagining his grandfather as he had seen him when he was first in Arusha. Balding and white haired in his early-forties when Stuart was eight, Atkinson chattered like a newsman, a story writing itself in his head and out loud.

Stuart opened the tiny photo album his grandfather had made of that trip and which he stashed in his briefcase on the way out of his Boston apartment. He stared at a photo of a grass-covered savannah and a trail marked with two large stones. He flipped over a photo, re-living his first view of the volcanoes along the Eastern Great Rift near Arusha. He closed his eyes remembering Africa through eight-year-old eyes. The volcano, Ol Doinyo Lengai, was, a native told him, the Mountain of God. *He had not forgotten that volcanoes housed god. When he returned to Seattle he had asked his parents if Mt. Rainier had a god. He remembered no one had a satisfactory answer for an eight-year-old.* And then he grew up and didn't think about it again until now, as he looked at the volcano, wondering if god was a fire-breathing volcano-like monster. On that same trip, an old native had told him his grandfather was cursed. When he and his grandfather hiked up a trail to meet a Maasai source, his grandfather had shrugged and told him that not all curses were bad.

Stuart opened his eyes, gazed at the beautiful Arusha gardens and the smiling Tuskers elephant. He took a long swig of his IPA and wondered, *was Atkinson cursed? Was that why he was dead?* Glad to have recovered an early clue he walked back to his room and fell asleep wondering about curses, Maasai spears and tiny tattooed curves.

CHAPTER FOUR

He was outside when the man dropped the car off at seven the next morning. The rental car man snapped his photo.

"Sir," Stuart asked, "I showed my passport and driver's license. Why a photo?"

"Pro forma technique," the man grumbled. "Boss requires photos of all car rental clients." He reached in his pocket and handed Stuart a mango and walked away from the hotel. "Wild mango—boss's gift."

The hotel doorman grabbed the fruit before Stuart could take a bite. "Wild mango is poisonous. Never eat."

Stuart frowned. Was he also a target? "How can you tell the difference between a wild and a farm-raised mango?"

"Most tourists can't. My advice," the doorman said, "don't eat mangos that you don't find on a hotel or restaurant table." He saluted. "Safe travels, sir."

Stuart climbed into the deteriorating car. Everything took a beating in his country—heat, mangos, people. He texted his mother for directions and wove down Arusha's main road, figuring he'd remember before she replied.

The head of his household at birth—sometimes gratefully

but cautiously because his life was so alone, Stuart frowned at the irony of his present mission. He was to go into this unusual land where landscape was deceptive and where one of his three remaining relatives had been murdered, where people were unwilling to answer questions about his grandfather and Stuart, the bookish one, was charged with finding George Atkinson's assassin. True, his sister had "disowned" herself. His mother had no time. And again the irony slid away as he remembered his own analytic abilities. Nonetheless, he thought, who or in what places besides the leads his mother intimated would George's assassin be or hide? That he was murdered was not a surprise, somehow. It was the "by whom" that mystified. George wrote stories that brought down regimes. Stories that saved Africa's children and some of its endangered species. People loved him or hated him. Perhaps George's house hid a few revelatory clues. He was, after all, killed at home, not working on a story in some remote African town.

He knew Africans were kind and believed that lightning would not strike twice in the same place. Additionally, the main tribe in this part of Africa was Maasai. Omega and Dalik were Maasai; his grandfather's sources here were Maasai. The old man he met years ago who gave George the antique spear owned by some long dead relative, a friend, was Maasai. This tribe killed animals, not people, and loved tourists. The man who dropped off the car— what tribe was he? *Stuart*, he thought, *it's not about tribalism, the Maasai, the Erak, the Northern tribes. George was on to information that would harm someone. Why his own spear? And given its weight, was it really the murder weapon? Was there another weapon floating around the house?*

He arrived on the outskirts of Arusha near the path to his grandfather's home and realized he hadn't eaten since morning. The outskirts of Arusha, away from the bustling tourist town, had few promising buildings, mostly small buildings with food and signs in Swahili. At last he found, "Maisie's Conference Hotel," a high rise building attached to a small commercial market that advertised "English food and language available here." He pulled into the parking lot, went into the hotel and asked, "English?"

A tall African pointed to a plump shopkeeper standing at the ready behind her cash register, who said, "Need groceries? We have them."

Stuart handed the woman a list. Wordlessly, she scuttled about the store like a rodent, collecting everything on his list, including several bottles of local wine. He ordered provisions for a day or two. He thought that two days at his grandfather's house to search it for whatever remained of evidence about his grandfather's murder, a day to visit Farouk and a few days in Nairobi to hold his grandfather's memorial ceremony, to chase the gamers and together with about two days to figure out what the Dar Es Salaam man-- George's former news partner-- might know, would be sufficient to discover what someone of his limited investigative skills could learn about his grandfather's murder. He had booked a flight departing from Dar Es-Salaam to Boston in ten days He would hire Omega for his Nairobi detour and the trip to Dar. That left him only three solo days to dodge mangos, Maasai spears and any other means of death. He handed a collection of American and Tanzanian coins to the shopkeeper for the food, ready to get on with his investigation.

The woman shook her head, her tight white curls moving slightly. "No charge. Nice to have a stranger here. Most days are empty. And boring. Everyone shop in town." She paused, studying his face and build, "You an Atkinson?"

He gasped, startled by the question. "What do you know about George Atkinson, ma'am?" he said slowly.

The short African pounded her chest and said, "I'm Maisie,

not ma'am. I tell you nothing. I die if I talk."

Stuart's eyes widened. "Die, why? And, yes, I'm an Atkinson, George Atkinson's grandson, the judge's son."

"You here as boy?"

Stuart nodded.

"Sometime when you stay a long time in Maisie's store, I tell you a few things about your grandfather." She grinned. "Not enough to get me murdered."

"Now's a good time," Stuart replied, pointing to an outlet. "I'm here for only a few days. Tell me about Atkinson while I charge my phone at your outlet. Mom said the house may have no water, electricity or heat. I might need one of your rooms if the place is uninhabitable."

Maisie shuddered. "House is haunted, you know. I wouldn't stay there if I was you. Maisie's rooms nice, clean." She winked. "Indoor plumbing. Foreign entrepreneurs live here when not making African deals. Threatening world out there."

Foreign entrepreneurs? Here for Dalik's game and other African opportunities? He took a minute to email this information jewel to Roz then looked up at Maisie. "You were going to tell me about my grandfather. And who's threatening you?"

"No say who is threat—they kill me." Maisie paused and continued, "Alphonse Britz identify body. I confirm." She paused, studying Stuart's face. "Alphonse not know grandfather. I worked for George years ago."

"What?" Stuart asked.

"I spent hours on phone trying to get an investigator here from the American consulate. No one come. I fill out form, Britz read. Sign, then leave."

"That's all?" Stuart asked, thinking at least the police were diligent enough to ask for kin confirmation before giving reporters

Atkinson's name.

"Police came, interrogated two men. They dead now."

"What exactly do the police know? Who is Alphonse Britz? I thought his name was Anton?"

"I not hear all conversation. Alphonse? He Anton's son. Lives in Nairobi sometimes. Was in Arusha on business. Anton not travel."

Stuart was intrigued. A riddle to solve and perhaps, other contracts to be won. *Did his grandfather know about them* thinking, *Caution, man, you could get killed. People getting killed for talking to cops about Atkinson. Curious. Why Britz and Maisie for I.D. purposes? Why not Ian? Or someone here in Arusha?*

Turning to Maisie he said, "Who comes here? It's mid-morning and the place is empty."

"Tourists. During safari season, not now."

"How can you keep it open? Where do Africans shop?"

"Africans shop in local markets. They wouldn't eat this stuff. Food, like you buy not sold in Arusha, too expensive, too foreign, and guaranteed disease free."

Stuart examined his pile of Western packaged goods—soup, saltines, all imports and wine—only the wine was from Tanzania. "So how do you pay the bills? How do you buy this stuff?"

Maisie blushed. "I don't."

"Who does?"

"Foreign man send check by courier each month. Checks cover utilities and monthly supplies. I have P.O. Box number, no name. I don't know them." She shook her head emphatically. "And no, I not talking."

Forehead wrinkled, Stuart asked, "Why won't anyone investigate Atkinson's death?"

"Police treat reporters like soldiers; bag, tag and notify

family. Classified material," Maisie said and continued, "only people who try to talk to investigator are now dead with notes on chests saying 'Other talkers will die.'"

"What else do you know?" Stuart asked.

Maisie shook her head, motioned Stuart outside. "Nothing. Forget it, young man. Go home. After you empty your grandfather's house of hate. Now that his family has come, the house will release him to God." She glanced quickly from side to side, then added, "Clean the home and go back to United States."

Stuart walked toward his car. He turned on his heels, remembering he would need a tool to pry open the studio door that his mother had said George kept bolted shut. Maisie's brown eyes opened wide when she charged him for the crowbar. "Big game hunting?"

"I hope not. Why do you sell crowbars?"

"Africans like them," Maisie said. "More useful than spears. Unlock doors."

"Unlock doors to their own homes?"

Maisie whispered, "Cars, mostly."

"Mm. Nearest cop back in Arusha?"

Maisie nodded. "Cops act funny when you ask them about the Atkinson murder. Like they affirm, 'foreign correspondents are classified, like soldiers, not their business to investigate, just catalog body and notify family.'"

"Wonder why they didn't tell me that," Stuart mused aloud. "Why they just told me 'an investigation' would not take place."

Maisie nodded. "Welcome to Africa."

Stuart threw his pack in the backseat of the subcompact rental and drove back onto the main road, following it until it ended, forking into multiple narrow roads. Using memory and his mother's text directions he parked on a desolate side street, found the pathway to his grandfather's house marked "Atkinson Lane." He locked the car, put on his backpack filled with provisions. He slid the crowbar down one side and started up the walk, nearly reclaimed by the jungle, carefully sidestepping divots in the ancient concrete drive. He imagined the place two days ago-- roped off, sirens blaring, filled with cops and investigators. Or maybe only his dead grandfather and the assassin.

Maisie, a clue or a puzzle? Employed by foreigners… But to what end? He sorted out a few facts from Maisie's circumlocution:

1) Cops had done no investigation, simply walked around the property and prodded with their sticks to be certain there were no more dead bodies; probably, like his mom had assumed, they had not opened his grandfather's blocked off studio, simply collected the body, called Madeleine and closed the case.

2) Natives use crowbars for auto or other locked doors.

Crowbars and cars, he thought again and stopped, closed his backpack, placing it on a high tuft of jungle grass so he could see it on his return, then retraced his steps to check the car—all doors and trunk locked. Would it be here intact in two days? he wondered.

He headed back down the path, picked up his backpack and saw the place ahead—the old man's last stand. Hidden behind acacia trees it was a large low house, rustic in appearance but with tall grass that was once a lawn where local animals wandered. An overgrown place whose uneven shape, odd corners and tilted roof created alcoves that were conducive to writing; the house was as he remembered it. Few in Arusha were similar. Most were stucco but George demanded wood. Madeleine engaged Stuart with wild tales of the house when he was a child. It lived and breathed George Atkinson and his many sides—New England clapboard, Puget Sound viewing windows—one bay window. When Stuart first saw it, he thought it belonged in Seattle or Boston. It was a view home. When he had asked his grandfather about its unusual design, George had said simply, 'I'm not trying to hide in a native design and I want a house that reminds me of what I like. As a writer I need a break from my thoughts so I look outside.'

A new chain link fence laced with yellow police tape surrounded the remains of a wooden fence. Could he break the tape and just enter? Unwilling to spend several days in a Tanzanian prison, he phoned the police in Arusha, advised them he was an Atkinson relative and wanted to enter his dead relative's house.

The officer in charge said, "Wait for police."

A motorcycle cop was at the house twenty minutes later. After he cut the tape, Stuart handed him a thousand U.S. dollars and said, "I'd like to enter alone, if you don't mind. Oh and please watch my car, I'll need it to return to town."

The cop saluted and screeched down the road toward Arusha. $1000 was a pretty heavy parking fee, Stuart thought, but ploughed through the tall grass and made his way around the old house. He stopped, wondering what disease he was likely to catch by launching headlong into the weeds that had once been a freshly groomed lawn. *Never mind, the pants are supposed to be bug proof.* On the front porch was a red blot glaring at him from a meticulously cleaned door step, the stubborn remains of George Atkinson, he supposed. He closed his eyes then straightened up.

Reaching into his pocket for the key, he prayed silently that it would fit. While still cognizant of his totally inadequate skillset as an investigator, he forged ahead, determined to find any clues about his grandfather's murder and perpetrator that might remain in the house. With a half-twist the door clicked open and a rodent the size of a chipmunk dashed outside. Stuart watched its departure with relief, thinking of the disease the little vermin carried.

He stuck one hand through the open door and groped around for a light switch. When dim overhead lights illuminated the foyer, Stuart stepped into the carpeted room and gasped, the wan light directed toward angry bright eyes and wide-spread ears of a charging elephant in Atkinson's prize-winning photo, "Charge." Animals peered at him from every surface. A graceful leopard raced toward the elephant. Circling them all on the ceiling was a large flock of vultures. Splits between the enlarged photos revealed faded damask wallpaper. None of these photos were here twenty years ago. George's legacy? He chuckled that the police already disinclined to walk through the house were probably terrified by these animals.

Removing his bag of groceries, Stuart pitched his backpack on the floor in the entry hall and walked through the home past his grandmother's mementoes, into what passed for the kitchen. He was surprised how much of the floor plan he remembered. On a carefully cleaned counter he found a clean glass and unused corkscrew, placed atop a new dish towel. *A clean glass in well-locked home of a dead man. Who had been here?* He opened Maisie's Tanzanian wine, filled the glass and took a sip. Not bad. He finished the glass and looked around at the otherwise disorganized room. He set down the glass and drank a third of the bottle from the jug. Fortified, he picked up the crowbar from his back pack and strode quickly across the foyer to the room with the bolted door, considering how he would detach the bolt on his grandfather's studio. He wondered if the police had moved it; then he remembered that reporters were classified, so all they had to do was bag and tag the body and notify next of kin.

When he pried the last board loose he gently pushed on the door, first an inch, a foot, then flung it wide open. A brilliant blast of light and noise shattered the silence.

CHAPTER FIVE

Stuart awoke on his back, enveloped in dust. Covered with shattered plywood, and furniture pieces in a dark room, he couldn't see his body, couldn't find his hands, arms or legs. He tried to focus, blinking until the dust was gone from his eyelashes. Ears ringing from the loud report, head throbbing from undefined pain, he lay quietly, eyes circling the room, head immobile. Light shone faintly from a hole in the ceiling. Red dust drifted through it like gently falling rain. He breathed it in, comforted by the mix of sweat and African air that called up memories of his grandfather's dark room and storage basement.

As his eyes adjusted to the dim light, he could see that several black cabinets covered the closest wall. Propped against one was a large leather bag with pockets on all sides. Peeking out of one pocket was a spotlight that his grandfather used to photograph animals or landscape on assignment. A dark lamp swung in the corner. Yes—the dark room. His grandfather's basement. The room was carpeted and wood-paneled; it had been nothing but a cement basement and cool refuge when Stuart was a child, used for developing photographs and hiding out on particularly hot days. Watching the falling dust cover him and the dark brown carpet,

Stuart fought to stay awake by remembering everything he could about his grandfather and why his studio lights might flash when he unbolted the door. The room was clearly untouched by the police but was intended to light up when opened. Why? A trap set by his grandfather to frighten people from precious work? But the rifle, not his pacifist grandfather's doing, he was certain. He focused on all the good things about his grandfather, but Atkinson's cold sightless corpse and the jagged stomach hole invaded every pleasant memory he conjured up.

Bit by piece, he tried to create a real and plausible reason for his being on his back in the basement. He remembered the lights and noise, but the fall was lost to memory.

His left side started tingling. He wiggled the fingers on his left hand and moved his arm. Head throbbing, he tasted tin, a mix of sweat and blood. He used his index finger to trace a watery trail from his chin to the top of his head. He flinched when he found the source. A narrow bloody tunnel ran from his right temple to the back of his head; he inspected the wound with his fingers. Deeper than a scratch and shallower than a hole. "Any other damage?" he said aloud to see if his voice worked. Furniture splinters covered his right arm. He pushed them off. Now able to see the floor, he caught a glimpse of his spectacles resting miraculously unharmed. He leaned back. Free of its burden his right side began to tingle until it, too, was awake.

Like a marionette, he unfolded himself woodenly, put one leg by the other. He reached for his eyeglasses, grasped them, wincing when they touched his temple. The pain of sight. His palms flat behind him, he pushed himself to a seated position, one vertebrae at a time, and surveyed the room. The black filing cabinets and photographer's pouch were at the far end. Nothing else was visible in the dim half-light of the basement.

Erect but still seated, eyeglasses at half-mast, Stuart inched forward slowly limb by limb, arriving at a cabinet base. Using his fully-awakened left hand, he pulled himself erect on the drawers, one handle at a time. He shifted his weight to both feet, his legs wobbling in and out.

Breathing slowly, sneezing from the dust embedded in his nostrils, he moved to the room's interior wall and guided himself to a lighter area, one hand on the wall to keep steady. Why so much dust in the police swept house? The afternoon windstorms?

There was a trapdoor entrance from the studio to the darkroom in the studio somewhere, and the dust was circulating through the studio like it was a secluded desert. The connection between rooms doubtless accounted for the dust falling into the basement. Using the faint light from the ceiling hole he moved his hands slowly along the wall and clasped a casement—an opening. Perhaps a door out? His mother said there was another entrance to the basement, not just the studio hole above. Holding the casement with his left hand to steady himself, he moved his right hand down the casement and found a step. *A way out,* he thought. Curious about the room layout and the gradually settling dust, he resisted the temptation to run, and leave all this wreckage and pain behind him. But then—what would he have learned that he did not already know? George was dead—causes unknown. Perhaps analysis of the house, floor by floor would reveal why his grandfather was murdered on his own front porch. So he was downstairs and he had discovered the way out, why not start here?

He steadied his left hand on the casement, moved his right hand from the step and ran it along the adjacent wall. He stopped when his fingers touched a furry object. He traced around the furry shape. When he found cold pointed objects that met his fingers, he ran his tongue along his teeth, using his tongue to mirror his hand actions around the furry shape. *It must be a head, a trophy, but why here?* His fingers continued to trace past the pointed teeth until he found a toggle switch and light panel. When he switched the toggle up, the dark basement brightened, dust illumined by both the dark room amber light and open hole overhead. Stuart laughed as the furry bump and hole turned into the bright marble eyes of a lion's head whose mouth engulfed his now visible right hand.

"Hello," he said.

Shifting to face the side wall, he saw two slender white tusks, curved toward one another as though still attached to an elephant, another of the remains of Stuart's great-grandfather's safari animal trophies. The elder Atkinson was a great white hunter who led safaris. His mother had said that George was so disgusted with his father's trade that he had sworn never to kill an African animal, only to photograph them and write stories about African people and their struggles.

When Stuart discovered the heads in a corner of the basement under crossed elephant tusks he had asked George why he didn't get rid of the rotting corpses. George had replied, "Heritage, memory, all that is left of the old man." *Stuart's heritage also, along with his grandfather's photos of living animals upstairs,* Stuart thought, as he looked at the dense collection of dead animal heads surrounding him.

His hand on the lion's nose, he looked through the falling dust and discovered the crossed elephant tusks across the room. The elephant ivory was chained to the ground, its value in dollars greater than its value in memory, hence the need for chains. Apart from the fact the front door lock had not been tampered with this might be proof, Stuart thought, that the murderer had not entered the house. He studied the tusks carefully, blue-lined, quality ivory. *Yes, amazing that they were still here. Clearly the assassin was only after his grandfather and perhaps some papers?* Giant kudo and other antelope horns guarded the ivory from above. In this refinished basement he had mounted them, set them up as illusions: the head as light switch, the tusks curved but locked like treasures. Stuart walked slowly to the huge semi-circle formed by the several hundred pound tusks and saw an irregularity in the wall. The paneling was flawed. The knotty pine paneling had several knots, not irregular as was typical, but in line. He touched it. It moved. A square about twelve inches across slipped back. He sneezed as fungal dirt from the hole seeped into the open air.

He waited for anything living or dead to crawl or fall out. When nothing did, he put his hands inside the wall and stared into the hole. An object glinted. *Slow, Stu, slow,* he said to himself. *You're surrounded by dead animals and people die in this house. You've been a target.* Head throbbing, he stepped back toward the staircase, eyeing the shiny object with suspicion. The staircase tempted him. Should he simply ignore the hole and glinting object and race back to the studio to find out why he had crashed through? A good next step, he thought and pushed one foot through the opening on a shallow stair. He stopped suddenly, retreating to the lion's head.

Remembering their eyes--his mother's pleading, his grandfather's sightless--he returned to the ivory semicircle. Wondering if he were entering a sacred, numinous space, Stuart reached into the open wall panel for the sparkling object. Feeling a cold handle on a rectangular box, he imagined it to be a cashbox—a place for storing valuables. He put his fingers through the handle and lifted the object until the basement light shone on it. It *was* a cashbox. One made in the fifties with a single keyhole for oddly shaped keys. Having moved it, he breathed out, realizing he had been holding his breath. Unremarkable and locked. He took out the second key his mother had sent him, an irregular one that was long and skinny almost like a nail. A perfect fit. It sprung the latch in the back of the box and the top popped open slightly.

He opened the box expecting documents and a few slides of favorite animals. Instead it contained several black books tied together, each intercalated by fading yellow newsprint, ripped in half, covered front and back with narrow lines of neat handwriting. *A diary? And another of his grandfather's stories—destroyed before filed?* No, he thought, two stories had already been filed. They had got Atkinson killed. What further harm could any more do? His mother had said something about a third and fourth story in progress and a final one that would ensure George Atkinson's death. He could only imagine the content of these three stories, if his grandfather was dead after Story One.

Stuart paused and looked at the collection of heads, the refinished basement and the curving tusks. What fun George must have had hanging the trophy heads, then using them as strategic places to bury fresh controversial stories. George's father had collected only the best lion heads, killed the largest lions, bagged the best elephants and here they were stuffed in George's basement, so that George was not confronted with the constant presence of death. To combat his father's violent desecration of the continent, George wrote stories, Atkinson truths about Africa. Given the drama portrayed in the first and, Stuart supposed, the sequel to come, whoever was after his life might have seen the other half of the torn story and not wanted it or any other work by George Atkinson published.

Diaries and torn story in hand, Stuart shook the cashbox for anything else. It was empty except for a hand-held Leica camera, an oddly shaped seashell and a few African coins. He looked back in the hole and almost out of his reach, deep in the hole was a hollow tube. He reached for it, removed it and read "filed but unpublished." Satisfied with the diaries he put the tube back in the hole determined to come back for the tube after he studied the diaries.

He pocketed the camera, shell and coins, put the diaries under his arm and replaced the cashbox, carefully closing the sliding panel. He wondered if anyone knew it was here.

Stuart walked quickly to the exit and climbed, one step at a time, until he ran into strings of beads—the basement door, the pain of which was too great for his wounded head today. Stuart ran his hand across his throbbing head. He had to get through these beads, each step causing pain, and walk half a house away to the entry hall where he had thrown his sleeping bag. He shrugged and decided to sleep downstairs with the animals. He would climb out of the hole tomorrow when his mind was fresh and perhaps the head pain would have eased. He found a scarred lion skin and pulled a ragged grey camp blanket over his body, shaking his head at the slaughter. He was mystified that George had hung his father's trophies in the refinished basement while he himself was taking photos of living animals and researching great white hunters whose shady pasts he later exposed in his articles. These princes and sheikhs, wealthy Californians and what George called the dimwit wealthy shot animals on savannahs, mountains and plains, often in numbers over their hunting license allowance. George immortalized the animals in photographs and ridiculed the great white hunters in his articles. Heritage. Legacy. Weak reasons, Stuart had thought at the time. Reflecting back, this "evening the score" could have caused George's murder.

Blocking out the dead bodies around him, Stuart closed his eyes, thinking through the pain, trying to remember what had possessed him to come here anyway— a VC with no experience at investigation come to sift through the living and dead threads of his grandfather's work and find out what his grandfather had called him here to do. Why had he arrived too late? Did someone know he was coming? If so, who? He drifted off to sleep.

* * *

Stuart woke to silence, darkness and a headache, worse now than it had been yesterday when he was still in shock. When the room lightened, he figured it was morning. Reaching for his phone, which had escaped damage in his fall, he texted Roz. He asked her to take a picture of his location and condition using the remote visit software system they'd funded for MGH and mail it back to him.

"Please tell me if anything other than me is alive in the house. I'm in the basement. You'll find a heartbeat there."

Roz answered in a blitz. "No sign of life except you. All vitals are normal. You okay?"

"Not sure. More later."

His phone signaled another text. He needed to urinate. He remembered the guest bathroom at the top of the stairs. Hands and legs working after a night's rest, Stuart took the steps as fast as he could, found the toilet and relieved himself of yesterday's wine. He then walked through the kitchen, under the vultures, and stopped by his backpack to stow the valuable diaries. He worked his way down the hall to examine his grandfather's ruined studio.

He scrutinized the broken door and shattered view window on the far wall, which was intact at one time and whose enormous hole explained the dust in the room and the dust that rained on him in the basement through the opening in the studio. He noticed fragments of furniture all over the floor. There was a trail of footsteps in the dust that entered through the broken windows and walked in a circle back to them. The footsteps stopped before each piece of pulverized furniture—to smash it up? They had made several trips, or maybe there were several people after something in the house who believed it to be in the studio that Stuart had opened.

Stuart bent toward the footprints, his knees flexed, his feet squarely under him. He fit his shoes into the stumbling footsteps toward the hole in the floor where he'd crashed through to the basement. His were not the only ones, however. There were a number of other footprints. Curious how numerous there were. And curious what different sizes. Several small footprints, one with a corrugated shoe shape, another odd one which was perhaps a thong? Funny that they entered the house after Stuart fell into the basement. Why did they want the studio door open? Did they want access to the basement and why pulverize the furniture? Were they after him or something else? The lights still shone in the bright fluorescent blue. Were the explosion and lights connected? Was the row of fluorescent floodlights he recognized as his grandfather's portrait lights a booby trap set up by his grandfather to protect George and his work when he was in the studio? The lights would flash on alerting him to a stranger's presence. Meanwhile the lights would blind the intruder, giving his grandfather time to respond.

The gun explosion, alternatively, was something entirely different, directed at Stuart through the now shattered window by the owners of the footsteps. His grandfather owned no guns. Were these footprints from George's assassin?

Blinking to be certain he was not hallucinating or that his injury was not giving him visions, he dropped to all fours and crawled over to a gaping hole he knew to be just inside the studio entrance, the one-time basement connection. The hinged door that covered the hole had been removed, allowing the red dust blowing in through the shattered windows to fall on the room below. Covering it now was a thin piece of plywood that had shattered under Stuart's weight—where he fell and his footprints stopped. The half-covered hole had provided daylight to shine in the basement. Nearby was a rope ladder he remembered using to find his grandfather one afternoon when he was nowhere in sight or shouting distance. The stairs did not exist when Stuart was here as a child and the rope ladder was the only entrance to the windowless basement. Once George installed the stairs he did not destroy the connection between the two rooms, made possible by entrance through a rope ladder. Stuart wondered why. To make a quick exit? Paranoid thoughts, Why a thin, useless piece of plywood covering the hole, and not the original solid door?

Atkinson kept the room barred for some reason. To protect the secret entrance to the basement and to protect his privacy while writing, Stuart assumed. His mother had told him to purchase the crowbar. Unable to explain why the hole existed and what the basement studio connection had to do with his dead grandfather on the front porch, Stuart peered through the shattered wood to examine the room below.

The black cabinets, sink and even the tail end of the chains from the tusks were visible in the room. Beyond the studio outside the broken windows, shapes drifted like undetermined clouds. Watching them pass, living or vapor, Stuart remained flat on his stomach.

CHAPTER SIX

His phone broke into its Thelonious Monk ringtone as the fluorescent photography lights caught a glimmer on the wall. Carefully skirting the hole and remaining low on his hands and knees, Stuart crawled toward the studio wall. He stared at the sparkling ends of bullet slugs, several of which extended far enough outside the door casement so as to encourage removal for investigation. He examined the number of bullets shot--eight. How had they missed him, only grazing him as he fell?

Shadows moved across the wall. Was he no longer alone? One eye on the lights and the shattered windows behind them. He rose cautiously and scratched and scraped at the bullet. Using George's house and cashbox key like metal toothpicks, eyes flitting between wall and broken window, Stuart worked away at the most extended one and finally pried it loose. He put it in the change pocket of his ragged jeans and sat down.

From his seated position he noticed a strange tracing in the dust on the wall near where the bullets had been aimed. Stuart used the iphone video function to capture the long tracing, then tore a blank page from the back of his grandfather's diary, blessing the old man for owning a diary with an attached pen. To make the word small enough to put in the Google search engine, he traced what looked to be an Asian language character on the paper. Conversant in German and French, he'd never learned an Eastern language but had been to Chinatowns all over the world and could recognize but not understand the characters as an Asian word. He snapped a picture of the small drawing and put it in Google search. He scored two hits, one for the first character another for the combination. The first character "Xiangya" meant elephant ivory; the second was a warlord named Xiang Yu who had lived in the third century B.C. and liked killing people. Elephants were one of his grandfather's obsessions. The diaries were hidden between legal but valuable elephant tusks. The anti-ivory ban did not cover tusks acquired when his great-grandfather would have shot the tusker. Why were the tusks chained….clearly not only because of their value? Perhaps to frame the hole and to guard George's investigative work?

Stuart's iphone blasted again.

"Stuart," the tiny phone shrieked at him, "Maisie, here. You OK?"

"Yeah. I'm fine. Why?"

"I heard a noise, a loud explosion near your grandfather's house."

"You sure you're okay?"

"I'm fine. I'll call if I need anything," Stuart said curtly.

"The cops are coming to get you. Your partner phoned them."

"I'm fine. Tell them to give me the rest of the day." How did Maisie know everything? Stuart wondered. Did she work with someone who might have choreographed his grandfather's death?

He shut off his phone, interest focused on the curious Chinese character. *Would Omega know, would his mother know? More specifically, what did it have to do with the bullets, the footstep and the graze on his head? More importantly, why would anyone want to kill him also?*

Standing in the hall outside the studio, Stuart dialed Omega who was not there, but left a message about the Xiang Ya or Yu connection. He dialed Seattle.

"Mom," Stuart said patiently, knowing full well he had awakened his mother at 3 in the morning yesterday, "did Grandpa know any Chinese?"

"No, but the ivory artisans do."

"What?" Stuart shouted hopelessly, realizing his mother had fallen back to sleep. Cursing the African night when people sleep and the Seattle mornings when boats slip in and out of harbor, he turned to his own need for a shower to clean up before the cops came.

Desperate to get the tinny taste out of his mouth, the dirt off his body and rinse cold water across his throbbing head, Stuart scanned the hallway for another bathroom. He could see the full bathroom at the end of the hallway. In need of relief before he could reach the full bathroom, he urinated out the hole in the window, watering what remained of the roses in the backyard. Comfortable but discouraged that his cursory examination of the studio had yielded nothing but information about bullets fired at him, and a strange Asian name, he stared out the window until the cold morning air found a nerve pathway to chill his spine. The question remained, who was trying to stop him—first the mango now a gun?

He walked the rest of the hallway to the shower, steadying himself with one finger against the corridor. Under the warm water, he was surprised he could feel nothing at first. Gradually, molecule by molecule his body warmed from the warm water falling onto it. He took his grandfather's recently used towel, dried himself and wrapped it around his waist. Two days ago, Stuart thought distractedly, the man was alive. *Why was he dead? What did he know? Was the assassin after all Atkinsons?"*

Refreshed, Stuart reviewed what he had experienced in his fall through to the basement and focused on the disarray he had seen in his grandfather's studio. He returned to the entry hall again, steadying himself with one finger sliding across the corridor.

The charging elephant and vultures watched over him while he rolled up his dirty pants, retrieving the bullet. He rummaged around in his backpack and found an oversized resealable bag he'd brought to stow evidence. Using his left hand, which had completely recovered from the fall, he collected fresh clothing, dressed himself and leaned against the wall. He shoved the bullet, shell and folded drawing in his clean pants' pocket, slid to the floor, and sat down. He removed the diaries he had found in the basement, and paged through his grandfather's most recent diary. Much of its content had appeared in article one; ivory information was featured in article two. He scanned through the pages again looking for places and names. "Maisie. Xiang Yu. Djibouti and Dar Es Salaam. Thursday." Bingo! One week before he died.

Stuart turned the page, his headache vanishing as his curiosity peaked. An entry of unrelated words: "Roots of Heaven. Alphonse. Neissa. Stuart. *Moroccan and NY Times.* What to do? Diaries and Leica in safe. Farouk and Maasai. Yu. Dar Es Salaam connection. Xiang story last. With H.B."

The next page was titled "Yu." and read, "The old Chinese faced off with the Maasai at Farouk's camera store. He passed him a large roll of bills. I heard the Maasai say, "Have you been to North Africa where the animals are gone? You and that Bantu rape our culture. Why would I help you?"

What was in Dar Es Salaam? The mediocre partner,

somebody Britz—the one who wrote lousy stories and took pictures so pedestrian even the local paper wouldn't print them. Didn't his mother say Britz lived in Dar Es Salaam? He thought of the curious word string of names in the diaries. His headache clouding his thinking, the word string ran together like bad crossword puzzle clues. Djibouti—quickest air lift to China he'd read. He reached into his backpack for his first aid kit, dug out the pain medications and swallowed a Tylenol without water, resigning himself to questions with no answers and dozed off. He was wakened by screeching tires.

CHAPTER SEVEN

A cop shook him awake, not noticing the head wound. Stuart held up his hand and screamed, "Stop! You're hurting me...."

"Stuart Atkinson," one said, "you must leave this place. We take you for questioning, our medic will fix your head at police station. You will stay elsewhere."

His iphone rang. "Omega," Stuart said, so relieved he almost laughed. "Meet me at the police station. I need your help."

Omega was waiting at the two-story colonial building when the cop car and Stuart pulled in. Everyone listened patiently as Stuart explained what he remembered.

"You cannot go to Atkinson house. Where you stay?"

Omega shifted nervously from foot to foot until Stuart asked, "Baby coming? I will stay at Maisie's overnight then I'll transfer directly to the Arusha Hotel. Call me there after the baby is born. Then we'll go to Nairobi to conduct my grandfather's service."

Omega nodded.

Mentally reviewing his mother's list, he turned to Omega. "Please take me to Farouk's camera shop, then you rush home. I'll taxi back to Maisie's. While at Maisie's I will check out what she knows and move directly back to the Hotel Arusha. Maisie knows more than she'll tell and I believe she was in on my grandfather's death. With a head wound it is wise to stay among people who are always watching you anyway. She's such a busy body she'll be camped outside my room. I don't think she, at least, will take her eyes off me. By staying in the hotel, when my head clears, I hope to unravel what she has been doing."

Stuart picked up his backpack, riffling through it to make certain the diaries and camera were still intact and texted his mother he would phone later.

As they drove to Farouk's, Omega said, "Tell me what you remember about your sister."

"She ran away from home before I was born, I met her years later. But why do you ask?"

"Just wondering," Omega said.

"She sought me out in Boston several years ago to go to a Red Sox game, meet me and meet with a client. Called me up, I told her I hated the local team, so she went off to her meeting. I never saw her again. Strangest woman I've ever met. Left me with no contact information so I haven't seen or heard from her since that time."

"I don't know what she looks like. Your grandfather told me he had tracked her down," Omega said slowly, "found out she ran a drug trafficking and illegal trading company based in Morocco. He told me he wouldn't expose her because he was concerned harm would come to you or your mother."

"The ripped story in the diaries," Stuart began, "was it the beginnings of an exposé on her and other trafficking rings?"

Omega shrugged. "I don't think so. However," he said slowly, "I wonder what she knows about your grandfather. Maybe we should try to track her down."

Stuart's phone buzzed. He showed Omega the text. "Speak of the bedeviled. You know this place?"

"Mm. Easy to lose you. Arusha market is dangerous. Say you will meet by coffee stalls in late afternoon. Aunt sells at one of them. I can be in back room."

"You go home and see your wife. I'll ask for a meeting around 4 in the afternoon in two days' time. What stall does your aunt use to sell coffee?" Stuart asked.

"The stalls have no numbers. Her bags are brown burlap with pink stripes and she is working on a needlepoint of your grandfather's face." Omega laughed. "You should recognize it. Your sister, who knows?"

When Omega drove him to Farouk's camera shop, Stuart observed, "After I talk with the camera man, I'll wander through the Arusha market, find the burlap bags and hope your baby is born!"

"Good ideas. All of them," Omega said. "Don't miss the woodcarver stalls."

Farouk's shop was down the street and around the corner from the clock tower. When Omega dropped him several blocks from the store, he pointed to the Kodak logo on Farouk's store and pointed to the clock tower. "Keep clock tower in mind. I send cousins to four corners. They can get to Farouk quickly from there. You look enough like George that they'll recognize you if you need their help."

Stuart looked around outside the camera shop before he entered. He was in the heart of Arusha. Downtown Arusha was lined with young men on motorcycles, poorly parked automobiles and Africa's lustrous dirt.

His iphone blasted. "Where are you, son? I just received two figures from the Tanzanian sculptress. Ideas yet?"

Stuart gasped and said, "Did the figures come with a note? Didn't Grandpa's figures have a note with them?"

"No, there is no note. If you recall the first note said "Send Stuart." You seem to have a critical role in this African adventure and are already in Africa, so why bother with a note? The figures appear to predict impending death. I want you to find out why I have them. I'm not finished on this earth," Madeleine said.

Stuart ran his hand through his healing wound. "I'm doing everything in order, Mom. Grandpa's house and my personal entanglement with murder. Farouk next. I'm at his shop now, the Nairobi service. Finally, I'll visit the Britzes and interrogate the sculptor.

"Please throw those figures in the garbage just in case they have something deadly in them. Africa is not a safe place. Seattle might not be either. I'm wondering if all Atkinsons are targets. On this voyage I've learned not to eat wild mangos and to avoid large windows. As for you, Mom, my Boston apartment is empty. Why don't you fly there?"

"That these figures are here does not bode well. Boston— good idea. I have your spare keys. Tell your partner where you are and to not phone me for your travel plans. She's concerned about your safety and your lack of communication. She phones for updates all the time."

Stuart laughed. "Not to worry. Her persistence, loyalty and tremendous family fortune keeps Erewhon running. Be nice to her."

His mother coughed and said, "She certainly is inquisitive— asking about our family, Africa and you. I don't know why she wants all the information and why she feels obliged to check in with me, but maybe she gets lonely. I guess your business is about nagging the client."

"That's it, Mom. I'm the good cop, she's the bad cop. Together we get the prize."

Madeleine laughed. "Sounds like you are making progress on two fronts—with the Erewhon contract and your murder investigation. I've booked an open-ended escape for you out of Africa at Dar Es Salaam. I'll email you my Boston travel plans. Don't bother telling Roz I'm in town."

"I'll phone the super. He's on the first floor across from the mailroom. Introduce yourself."

CHAPTER EIGHT

Outside the Indian camera shop a slender young woman was sweeping the dirt. *A futile task,* Stuart thought. But the woman was certainly beautiful. "Is this Farouk Sharma's shop?"

"It is," she inclined her head toward Stuart, "I am his daughter Rumila."

"Enchanted. Stuart Lehrman," he said, extending his hand, "George Atkinson's grandson."

"Our condolences."

Stuart said, "You knew George?"

"He was a frequent visitor here," Rumila said. "Newsmen use inordinate quantities of film, cameras and we used to develop his more difficult photographs. Have you read any of his recent stories, most especially the posthumous ones?"

Stuart nodded. "Yes, I've read his most recent story and noted several are to follow."

Rumila smiled. "The poacher in the next story is the warrior with the spear on the wall. It was a fabulous photo." She pointed to a poster-sized photo of the tiny one in the newspaper article. "Maasai in the photo that the world will see in Atkinson's next story, is so proud of it. He comes in here occasionally and poses by it."

"Where is your father?"

"He's resting now," the dark-haired woman said. "I do the day shift, clean up. He wakes and takes the evening shift around 6.30 in about one hour. I often relieve him later in the evening if business is good."

She looked at his head and eyes carefully. "What happened to your head?"

"My head is a long story. I'll tell you both when I return."

"Good idea."

"I thought he also might have some insight into who's after the Atkinsons. Mom said he was a valuable contact."

"Don't know about that," Rumila said.

Stuart scanned the rest of the tall narrow shop, lined with poster-sized reproductions of African photos and tightly organized shelves with camera equipment from Germany, Japan and the United States, stacked neatly but dangerously on the narrow shelves. He walked over to a yellow Kodak box and pushed it back so as to keep the entire stack from toppling.

Rumila laughed. "It's a giant jigsaw puzzle that gets re-organized every time someone drives by here too fast or when a client buys film or equipment."

"How's business?"

"Terrible. Tanzania's government wobbles in the wake of Kenya's. The recent bombings there have slowed tourism, the region's principle business. And the rebels on the Coast frighten traders and tourists away."

"I'll go have a coffee in the neighborhood and come back when your father is working."

Rumila shook her head. "Go back to your hotel. This is an Indian neighborhood and Indian coffee is terrible. We've always been a nation of tea-drinkers. Coffee was nearly laughed out of the country."

"But African coffee is wonderful."

"Try the Hitowa outdoor café down the road and beware the panhandlers," Rumila cautioned. "Your pale skin announces that you are not from this country and your head wound makes you appear vulnerable. Be safe between here and the café."

"Your skin is light also," Stuart said.

"Gene SLC24A5 and lower melanin production, but Indians have been merchants in Africa for a long time. Whites have only been colonizers or tourists—one oppressive, the other transient. I, like other Indian young people whose parents came here as traders, was born in Arusha," Rumila added.

"You a specialist in field history or genetics when you're not doing camera work?" Stuart asked.

"A bit of both. Social anthropology."

"African thing, I guess. So was George's wife. Working out at the Leakey site?"

She shook her head. "Only grad students are allowed out there. That's next, when my father doesn't need me anymore. The coffee shop is that way and do watch your pockets. Someday you'll have to tell me about your grandmother."

"Mm," Stuart said, shaking his head, "can't tell you a thing. I never met her."

He strode off in the direction she pointed. Almost immediately a pair of young Africans fell into stride with him. Shit, he thought, as he felt one hand near his waistband.

He turned and faced each of them, one at a time. "I'm here to find an assassin and if you people don't go back to wherever you came from, I'm calling the police and telling them you're after my wallet and are probably both killers."

"No problem," the darkest African said as they rushed away.

Stuart arrived at the coffee shop and ordered a double espresso, flushed with shame. *What an awful thing to do, but then he remembered even his grandfather lost patience with natives.*

He wondered if this Sharma family would be of any help to him. So far, beyond Omega and Maisie's ramblings, the diaries and his mother's memories were all he had.

The café lead had been a good one: the espresso was remarkably good. But then he noticed the tiny silver pots stacked one on another. He watched the native as she ground a cup of the darkest coffee he had seen since his college Paris trip. One cup at a time. No wonder it was delicious. He caught her eye, when she was watching him watching her, and signaled her over. "May I have another?"

"Sure, you don't want cappuccino?"

"No, it's so rare to find good espresso it's worth the extra time I spend tonight suffering from insomnia."

She smiled and prepared the cup while he watched.

"Don't you have good espresso in America?" she asked as she set the inky black liquid before him.

"Oh, I can find it at cheap chains for affordable prices but good French espresso is rare and expensive. I've had good coffee everywhere in Africa."

He pulled out his grandfather's recent diary, flipping past the pages he had read. His eye was caught by a short sentence in the middle of the diary: *Something is different outside the house,* Atkinson had scrawled, *Turning to an empty place in the brush, I took still photos of the empty shrubs. Could the telephoto lens reveal whatever my eyes can't see, but is rustling through the garden?*

What was this? Stuart thought. The Leica could have real

evidence!

He sipped on the espresso and turned on an ipad and connected to the internet, using the Hitowa connection. When he found Skype he stuffed in his earbuds, and phoned his mother. He used Skype for the initial connection to confirm the arrival of the figures had not damaged her yet.

"Hey, Mom? Roz sent an SOS that my computer and phone have been hacked. Must have happened in Grandpa's house. I have a new ipad and disposable phone and am in a coffee shop using their network for a few minutes of Skype and will switch to the phone in a moment."

She nodded and gasped at his appearance. "Your eyes, the bandage, what in god's name?"

"I forgot about Grandpa's studio darkroom connection."

His mother grimaced. "You fell through? But there's a door on the hole. And now there are actual stairs to the basement. A staircase near the lion's head."

Stuart blushed. "I had forgotten he had that built, but am well aware of it now. Strange the studio trapdoor was no longer there, but the hole was covered by thin plywood. I guess to remind Grandpa not to fall through." *Was its existence not known to the shooter?* he thought. *Perhaps that is why they never found the diaries?*

"Could it be the person who wanted Grandpa dead had no idea where the diaries and unpublished manuscripts were and that when they shot him and then wondered through the house opening in the studio, but found nothing, since everything of value was in the basement?"

"Stuart, the bandage? I suspect you are correct—the shooter's motivation was doubtless the diaries and unpublished stories in the basement wall. Clearly the assassin never found it. Why the studio was carefully closed up, I don't know. The open trapdoor and plywood appeared to have accelerated your basement entrance. Is all the damage to you from your fall?"

"Someone took a shot at me before I fell. Why would they shoot me in the studio unless they wanted in the house there where they thought the diaries and manuscripts were?" Stuart said. "The police picked me up, had my head wound bandaged—a few wraps of cloth, a bandage. That's all the visual you get on me. Let me have a look at you. Then I'm switching to a throwaway phone. Contact me through email only. I'm getting a new phone tomorrow and will have Roz upload all the programs from our office, including my ringtone. I'll switch between it and disposable phones for the rest of the trip."

Madeleine leaned into the screen and stuck her tongue out at her son. "This is so foolish. Of course, I'm well. Now, Stuart, about the head wound?"

"Last glance. I'm switching to voice." He shut off the computer and redialed his mother in Seattle.

"Stuart," she persisted, "the bandage, the hole in the studio?"

"I wandered into the studio," Stuart began. "If our theory is correct I did as they wished, found the diaries and manuscripts through luck not design. But after I fell into the basement, they never found me. After my shower this morning I wandered into the studio and found eight bullets in the casement where I was standing and a shattered view window. The shooters had terrible aim but did significant damage to the house. Besides breaking the window, in their search for something besides me they shot up every piece of furniture in the room. I have the diaries and manuscripts. They are well-hidden."

His mother gasped, "How did you get out of the house?"

"Roz called the police and these cops came screeching into

the front yard, just as I was settling down to read Grandpa's diaries. They hauled me to jail, told me they would deport me if I had no reason to be here. When I explained I was investigating Grandpa's death they treated me like visiting royalty and said, 'Glad someone wants to look into that complicated rat's nest. No one in the department will go near it.'" He paused and continued, "They were so grateful they even hired some medic to dress the wound."

"Anesthesia?"

"Of course not. But he handed me a fistful of painkillers and told me to change the bandages every other day. Left me with five extra bandages and some cream to cover the bruising. I guess that means I'll be fine in ten days. On my way the medic added, 'don't be telling anyone, now. These bandages and painkillers are in considerable demand here.'"

"So you have the diaries?" Madeleine said.

"They were in a cashbox stuffed in a hole behind the tusks in the basement."

"I thought so. The key fit?" Madeleine asked. "Are you being followed? And the cops, why were they there?"

"Clearly I'm being followed. Someone came to Grandpa's house to wound me, only to frighten, not kill me, I think. The cops? I told you. Roz called the police, Mom. She was concerned about the collapsed house and my hacked computer and iphone. And yes, the small key was a perfect fit for the metal cash box that held the diaries."

Stuart stared at the horizon, considered her last question and wondered how much she knew. "The only person that knows I'm in town is Roz and this weird lady who owns the store and high-rise dump I'm staying in tonight. Roz tells me there are a number of in-country competitors for the videogame. A few stay in my current dumpy hotel. I'm trying to confirm who the other competitors are. I think this weird lady might know." He paused. "I also hope to enlist the help of Grandpa's Maasai driver."

"Is the dumpy hotel owner named Maisie?"

"You know her?" Stuart asked. "Yes, and I think she was in on the murder—I'm working on the link. The driver, Omega, is Maasai. He's tall, skinny and speaks English well. Maisie's small; her English is fair."

"The Maasai you can trust. Maisie," his mother said, "she was my mother's translator for five years. We let her go."

"Why did you let her go?"

"Sticky fingers," Madeleine replied. "Unaccountable expenses in an NGO don't cut it with management. If we didn't get rid of her, mom would have lost her funding. We set her up in business and, from what I hear, I don't think everything she does now is strictly legal. Be careful Stuart. Please tell me how you got out of Grandpa's house."

Stuart studied the table where his closed computer lay and went on, "I told you. Roz phoned the police. Just as I'm slipping into my sleeping bag with Grandpa's diaries and the cops came screeching into the front yard. Have no idea what they did to the lawn."

"Never mind, sounds like the house is trashed anyway…"

"Mom, if you fired Maisie why does she keep contacting me? Would she have organized the gun shots into the office? Is it safe to stay at her hotel?" A strange flying something flew into his nose. Holding the phone away he sneezed, so loud he looked around to see if anyone was looking. The beginnings of a headache made its way into his eyes. He knew it would move from there to the wound. He dug his fingernails into his free palm.

"Maisie may be a crook," his mother said, "but she's a good business woman. She's tracking you and will rent you a room because you are a paying customer. And yes, get out of the hotel tomorrow. Now tell me about this videogame."

"So I need to solve Maisie's part in the crime?" Not waiting for an answer, he continued, "Omega's brother Dalik Oweke designed the game that Erewhon's trying to get funded. The research we've done indicates the games in Africa and worldwide have a huge clientele. Digital gaming gathers not only sports aficionados but also the betting crowd. Foreigners pay Maisie's bills and may be competing for the videogame contract."

"I have little doubt, Maisie has a bit part in this play and don't lose the diaries. I believe there are some unpublished stories in the wall safe."

"The diaries I have. The unpublished story copies are in a photo roll, out of reach; I'll get them later. A few other questions, Mom. All VC related. Do Africans like to bet? Why is Omega trustworthy? A Maasai antique spear killed Grandpa."

"Africans love to bet," Madeleine said, "I imagine your competitor does also. Isn't VC a sophisticated form of betting? I don't like videogames. People will steal to get them."

"They sell, Mom. Erewhon is about investing in profitable business. That's how I pay rent."

Madeleine coughed. "Omega—trustworthy, yes, he's Maasai, but his tribe has always been friendly to our family. Remember that Maasai relic was in Grandpa's house that police think killed him? It was a gift from a chieftain. Whoever got it knew it was there. Omega may have known it was there, but so did Grandpa's assassin. No Maasai would throw that spear. They have spirits surrounding them. It was in his stomach not his heart. Maasai go for the heart and they don't miss. Someone who didn't know that might have wanted to mislead us. Tell me more about Maisie."

"She told me she would be killed if she talked about Atkinson."

"How would you have answered that question if you were hiding something?"

"Good question, counselor. But what if it's true? How to find out?" Stuart asked. "Lying low reading Grandpa's diaries? Oh, and there was a funny seashell and Grandpa's Leica in the cashbox. And the Chinese word for elephant on the wall."

Madeleine gasped. "Any other words by that funny character 'Xiang?' Like 'Yu?'"

"How did you know this? Is there anything else you... Why aren't you telling me what you know about this murder, Mom?" Stuart asked, now espresso-alert, the fog lifted from his brain. "Grandpa also had a meeting with Xiang Yu the week before he was killed."

The line went dead, but did not return to the dial tone. He checked the throwaway phone, there were twenty minutes left. Stuart asked, "Mom, are you there?"

When she spoke she used her "explain it to the jury tone," each word separated by lengthy pauses for emphasis. "Your grandfather had another story about some crime gang with that character tattooed on members' chests. As to what I haven't said, only your investigation makes seemingly irrelevant facts useful. I can't promise you there is nothing else—I have given you names and places I remember or have heard your grandfather speak about and am trusting to my long life and memory that I can fill in blanks if you find any. What's next, Stuart?"

"As to what's next, several important open ends. First back to Farouk and find out what he knows, then on to Nairobi for the memorial and then to Grandpa's first partner Anton Britz's house in Dar Es Salaam where—barring any other unforeseen difficulties—I can catch a plane to the States or at least to Europe. Grandpa's ashes are on their way to the Sarova Stanley, you said?" Stuart replied.

"I've set the memorial for three days from now. You should meet people there who have ideas about his death and his editor Ian knows all the scuttlebutt in Africa. Not only will you find more clues about Grandpa's odd partner, you may find funds for your gaming venture from his colleagues and in Dar Es Salaam. Dar Es Salaam is a port town with lots of rich people," Madeleine said. "I've already phoned the Britzes. They're expecting you after the memorial. Let's hope you are presentable by then. Don't lose the seashell. It's mine. Grandpa and I found it when he took me to the beach after my mother died. He said hers and thousands of other souls were in there and I would never be without her. I lost it."

Or the drawing, the bullet, or the camera, Stuart said, "Mom, the guy told me I can't drive for a week. He also said the bruises around my eyes, which accompany head wounds, will fade in a few days. The cream he gave me is also "make-up" to cover the bruising. I'll be presentable for the service."

"Never mind. It will make for interesting conversation with a group of people you don't know," Madeline said and continued, "Hire the Maasai and leave day after tomorrow. Please collect the rest of the Arusha area investigation information and move on to Nairobi for Grandpa's service. I think it would be wise for you to get out of town."

"Mom, the solution to the mystery is somewhere in Arusha and the wound? It's a light scrape, slight abrasion. May scar, but I have lots of hair. I still have Farouk and the Arusha market to visit then I'm off to do the service."

"Why the hurry?" Stuart rubbed his neck, trying to alleviate his headache.

"These two figures," she said. "Nice enough, but frightening to own. Please don't tell Roz I'm in Boston. You do need a maid,

Stuart."

"I'm a bachelor and I enjoy my dirt."

"Well, never mind, son," Madeleine said. "I've been on my hands and knees scrubbing the crud off the boards and have bombs out for the silverfish who love your leftovers."

"Why do I need a maid when I have a mother in residence?" he said, laughing.

"Not for long! I'm shivering in your snow," his mother said.

"It is cold, no doubt about it."

"I won't tell Roz you are in town but remember we do owe her my life. She found me when I fell through the hole and took it upon herself to phone the cops to haul me out of the debris. Yeah, it's cold in Boston but it's winter. It's probably raining in Seattle."

"Yes, it's raining at home. I'll try to remember Roz did save your life, and that her family wealth supports your firm in dark times, but that does not explain what she wants with me," Madeleine said, "she wasn't there, but she phoned me saying, 'Stuart might be in trouble. Have you heard from him?'"

"She wants to find out where I am now because she knows my phone has been hacked and she knows I can't contact her. We agreed I would use it only in times of desperation. I'll buy a new one soon and switch between the new one and disposables. The old one is officially dead."

Madeleine said, "That explains her comment, Stuart cannot phone or text. From the satellite photos I was able to obtain from the GPS on his phone and a hi-tech camera attachment made by a company that Erewhon funded which can photograph into remote locations…"

"Mom, how long has it been since you've been to Africa?" Stuart interrupted.

"About fifty years. The last time I saw your grandfather was at your father's funeral. I have not seen the house since I left it as a child. When he was here in Seattle we talked about blowing up some of his best photos for wallpaper." She paused, a slight hiccough in her voice. "The work was installed last week, just before he died."

"The photos looked great. Terrifying, but what a tribute." Stuart paused. "The strangest thing about the house, Mom, there was one clean wine glass and one clean counter. Dust covered the other counters. The shooter left small footprints in the studio. Obvious why the dust was in the studio after the window was broken. Why was dust everywhere else?"

"The dust? Grandpa loved the open air so he let the winds blow through the house all day long. There are hidden open air vents all over the house. I had trouble holding onto housekeepers because they don't like to work that hard, but I found a service that would help him out occasionally. I asked the service to send a housekeeper by when you were en route. The police tape would have stopped her, but they must have asked her to come by after they collected your grandfather's body and cleaned the porch. I had told her to clean a wine glass and set it on a clean towel two days ago. Good news is that the dusty footprints might help you find the killer."

Madeleine paused and continued, "I think the Chinese man may be somehow connected to your grandfather's death. I can't remember what Grandpa emailed....Find out what you can about Xiang Yu. Study his feet when you go back to see him."

"But more on your filthy apartment. Why didn't you tell me about the great food in Brookline?" she asked.

"You never asked." Stuart grinned.

"French, Italian, Lebanese."

"I know. I've lived there for ten years. Talk to you later.

Tonight while I'm focusing on Asian types here in Africa, head to the Thai restaurant around the corner."

"But I'm staying out of the Chinese restaurant in Cambridge. Now get back to work."

"I'm off to get another iphone and will text you the number. Roz and I are trying to figure out how to acquire some Apple stock since I go through so many of their goods."

Stuart walked outside, thinking of his mother's seashell, the insular life she and his grandparents had here and wondered about the place. He stared at the absolutely clear blue African sky beginning to be fringed with the rose of sunset and began to understand why his grandfather returned. Certainly not Brookline, he thought.

His new iphone buzzed. "How's it going, Roz? Testing the new phone?"

"Nice to have a contact number again."

Stuart looked again at the waning light and the beautiful landscape, reminding himself that Roz was not always interrupting, she was sometimes saving his life. "I understand you are treating my mom like Erewhon's new best deal. She asked you to connect with me now that you've found me. She's got problems of her own.

"I'm staying at Maisie's after I meet with the Indian camera man. With the new phone I'm clean for the moment. Text anytime you want and thanks for the SOS. How did you know?

" The programmers. Their videogame started going haywire. And about the programmers," she went on, "we need to close with Dalik and crew. I hear there are some powerful African bidders pressuring the group to sell to them. And we could use their expertise in other ways. Some of the electronic packages we get are full of worms."

"That's a truth," Stuart said. "Who's more powerful than

Erewhon?"

"Couple of local traders," Roz replied.

"Where do you get your information, genius lady?"

Roz laughed. "I'm tapped into Maisie's phone."

Roz was silent, then said, "Might pay to be her new best friend."

"Maisie's best friend—that will take some doing," Stuart advised, "and a considerable number of shillings over and above my room cost. My family fired her because she was taking money from my grandmother's grant. Further, she pointed out that Africans are killed if they talk about Atkinson, so her lips are sealed. I think she's connected with my grandfather's killers and the guy or guys who shot at me."

"Well, let's not lose you also. Be discreet. What did your grandmother study?"

"Socio-anthropology," Stuart said.

Roz sighed. "We could use her help now."

"No kidding. And I could use an Erewhon advance."

"I'll get on it. Check the BNP outlet near you tomorrow. Only honorable outfit over there."

"I'll chase after Dalik in Nairobi. My grandfather's service is at the Sarova Stanley there in three days. Make certain Dalik attends. I'm moving to the Arusha hotel after tonight. I'll phone you from there.

"No bothering my mom. She wants you checking in with me not her. Deal?"

"Deal! I have family too."

"Now that both you and Mom know the new iphone number, I'll use it and occasionally mix it with use of throwaways. I also plan to buy another iphone. I'll text every time I change."

"Not a good idea," Roz said, "what if one of the creeps

wants to reach you?"

"Good point. So I'll hang on to the sucker and please get Dalik to my grandfather's service?"

"Will do. I have a sense of your voyage and realize communication is a problem. I promise to leave dear Madeleine alone."

"Thanks, bye."

How is it I could be taking orders from two women? Stuart thought. Maybe his grandfather was on to something. Maybe he should stay here in Africa where no one could touch him. Solve this case and hang out a shingle as a private investigator. Ah, but he loved his business and he would miss the Cambridge snowfall.

Stuart checked his watch. He had wasted enough time. He stood, waved at the friendly waitress, who said, "Please come back. The manager likes to showcase his coffee."

"I'll make it a point to stop by when I leave the market."

"You're headed the wrong way."

"I'm headed to a camera shop."

"That Farouk?" The waitress shook her head. "Strange people go in there."

Stuart moved closer. "Describe them."

"White South Africans and traders from North Africa, I think."

"How do you tell who is a South African?"

"Language. If they are silent, nose shape. North African peoples look more European, with slender noses, narrow faces. South African people look Nordic or Dutch, broad faced with larger features."

"I have to go now. I will stop early tomorrow."

"I do not work tomorrow."

"What time do you leave today?"

"5 PM."

"I will see you before 5 PM or the day after tomorrow."

Outside the coffee house, the hustlers were waiting for him. They hurried to fall into his stride and were running to catch up with him.

"What, no luck?" he asked the closest native.

"We try but you are more fun and we decide to wait for you."

"Why don't you go to college and get jobs?"

"Education expensive," the chubby native said.

"No money from your people or the government?" Stuart asked.

"All Tanzania is poor," asserted the taller native. "But you look, you look at my drawings. I work hard on these. Many foreigners buy." He started to roll out a cloth roll filled with ink drawings.

Stuart held up his phone. "I call police."

The man rolled up the cloth. "Please, no police. We just walk with you, mister."

When the trio arrived at the camera store, Stuart faced the natives and said, "Shove off. I've got an appointment."

The pair strode back toward the Arusha hotel clock tower. As he watched their receding forms, their almost Mutt and Jeff like appearance, Stuart thought natives, come in all shapes and sizes. Omega was tall. His kinsmen were tall. These two were smaller than all Omega's people, four of which were standing, as promised, at all four corners of the clock.

(HAPTER NINE

Stuart had not noticed the dark bronze statue in front of the shop when he was there before. It was a small boy holding a fez and a camera. The arm with the camera reached into the camera shop. He saw an elderly Indian behind the counter and flipped to the one page in his grandfather's diary he remembered...something about the best informant in all of Africa.

Rumila had changed to another sari that matched her father's light blue shirt. "This is the gentleman I told you about, Father," Rumila said. "Stuart Lehrman, please meet my father Farouk."

"Enchanted I'm sure. Your grandfather was a good man and we are sorry for your loss."

"As are we, Farouk, which is why I am here. Thank you for agreeing to meet me. My mother believes you were one of the last people my grandfather saw before he sent for me. Can you tell me about your last meeting?"

"He told me something of the story he was working on and I cautioned him against the traders. He asked for the best telephoto lens I had to fit his tiny camera. He had very little time as someone was waiting for him in a camp and another in a hospital. He said he hoped the stories would break in Nairobi before the awful damage they described was compounded. He also hoped to photograph some people he believed were following him. Said something curious," the Indian said thoughtfully, "if he could find faces in the empty spaces of his photographs he would be able to expose them. He thought it might be someone, like Britz, who was after his story ideas."

Stuart wrote Farouk's thoughts in his notebook and retrieved the Leica from his backpack.

He handed the camera to Farouk. "I retrieved this camera, his diaries, and notes about his unpublished stories. I think I have the scraps of a missing link that may be more useful and notes that will be invaluable to finding out why and who murdered him. Additionally, I have pieces of one of his stories that was ripped in half. Is there anyone to whom he would entrust the other half? His diaries also contain information about a Chinese. My mother believes this was a story in the works. Would you know anything about any of these missing links? Further, can you remove photos from a camera?"

Farouk rubbed his chin thoughtfully. "I will think about your questions. After a number of friends had betrayed him I believe your grandfather trusted no one. I will send my daughter with a message if I think of something. As for the photos—your grandfather's last, I guess, yes I can remove them, but it will take several days to a week. I will give them, my closest attention, knowing they are important."

"Thank you, take your time. Another question—you are my mother's age," Stuart said. "You must have been a teenager when you opened this shop."

Farouk nodded. "We brought the bronze in front of the store with us when we left India. I had finished high school at age fifteen and we heard people were doing photo safaris so my parents' near eastern and Commonwealth connections could fill the store with all the camera gear that the safari excursion people would want. I attended the Arusha technical school for several months but had already done the classwork they were teaching. I went to work for my parents and never completed my college degree.

"Rumila has already finished a masters here and will do graduate school next year in England, her field work concentrated here in Africa so she can be with me."

Rumila flushed. "I like it here, father."

"How did you come to know my grandfather?" Stuart interrupted.

"He liked asking questions and I like to talk," Farouk said, turning bright red. "Sometimes to my disadvantage."

Stuart wrinkled his nose in confusion. Farouk pointed to the fez tassel on the bronze statue. It was blown in half.

"Someone did not like what I said about the gunrunners in the Congo. But, never mind, because I like to talk, people from all over the continent stop here to buy camera parts. I often hear where the best animals are, who the best guides are and can point them to the right people. Your grandfather always came here for stories. I gave your grandfather the child exploitation lead, the one published on the day he died. The Red Cross refugee site was supposed to be safe. I don't know if the visitation caused his death and it troubles me so much that an old man's leads could cause a good friend's death."

"I don't think that one story brought him down, but do you remember how you first heard about it? Remember that he was shot on his own front porch, not at the NGO. There was nothing my grandfather would have liked better than to have saved an African life even if it meant losing his own life. It's my understanding the subject of the story is now safe. So please, do not give it a second thought, Farouk. Do you happen to remember what lead you gave my grandfather and I can follow that thread?"

"An aide worker whose card I might still have visited from an NGO. I doubt that her group is still in the country. Each group lasts about two years, then go back to wherever they came from. I gave your grandfather her card then." He shuffled through some papers in a long narrow drawer below the cash register and brought out a business card.

Stuart studied it. "Man or woman?"

"Woman," Farouk replied, "now Alphonse Britz's second wife."

Stuart tried to mask the nausea he was feeling—at every corner of this mysterious murder he found a Britz—a figurine sculptor, a second wife, a lousy reporter.

"Thanks and don't worry that this is old. It's a lead and I have precious few of those."

The Indian scratched his grey-black hair. "I will try to remember who he trusted. There were not many of us. Fact is," the man said archly, "it's a wonder he lived as long as he did. I'll phone when the photos are ready."

Stuart nodded gratefully. "Finally, can you point me in the right direction to the daily market? I'm told it's not easy to find."

"Rumila," Farouk said, "take him there. I will be fine. Please keep in touch with us, son. I want to know what happened to my friend."

Stuart and Rumila stepped outside into the heat. Several blocks beyond her father's store, Rumila slipped her arm under Stuart's, saying, "Forgive the forwardness, but as I'm certain you noticed, the streets roam in donkey cart paths throughout Arusha. It is easy to lose track of people in this small town."

"Why did you change your clothes?"

"My father does not like the dull colors of my work saris. Says I should change after I clean up. Your grandfather once asked me how many colors I had. Curious man, he was."

"You should have seen him a decade ago before he returned to Africa for good. He would travel to Africa or other countries nearby to chase stories near his beloved Tanzania. He would show up at various ages in my life, an itinerant journalist and loyal grandfather."

Stuart recounted the tale of George's arrival at Harvard Square on Stuart's twenty-first birthday. "George was both observant and naïve, a winning combination, I think, for an award winning journalist. While sitting at the T stop he stopped every passerby and learned more about Cambridge in the twenty minutes it took me to discover he was in town than I had learned in four years. Most interesting part of that story is that his visit was a surprise. Because he did not always phone when he was in the country even my mother was unaware he was sitting near a well-known Cambridge newsstand. Fortunately, I had a class outside the quad and had to walk by the T stop or I might never have found him to come to my birthday celebration."

Rumila laughed.

Stuart continued, "My friends could not get enough of the old man. The one who now works for the *New Yorker* interviewed him asking how he worked, told him he had read one of his stories and loved the old man's style. Grandpa told him how he followed leads and described his interview technique. My friends told him they had never seen a Tuskers beer. He sent us a case from Kenya when he returned. But, no doubt his best coup of the evening was when my mother called to wish me Happy Birthday, he picked up my phone and said, "Madeleine, not now, we'll call you after we place our orders."

"My mother phoned the front desk at Anthony's where we were eating, and the maître d'hotel called him over to the desk, "Mr. Atkinson, your editor."

"Madeleine," he had said gently, "I was about to call back."

Rumila grinned and walked them past blocks of the "new" Tanzanian marketplace, the several story glass buildings filled with Western clothes and cosmetics. One of the shops had a shiny new escalator between floors.

Confused by the expense involved and aware of the low Tanzanian GDP, Stuart asked, "Now that hunting is no longer big business, where does Arusha get its money? That's a new and highly complicated escalator inside that department store."

"China is dumping big money into the African continent, but with our and Kenya's unstable governments, much of the funding has been cut back. America sent the escalator parts," Rumila said drily, "to Colombia for assembly then crated it to be reassembled here."

"Too bad someone lacked the foresight to establish a factory here."

"I guess they tried," Rumila said, "but the cost was so great and the salaries so overwhelming the base company could make no profit."

"Why?" Stuart asked.

"Factories require such protection from native governments and rebels, it's too costly to maintain them…" Rumila released his arm and pointed to an alley framed by two open market stalls. "We're here. Arusha's original market place. You'll find the coffee stalls and food stuffs on the inner ring of the labyrinth. The outer ring is filled with tourist tantalizers, photographs of Africa, postcards, safari heads."

"Want to come?"

She shook her head. "This is your war and I'd rather live to start graduate school."

She took out a card. "This is the camera shop." She scribbled a number on the back. "This is my cell. Call me when you are back at the hotel. I'll take you to a good Indian restaurant nearby."

CHAPTER TEN

Stuart headed into the dark alley. He looked at the curios and saw nothing that tempted him. This all-purpose one stop shopping was for those who needed to prove that they'd been to Africa.

He had been willed his grandfather's walking staff—a one of a kind curio. He had not seen the staff and wondered if it lay at the bottom of the house rubble. He was anxious to retrieve it by searching through the remains of the fallen house.

He rounded the bend of visitor enticements and entered the market itself. Dead fish stared at him with their sightless eyes. Piles of meat were scattered unceremoniously in various booths.

Incense emanated from a booth stacked high with apothecary glass bottles and dark plastic stoppers. The African medicine booth, he presumed. He wondered if Africans received some of their training from the Chinese.

He passed booth after booth of fine wood carvings. Some of bowls, some of animals and several peculiar tall poles, with intricate carving up and down them of people, animals, village huts, the African thorn tree. While the animals and bowls sold for twenty to thirty thousand shillings, the poles sold for as much as 500,000 shillings. Stuart stopped in front of one man working on a pole and said, "Why do these cost so much and what is it?"

The black carver grinned. "I make you good price."

"Not interested," Stuart replied.

When the man turned away he said, "Why so expensive?"

"My family tree. Each small face is modelled on a real person. Take long time. Use special techniques Chinese teach."

Stuart wandered deeper into the market until he found a wooden piece he couldn't resist—a spotted leopard. When he paid, he noticed a closed shop nearby with a large elephant and some Chinese characters underneath it.

A cop stood at the entrance to the hallway. Stuart approached and asked, "What is that place?" He recognized the characters as those in his grandfather's study. He pulled the diary with his crude drawing out of his backpack and compared them. They were the same.

"That part of market not open to public," the cop replied. "Chinese carvers work there. They don't like tourists." The cop scrutinized Stuart's face. "Are you the American Atkinson?"

When Stuart looked at the man curiously the cop explained, "I let you into your grandfather's house."

Stuart nodded. "I'm trying to find out who killed my grandfather. I think it's important that I enter."

"Proceed at your peril. It appears, like your grandfather, you have an interest in tragedy." The cop stepped aside.

Stuart shrugged and rang the shop bell outside the Chinese carver's shop.

"Come in," the carver said. He looked Stuart up and down. "I was expecting you. You look just like your sister. Name's San Xiang Yu." He grinned lasciviously. "Nice body, that Neissa."

Stuart ignored his last remark and examined the dark

corners of the shop littered with smuggled ivory, ivory shavings and exquisite carvings made from tusks. One in the shape of a boat had sails, was filled with animals and was entitled, "Noah." Another case held jewelry ranging from simple round bangles to intricately carved earrings. "How much for the earrings?" he said.

"$15,000 American dollars."

"Contraband?"

"Some ivory in store legal but much is illegal. Easier to carve fresh ivory. Asian artisans like it better," Xiang said matter-of-factly. The Chinese looked thoughtfully at Stuart. "Guess someone took a shot at you. Might want to watch out for Neissa's competitor, tall blond guy. I need to make a visit in town. I will be back," Xiang Yu said.

"I'll see you another time then," Stuart responded, looking carefully around the shop noticing half a dozen men with Xiang Yu's name tattooed across their chests. Each was carving small ivory pieces. Xiang Yu signaled to one of his workers and rose to leave.

"My men escort you out of shop and market. See you another time."

Stuart nodded as an armed man came toward him, pistol pointed at his head. "Allow me to guide you out the door."

Stuart ran out of the ivory store into the woodcarver's market where he plunged into the center of a crowd of Tanzanian school children. He was immediately surrounded by a sea of unsuspecting black faces. He had bent to their level and was deep in the midst of them. The gunman, also crouched low was distracted by the children.

Their teacher saw the man and gun behind Stuart and said, "It is time to go, children. This white man will not hurt you."

The children turned to stare at Stuart's white face but

apparently did not notice the man behind him who retreated toward the market when he lost track of Stuart. When the children entered their cloistered school several blocks away, the gunman had vanished. The teacher showed Stuart a back entrance and gave him circuitous directions to find a nearby taxi stand.

Stuart had the driver take him to his room at Maisie's conference hotel.

CHAPTER ELEVEN

Stuart walked outside the complex, still wary of phone tapping, and bought another cheap disposable phone card at one of the department stores. He texted his mother and Roz everything he had learned. He pulled Farouk's card from deep in his pocket and dialed Rumila's cell.

She picked up after one ring. "Safe?"

"Safe," Stuart said. "Dinner at eight? Phone runs out in two minutes."

"Meet me at the Arusha Hotel clock at 7.30," Rumila replied.

"Go to the lobby. Sit down. I'll phone the concierge to inform him I'm moving there tomorrow." Stuart went back to his room at Maisie's, washed his face and changed his shirt. He phoned the concierge at the Arusha Hotel, asked to have his old room back tomorrow morning and said he'd taxi to the Hotel in fifteen minutes. "A beautiful Indian woman will be waiting for me, be nice to her," Stuart added.

"Farouk's daughter. She's a nice one, that one."

Small town, Stuart thought and slipped on his pullover.

He walked into the desk to settle with Maisie. She was engaged in a conversation with Xiang Yu which he could barely hear.

"The packages and Bills of Lading?" the Asian asked.

"Here," Maisie said and pointed to two boxes in the back.

Stuart's height and proximity to the counter enabled him to see the top line on both shipping labels: One was Djibouti; the other Tangiers.

Seeing Stuart, Maisie said, terror in her voice, "Business, now. Time to go."

"I will send men later," Xiang Yu said, bowing to Maisie and to Stuart as he turned away from the counter, moving quickly out of the hotel.

Stuart settled with Maisie, saying he would leave after breakfast tomorrow. "What did Xiang Yu want?"

"Packages. I collect them for him." Maisie said. "He pays rent occasionally. Checks from him are all drawn on New York banks."

Stuart hailed a taxi, digesting this piece of information, wondering which New York banks were owned by Chinese and wondering how many other line items Maisie had provided him were lies. Hotel not paid for by "entrepreneurs who used hotels" but by Xiang Yu. The conference was a way station for Xiang Yu's illegal transfers.

At the Arusha Hotel, he collected his thoughts and nodded at Rumila who was waiting for him in one of the large chairs by the registrar.

She was still in the blue sari but her face was lightly colored with cosmetics. She walked toward him and took both his hands. "Glad you could spare me the evening," Rumila said. "You have a difficult task ahead of you and an unsolved crime to solve. Let us start the next part of your adventure with a good meal."

"My pleasure, I'm sure. Who knows when we'll meet again?" Stuart said, lightly squeezing her hands.

"We will hope to see you at the service in two days and remember we have your camera," Rumila said. "Don't forget my father's store is a veritable post office for out of towners and we will post the service notice when it comes out in the *Tribune*. Come," she went on, "the restaurant is just past the park in the town center."

They walked along the broken cobblestone path that followed the concrete bound park below them where Africans stood singing hymns and swaying softly to the gentle rhythm.

Stuart was struck by the uniformity of their movement and its similarity to what he had read of Africans in America in the enslaved South. These Africans were free but a black person's rhythm when singing or when listening to music appeared to be innate. The major difference between these hymns and plantation hymns were the composers—in the service below the choir was singing familiar hymns composed by English musicians whose names could be found in hymnals the world over, instead of unknown Southern composers whose hymns rarely if ever, left American shores.

"Shame they don't know hymns from other countries," Stuart remarked. "Composers whose works are black African in origin."

"In India we sing them all," Rumila offered. "I love your southern tunes."

"Who brought Christianity to Africa?"

"Colonizers, just as in India," Rumila responded.

"Meaning it's here in all its derivations? Lutheran, Methodist, the works?" Stuart asked.

"Yes," Rumila said. "Your apostolic churches and Mormons have been here, but Africans prefer the continental religions. The

Mormons and apostolics are too harsh, not simply ordered song-filled services. Africans love their movement, to raise their voices in song. Many learn English from church music."

"Don't Africans have their own religions?"

"Oh, you know the theory," Rumila said, a grim smile on her face. "All religions are wrong if they are not your own—in the colonizers' case, that's Christianity. And the missionaries also set up schools. Traditional African religions are simple, with single creators and occasional special gods; not dramatically different from Christianity and its apostles. Their own religion—animism mixes with the landscape in a curious way. For example, combining the Hebrew bible's "ashes to ashes" and animism, Africans make the circle of life complete by leaving their dead outside to be consumed by hyenas. Regarding Africans and Christianity, Africans converted to please colonizers then cognized they were gaining education and a grasp of language at church so they attended church to learn English. Fortunately, if they walk in the camera shop and see our scattered Hindu gods on the shelves, they leave us alone." She sighed.

Stuart shuddered, the visual of a dog-like animal eating a human too much to stomach when he was faced with a burial service for his grandfather to plan in the near future. At least his grandfather's ashes were already in a burial urn. "Must be tough being an expat," Stuart observed.

"Africa is my home. I've only visited India," Rumila said and paused. "My father would like to go to India more often but his business is here. He has saved my mother's ashes. We will take them back by boat soon and scatter them in her home state. We've been home several times, but not since she died."

"Why not fly?"

"My father is old and our last experience with airplane

security was horrifying. The travel to our country needs to be easy because our mission there will be difficult. My mother and he were close. Unlike many Indians, they found each other at University and chose to marry." Rumila's eyes filled.

She slipped her arm under his again. "It's time to cut off the main drag. I want you to meet my cousin." She guided him to a small cobblestone and dirt street, where a back door was open on a restaurant kitchen.

A short slender Indian handed his whisk to the man next to him and approached the pair. "Rumila, such a joy," he said and kissed her on both cheeks.

"Cousin, meet Stuart Lehrman, George Atkinson's grandson."

"Oh, my dear boy," the grey-haired Indian said, extending his hand to Stuart. "My condolences. Your dear grandfather loved our food. Ate here often." The man took them up to the swinging doors to the kitchen and pointed at a small table in the corner. "Ate there. Table is always set for two. Your grandfather was always alone. Brought his notepad and scribbled notes. You two take the table. I have let no one sit there since your grandfather was killed." He turned to Stuart. "Have you a favorite dish?"

"Chicken Vindaloo," Stuart said, wondering if there were clues at his grandfather's table.

"Our house specialty," the man said, his face brightening.

"Rumila. The vegetables as always?"

"Please, cousin," Rumila answered.

Once they were seated, Stuart examined the restaurant. He looked at the view from his grandfather's table. Both chairs faced the door. Whichever one he sat in would enable him to see friends or foes. *Had George known his life was in danger for a long time?*

"I wonder," Stuart said aloud, "can you be an investigative

journalist and not fear for your life?"

Rumila reached for his hand. "I don't know, but you want to know what I think?"

"Yes," Stuart said, the desperation echoed through his soft voice. "I think your grandfather knew he was in danger all the time, but that he would come here to my cousin's restaurant or he would go driving among the animals and he would relax. I think he would find time for his mind to empty of fear, of leads and, after his wife died, would lose himself in his mistress. When none of that worked anymore, and when someone told him the threat to his life was imminent, he called for you. Your grandfather enjoyed his life. He did not want to die. But he was tired of watching, always watching and waiting. That made him vulnerable."

Stuart sighed, smiling thoughtfully. "Seems you knew him well." He looked at the reflection of his face in her dark eyes and could see his grin mirrored on her finely chiseled face. He took her other hand and said, "Heaven spared no grace when it created the Indian woman, did it?"

Rumila blushed.

Her cousin approached with some starter salads and appetizers. "Am I interrupting anything?" he asked.

Rumila released Stuart's hand and said, "No cousin, we are trying to understand George Atkinson's last thoughts." "I would imagine they were distilled to what will become of my family and my work when I am gone?" her cousin replied.

Stuart looked up at the grey-haired Indian. "Do you hear of him or of his death here in the café?" Stuart asked. "Does anyone miss him?"

"No," the man replied quietly. "So many people die in Africa—of disease, of gunshot wound, in traffic accidents—that no one person is kept in community memory for long. The family--but you are the first one I have seen--never stop talking or thinking of recent death."

"Do you remember what people said immediately after his murder?" Stuart asked.

The elder Indian rubbed his stubbled chin. "Some said he deserved it; some said Africa's people would suffer—its corrupt government and ever-present foreign criminals and its people's resultant misery would not be revealed."

Stuart's face brightened. "You liked his stories."

"All of Africa liked his stories. They signaled problems Africa has. We have fixed a few. His honesty was always a risk."

"Thank you. He was an important part of my life. I'm sorry Africa took him away from us. May we have the check?"

"I'm sorry for your loss. The check? On the house. Joy to see my niece."

Stuart flagged two taxis. He sent one with Rumila to her home and took the other back to Maisie's hotel.

In his room he found Omega's card and smiled at the peaceful leopard facing him. Maybe he should have something like this on his business card.

Once connected, he asked, "Is the baby here?

"Great and healthy, too? How's your wife? And it's your watch? How are you?"

"I feel so useless. Baby only wants mom." Omega said, a yawn in his voice.

"Super. Does your wife have family nearby? I need your help."

"I told her I'd stay for one week," the African replied, "but she knows your time is short."

"I need you tomorrow. We need to set up for Grandpa's service."

"Tomorrow's Sunday and the relatives are all coming."

"Two days, then? You'll find me at the Arusha Hotel. I'm moving there tomorrow."

"Are you not safe at Maisie's?"

"I don't know. Oh and Omega, do you have a weapon?" Stuart asked, "Yeah, you told me you learned to throw a spear and that you have cousins who can save us if necessary. The knife's fine. Remember, I'm asking you to help me find my grandfather's killer. Whoever it was used his antique Maasai spear. Clearly some clue there. Although, other than the person who knew George well enough to enter his house without suspicion, I have no idea whether he or she used the spear or another equally complex tool.

"See you Monday. Give Georgina and your wife my best wishes."

After he hung up, Stuart left the room, entered the lobby and stepped out onto Maisie's 'conference hotel' front porch. He pulled out his packet of photos from his eight-year-old visit and studied a photograph of a cow, two small boys, one black, one white, and the staff with a carved cobra's head at the top he still hoped to find. The white child was Stuart, the black child's face resembled the poster Maasai at Farouk's. He groped for memories buried in this twenty-year old photograph that would help him now.

Mystified by these interlacing clues, he shook his head, a few drops of liquid escaping his nearly healed wound. The gun graze was leaking and his head ached. He typed Red Cross Arusha in his phone and scoured the myriad bubbles that showed up throughout Tanzania. There was a clinic nearby. He called for a taxi and headed to Njira Road.

He was examined by a Russian physician who was a female double for Vladimir Putin. The woman stitched it closed again, handed him more pain pills and hailed him a taxi outside the fence.

"Marta's my name if the stitches break open again."

Stuart muttered thank you and tried to pass her a few coins.

She shook her head. "Americans pay for this post."

Hailing a taxi to return to the hotel, he heard his phone buzz and read the text, "Call home."

He called immediately.

His mother did not wait for the customary greeting but began speaking immediately, "Stuart, it is critical that you get out of Arusha. Hold your grandfather's service and race to Dar Es Salaam."

"Mom, I cannot drive for a week. Head injury just re-treated by Red Cross physician who cautioned against driving."

"Leave as soon as you can."

"Relax, Mom. Why the hurry? I planned to hire Omega. His baby was born this morning after I met with Xiang Yu. He can leave in two days."

Finally, Madeleine said, "Xiang Yu, Stuart?"

"He told me Neissa is beautiful. Still beautiful and still in trouble I guess. I'm meeting with her in a few days so please email the Britzes that I'll be awhile. I think she wants to attend Atkinson's funeral so that's good. I'll text you date, time and place and give her your love."

Stuart groaned, thinking of the countless open ends and that he would soon be meeting with Neissa, his runaway sister.

Stuart hadn't thought of her for years. She rarely made contact with the family. She phoned him once from Logan Airport while he was at work, said she had a meeting in Boston. Could they get together?

It was a curious encounter. He remembered it in detail—

they were bidding to get a technology for an extra powerful electron microscopy lens. Erewhon was still quite a young company.

Bidding against unknown established VC firms in Boston and New York, Stuart had focused his attention on this bid. Roz hated science and maths—these were his strengths.

In their warehouse-like building, Stuart was head down, legal pad on one side and computer screen open, extracting relevant numbers from the project to see what was the real possibility of Erewhon's bidding on this expensive piece of technology. A grey-haired woman they had inherited from a closed department and who served as their receptionist touched his arm softly and left a note where he could not miss it.

Stuart glanced away from his column of numbers and read, "Sister Neissa (sp?) is passing through. Wants to know if you have time to see her. Left this number."

Stuart stared at the computer screen, saw his eyes staring back at him. Yes, he was all there. Sister Neissa. Gone before his birth. He dialed, thinking apart from Madeleine, and his then living grandfather, she was his only blood kin. Ran away. No address. No contact. Why now?

"Hello, Neissa. This is Stuart."

"Do you have time to meet up with me?" she said with no preamble. "I have tickets to the Red Sox…but then, internet says your firm is in its early stages. You probably work all night.

Rubbing his eyes and trying to keep his voice calm, he said, "We are busy but my partner and I make exceptions for family."

"Meet at the ball park?" Neissa said.

"I hate the Red Sox. Where are you now?"

"Ritz Carlton near the park."

"I'm in Brookline. That's twenty minutes away."

"I'll meet you in the lobby. I look like a tall Madeleine with blue eyes. Our dad's eyes."

"I never met him." Stuart said and waved at Roz. "Appointment downtown." He walked out of the building and headed to the Ritz.

Stuart had found Neissa leaning against a post, looking much as he had expected, aloof but resembling the rest of them. Same dark blonde hair, strands of grey. Like Stuart, she had an easy laugh.

Until that meeting, he only knew her by the pain she caused. When he was a teenager he had been rummaging in an old costume trunk and found all her childhood pictures from public school. When he brought the box to his mother, she had started crying immediately, motioning him to wait for an explanation. She breathed deeply and told him that this child named Neissa was his sister. She ran away after their father died and had not been seen since her brother's birth. She was fourteen years old when she ran away. He remembered being puzzled at the time and wondered why anyone would run away from his mother.

And now here, he had thought to himself, as he wandered into the Hotel Lobby she was. Would he find out why she ran away?

"Hello," she had said abruptly. "Except for Mom, we're all we have and since I've never seen you I wanted to meet you. Who knows when we'll be in need of kin?"

Curious reason, Stuart had thought, but what did he know about her.

"My trade is illegal; yours relies on luck. I might need your help someday. You may find need of mine."

"Want a coffee?" Stuart asked as the lobby bar waitress passed by.

"No time," Neissa had said. "I'm here to meet with some

clients. Since you're not into baseball, I'll move my meeting with them so I can go home. Just wanted to introduce myself in case we meet again."

"Where's home?"

"Africa." She had turned on her heel and Stuart still remembered staring at the space she had left behind.

He took the train home feeling like he'd been horse whipped. A friendly visit, he thought bitterly. He had no idea what she did. Back at the office he fired up his computer and Googled Neissa Lehrman. Nothing.

He never heard from her again and never told his mother she had visited him.

He brushed his hair off his forehead and tried to block this memory and focus on his mother. "Why only the three stories for the *Tribune*?"

"His last stories were designated for other papers. He gave the first of his ivory series to Ian but wanted one in the *Moroccan Times* and one in the *New York Times*."

"Did he know they would all be published posthumously?"

Madeleine sighed. "I think he hoped you'd help him unravel his problems with the traders. Other stories could be extrapolated from notes in his diaries. One is ripped and in the diaries; the others are fragments buried in his notes."

"The diaries in my hands?"

"Perhaps, if published, the memoir would be more dangerous to him personally than the two articles in the *Tribune*, the torn article and the article about a Chinese gang," Madeleine continued. "Read the diaries. They should make you smile. His writing, while pessimistic about the present state of humans, held out hope for the future. He wrote me once that he would like his memoir to be a tribute to the Africa and the people he loved, the freedom of the animals, the freedom that was not always reflected in tribalism and government figureheads and was, in fact, undermined by many powerful leaders and corrupt officials. The diaries also have derogatory facts about community leaders and merchants. The Xiang Yu notes are in one of the books, I think."

"What did Grandpa know that he wouldn't share?" Stuart asked. "I have half of an unfiled story, the oblique reference to Xiang Yu and our family. The torn story reads more like a diary entry than a story."

"Stuart, in the ripped article, I think he was hiding some idea, something or someone. In the Chinese article he was gathering information to explain what was happening to the Africa he loved."

"I received a letter last year on my birthday saying he was writing the book on an Africa we both loved that I would remember from my visit."

"That's why his last gasp was a call for you, Stuart. He knew you could help."

Stuart was quiet, absorbing the silence of Africa as tears eked out of the corners of his eyes. He pulled out a diary cum memoir segment he'd been reading, wiped his eyes with the back of his hand and cleared his voice. "Listen to this. You can almost see him pulling on his neatly trimmed moustache and grinning from ear to ear."

Nairobi

Omega picked me up at the New Stanley Hotel. We catalogued our gear. I was lacking the correct lens for our assignment. The Herald Tribune needed the story when the next world issue hit the stands in 36 hours. We had two hours to travel to the source. Omega signaled to the passenger seat in the Rover to Farouk's store. I knew I would not find an exact replacement but he would have a used lens for the Leica that would fit. Farouk always had a replacement—be it German, Japanese or African. "Atkinson, back so soon?" Farouk said.

I paid and turned abruptly, ending what was, on other days, an informative conversation with one of the most visited merchants in Arusha.

Omega and I stuffed enough food and ammunition for the several days' journey in the Land Rover and took off, arriving at a camp, by nightfall.

In the dusk we saw a herd of hartebeest, two giraffes, two herds of Thomsen and Grant gazelle. The "Thomies" with their white and tan stripes were so beautiful in motion that I could not resist wasting precious film as they ran across the Serengeti. Omega accelerated the Rover playing "race the gazelle" while both the camera and I hit the roof.

The mission was not a pleasant one. It was time to quit enjoying the beauty of the landscape and consider what I would say to the man at the docks......

Stuart paused, listening to his mother's soft chuckle. "The New Stanley is now the Sarova Stanley, hence the Nairobi service. It was your grandfather's favorite spot in Kenya."

Stuart added, "Mom, when I arrived and bought groceries from Maisie, she cautioned me against going to his house saying that it was haunted by the ghosts of those that George had denounced. She told me I needed to 'release these spirits and my grandfather's spirit and leave the country immediately.'

"I asked her how the ghosts got inside locked doors.

"Her eyes widened and she reminded me that I was not yet thirty. Police and local investigators do not open doors of houses where people have died. They are, she told me, 'Too terrified of their remains.'

"If I'm a lousy investigator, she's an unfeeling woman. Her

bills are paid by Xiang Yu. She collects packages from North and East Africa for his group, which I think are not legal goods. I think they sicced the gunmen on me at Grandpa's house to frighten me away, so they can continue their illegal trading activity without anyone's knowledge. Proof, I lack but I'm working on it." Stuart finished, thinking, a published story about child exploitation, one about ivory poachers, another ripped but curious one in his possession; yet another about the desecration of the continent; there must be a thousand reasons Atkinson would be dead, a thousand possible killers. Is ivory the connection? These diaries and papers were framed by the elephant tusks, but framed so that they could be found by someone with a key to the cashbox, namely me or another Atkinson. The story I have inside the memoirs is ripped in half. It might hold some critical information since it's covered with what Arusha police confirmed was animal, not human blood. The segment of the title remaining on the paper appeared to read, "Animals as slaves or something…."

"Tell me about Anton, Mom—the early partner? Would he have the ripped half of the unfiled story?" Stuart, stop, he thought, you're a VC from Boston, not a police detective from nowhere northwest. "He's in Dar Es Salaam and evil? I won't have to confront him until the end of this journey. I'll be leaving Maisie's after breakfast tomorrow. Her connections are undesirable. I must confess that Xiang Yu was very open about his illegal trading.

"But back to George. So Grandpa was protecting someplace, perhaps where animals are empowered?" Stuart shook his head and having answered his own question, "Could there be a connection between ivory and his death? Was he mixed up with the Chinese? And Farouk? Is he mixed up in the whole thing? And why the Britzes?"

Madeleine almost whispered, "Son, I don't know. You have

a family service for your grandfather in Nairobi, a possible clue in the camera, which won't be ready for weeks, during which time you can go on to Dar Es Salaam. Service first, Dar second, home third. Find out for yourself who the Britzes are. Please exercise caution. They are merciless. The sculptress is Anton's granddaughter and Alphonse's daughter. The family knows everyone in Africa. Be careful, though, your grandfather never trusted Anton. You should remember Anton from your summer camp in the desert. They were working together at that time."

"That tall blond guy? You're thinking he might have the other half of the story? I never liked the guy. What do you know about Xiang Yu?"

His mother sighed. "First—the tall blond guy Anton will not have the ripped story. As I said, your grandfather didn't trust him. The sculptor. Beautiful woman, I'm told. Not so tall as her father, Alphonse, who mostly looked over the top of my head and occasionally picked me up at the airport. Fast driver. Asked me to marry him. You need to spend enough time in Africa to find Grandpa's killer before the assassin targets me. Seems you're already a target. Find out what all the Britzes are doing. And what the granddaughter's sculptures signify. Get a hotel in Dar Es Salaam. They'll insist you stay with them and they're not to be trusted. Anton's crippled, has his granddaughter for company and a housekeeper whose two sons live with them. Alphonse lives in Nairobi and Turkey; his daughter will have an address. I have no idea where the ripped half of the story is, but I would doubt Anton would have the ripped story. If I were you I would not reveal you have it. They may think it is some kind of wonderful puzzle to complete now that your grandfather is dead. Alternatively, it may provide one of the keys to your finding his assassin.

"Xiang Yu—the Chinese connection? Asia is across the

Indian Ocean from Africa. And remember the tattoo gang story I told you about?"

"Yes, and I saw their tattoos; now we have to find the story and hang the guilt on this man.

"We need to short cut this when we can. I have only a limited amount of time to spend here. Several of my VC deals are still open in Boston." Stuart said. "Is Britz necessary? I didn't like the man when I was a child. He's doubtless more disgusting by now. If you think the visit will help find Grandpa's killer? I still have no verifiable assassin or motive. Shall I give up and fly home?"

"Stuart," Madeleine said quietly. "He would never give up on you. The Britzes, Maisie and Xiang Yu have always been connected because of illegal ivory. So the Dar trip is for fact finding only."

Stuart sighed. "Fine, I'll arrange for another week here. Neissa has asked for a meeting here which has extended my stay in Arusha by two days and who knows what that meeting will entail. As for Britz—his most awful features were his pale blue dry eyes. Thanks for not marrying into the family. I find it hard to believe I'll find anything there. He was not very bright."

His mother laughed. "You're most welcome and, with respect to Erewhon, never mind. It was Roz's idea. She thinks gaming technology of an African Virtual Safari needs African business backers, which is, she believes, why your major competitors are local African traders. So hold the memorial, interview the Britzes and fly home.

"If you're really looking for help regarding your grandfather's murder, ask Ian Smith, George's editor. Ian will be at the memorial. He lives in the Sarova Stanley, the hotel where the service will be held. About Neissa—thanks for healing rifts, Stuart."

"Someday I guess you'll tell me her story?"

"Later, Son. Let's get my dad taken care of. Neissa is a deep-seated pain in my heart and I will need to figure how to tell you what went wrong. Back to your grandfather—Is Omega's baby here?" Madeleine asked.

"I told you his baby was born while I was meeting the Chinese man in the market. Beautiful girl they named Georgina, after Grandpa."

"So it's off to Nairobi. Meet with Ian. Perform the service. Greet your sister. Tell her I miss her, if it fits. Finally, the Dar Es Salaam Britzes. Alphonse will be at the Nairobi Memorial Service, which is set for day after tomorrow. You can see for yourself what I gave up for your brilliant father. Yes, he has waterless blue eyes. Your father's eyes were blue also. Compare Neissa's steady blue-eyed gaze with the wandering eyes of the Britz family. I put the memorial announcement in the *Tribune* yesterday and his was the first email I received. I'll email Anton that you will be at the memorial and that I've heard from Alphonse."

Stuart hung up and dialed Omega. "How's the baby? Head upright?"

"They don't do that yet," Omega said.

"I need your help. Can you get away today?" Stuart asked.

"Yeah," Omega said, "I was going to phone. We went to church last night."

"Wonderful. See you later. You'll find me at the Arusha Hotel," Stuart said.

"So you said," Omega confirmed.

"Give Georgina and your wife my best wishes," Stuart added.

After he hung up, Stuart walked upstairs to the lobby and stepped out onto the Arusha Hotel porch. He ordered an India Pale Ale and looked out over the beautiful gardens.

His cell buzzed. "I come now," Omega texted.

"I come to table. We leave tomorrow. I'm tired of crying baby. Adults more fun. On way to Nairobi we stop by Aunt Lou, your grandfather's friend/mistress. She give you good African medicine. Make certain your head healed. Maybe she will have clues about George's murder."

Stuart grinned, the idea of meeting his grandfather's mistress mildly distasteful, yet doubtless quite interesting. Five minutes later Omega sat next to Stuart. "That was fast. So how's the baby?"

Like every other parent or grandparent Stuart had met, Omega whipped out his phone and scrolled slowly through the photos of birth to living creature. This part of children had only been shown to Stuart on videos at his school's "sex camp" in 8th grade. The tiny creature was covered with water and disappeared when placed on her father's shoulder. *Really, he thought, she looked like a slime covered toy.* As he watched Omega's smile deepen and broaden, he searched for the right words. "Her hands are so tiny."

Omega nodded. "We Maasai men—we large like lion king. Our wives are slender and fast like female lioness. Alice is tiny. When she is well, I bring baby Georgina and wife to meet you. But I warn you now, baby is noisy."

Stuart shrugged and said, "I'd like that," surprised that he actually meant it. He endured other peoples' kids. Some of his clients named their innovations after their children. The crazy African safari programmers had named each animal after a kid. But then, he thought, pitching your game to kids maybe it's good to call the hyena, "Ray," not Hyena.

"My grandfather would be honored to have a girl with his name."

Omega blushed. "We know other Georges too. We thought

about Madeleine because your mother loved my people. I never met Madeleine, but Aunt Lou knew your mother. My wife said no Madeleine for first child because then we would be cursed with twelve little girls who walk in two straight lines."

Stuart smiled. "My mother does not like her name. Children taunted her at school; even graduate students teased her with verse."

Stuart began and Omega chimed in when he knew the words. "In an old house in Paris all covered with vines...." Stuart interrupted the flow and said, "Enough. I need some time to myself. I'll find you in front of the hotel tomorrow. I'll go repack my stuff. We have a long drive to Nairobi and a memorial to prepare. And where, on earth, do you learn all these American stories? Certainly not in school."

Omega grinned. "We do have your textbooks, but mostly learn English language in school. When I start working, I learn about Americans and their stories. I pick up Americans in taxi and I listen to them read to their children. Europeans too stuffy. They colonize us and sometimes still treat us like their slaves. Americans wear crazy clothes, laugh and joke in taxi. They more like us. Funny, though, they all carry water bottles. Even you."

"Used to clean water," Stuart said, his hands on the bottle on his belt. "See you in the morning."

CHAPTER TWELVE

Tangiers, Morocco

The sun was setting into the Mediterranean when Neissa squared her toes, sprang into the air, and executed a perfect swan dive. As she spread her arms wide, she hovered in the air like a glider on a thermal, snapped her legs and arms into a perfect line inches before the small peaceful sea below. She smiled as she splashed through the low waves in the calm water and swam vigorously toward the sinking yellow orb on the horizon. As the sun disappeared from sight she turned quickly and swam vigorously to the shore, putting on her warm robe and slippers before the darkness became cool.

Nipples erect, she strode toward the grey Toyota that had been her only vehicle for thirty years. She dressed in the warmth of the car and was unlocking the padlock on her home office gates before the blackness of the African night enveloped every tree house and business that wasn't lit. Her own home, well-lighted and large, was inconspicuous in the line of other mansions along the waterfront.

Her journey had followed a path that facilitated her current occupation. She had lived most of her life as an expatriate using her given name, first in France, then in Morocco using her African name. In Morocco she was adopted by a French-Moroccan family, the Abencours and carried a French passport. She acquired an English literature certificate from the University of Kenya. University had been a challenge because her English was imperfect and it was the principal language of the former English colony. However, she was not the only white face there and many did not have the mastery of Africa that she had. A small private college in Oregon had an exchange program in Kenya each year. She made certain she attended their classes. Fortunately, many were literature oriented.

She chose Kenya for University because she wanted to improve her English and she was eager to attend large lectures run by Alphonse Britz, the son of her grandfather's partner. Neissa's thesis was a negative response to her father's academic work, which focused on amelioration of societal structure inherent in utopic novels. Her honors thesis, "Utopia: Art at its Worst," was grounded in Alphonse Britz's sociology courses, which she used to prove the governmental disaster wreaked by harboring hope. One professor actually asked her if she'd studied Professor Lehrman's work, so she mentioned several of his articles in a turgid prose footnote.

At first she tried to befriend other students from America, Britain, and other English-speaking countries, but her abrupt manner and demanding questions were off-putting to the easy-going men and women from the U.S. Additionally, her mastery of Swahili and several other tribal languages, and her height intimidated most students she encountered. At six feet, the svelte muscular woman was as strong, and only a few inches shorter than her brother Stuart.

Friendless, she retreated to isolation in her first apartment, then after well-launched in trade, into the large mansion she had built in Tangiers. When she was well-enough connected to start her own business, she was glad she had managed to learn English—Americans and European Union members were among her most frequent callers. Her trade was not only valuable to them and their intelligence agencies, her ability to maneuver quietly and efficiently through the African countries was worth money to them. This side business funded her import-export business and provided her with protection throughout the continent. It amused her to serve as informant to Western countries who decried the poaching of ivory, set up the rules against its trade, causing her lucrative tusk trade to be illegal. She was breaking the law. Like her masters thesis that was skeptical of her father's focus on Utopian futures, her daily living enabled her to get back at her mother. Daily she proved that the "rule of law" did not touch her trade of tusks, drugs and guns. Her connection with African and Western intelligence agencies perversely shielded her and helped her business. She gave tips regarding her competitors and alerted officials to any activity in East Africa where the elephants and rifle and pistol trade flourished. She learned to fly so that she could trace her tusks and firearms shipments throughout the continent. She was cleared to land in Nairobi, Arusha and Dar Es Salaam.

She had little interest in her birth family. She never contacted her grandfather in East Africa, but harbored no ill feelings toward George. She visited her brother to confirm she resembled the rest of her family, but never appeared at the old man's house. It was Seattle and her parents she had hated and had run away from. She was religious about reading all of George Atkinson's articles and grinned as she thought how helpful they had proven when moving goods through the continent. She was particularly interested in a posthumous article advertised to appear today as it featured an interview with a man now in her employ. Curious his remaining articles were being parceled out posthumously. Perhaps willing readers to believe the writer was still alive, she thought. Or perhaps it was the *Herald Tribune's* own means of memorializing the man.

The absence of personal friendships or connections was necessary in her trade, but her biting sarcasm was an angry spitefulness that distinguished her from the rest of her family. Her African born mother used her skills of survival to win court cases; Neissa used hers to outsmart the law. Her brother Stuart combined his family members' different intelligences and set up a business with Utopian dreams for fledgling startup companies' success, based on contract and the rule of law.

Neissa's occasional need for human contact and innate curiosity sent her to Fenway to seek out this brother she had never seen. Otherwise, she worked only among trusted Africans in her employ and had no personal friends. Sometimes she would drop in unannounced at employees' homes to play with their children or chat with their spouses. A runner and swimmer, she was strong and capable of moving product alone, if no one was on hand. Her few luxuries included her house and her cuisine.

She pulled her compact Toyota into the three car garage adjacent to the brightly lit multi-storied Mediterranean villa and strode to the front door where the maid already was standing in front of an open door. The maid handed her the mail and said, "What time is dinner, ma'am?"

"Eight o'clock, as usual. On the terrace, please. It's warm." Leaving the efficient woman behind to prepare her eight course meal of mini-dishes, Neissa entered the open double door that was her office, closing the doors behind her. A computer screen as large as the desk it was on, faced her, but did not eclipse the coastal view.

She turned the spotless new machine on, groaned when the

overhead lights flickered, while the lights and computer battled for the weak power that the emergency generator provided. Since no one in her aristocratic neighborhood, including herself, would consider being without air conditioning, the emergency generator was on more during the summer than the winter when the sea was temperate, not boiling.

She removed the iphone from her pocket and downloaded the most recent updates from Tanzania, Republic of Congo and South Africa. She traced her fingers along the caravan that had started at Capetown and was headed to a Tanzanian border town near the Congo.

She phoned her foreman and asked where they were now. He sent her an image: the boat was in a queue waiting to offload its cargo at Dar Es Salaam, Tanzania.

"Excellent," she muttered. "They'll arrive in time."

She checked another screen then split them to see what was coming out of the Congo. Nothing. Where was it? She sent several emails, then opened the *Herald Tribune*. Her grandfather's second posthumous story. Scanning through it, she wondered, had he known about her? How his stories ran her business? There was always something left unsaid in his stories about ivory. Was the old man protecting her? She tried to read between the lines as she had learned to do in the former French colony of Morocco where much was left unsaid to confuse the natives. Did he know the featured men in some of his stories were in her employ? Had they told him? He must know something. His renown as an "Africa-first" journalist was legendary. He would expose her if he knew. Or did blood run thicker than water? Stop, Neissa, her unconscious shouted, "Your business is making you paranoid."

She opened the paper, wondering about Ian Smith, the editor who found all these wonderful stories for her grandfather, and turned to Atkinson's story to read:

[Ed. Note: George Atkinson was murdered two weeks ago. This is the first of several posthumous stories sent to us by relatives. Look for reprints of "Elephants Survive" and "Asian Tongs" over the next month]

[…Republic of Congo]

Blood and Ivory: The Nature of Animal Subjugation

I hadn't seen the elephant or I would have had time to move. It was charging and was now 30.5 meters (100 feet) from the car. A shot rang in my ears and before I could photograph her charge, the ancient cow was lying on her side, her tiny tusks sawed off at the roots. Remembering the initial pain of tooth-pulling even after the anesthetic had kicked in, my heart went out to the old girl. But where was the culprit? My driver and I walked the area and it occurred to me that perhaps it was her or us. We would have been lunch if that precise shot had not been fired between her eyes. So what do they claim in court? Self-defense and illegal slaughter? We wandered around the plains trying to find the rest of the herd. Surely there was a tusker belonging to this female. We let the sun set and went out again near the water but saw no herds.

Two days later

A shot rang out in the distance. Wallowing in the water was a wart hog that had had reasonable tusks and whose bulk displaced the water in the stream as though it were a tiny tugboat. Like the elephants' tusks, the hogs' tusks were also sawed off at the roots. No self-defense here. Just murder and burglary. But surely there was something else? We weren't even on safari. The murderers were taking nothing from us. We were trying to decipher the nature of poaching. Were these deaths leading us to the answer? Was all the ivory taken just as we arrived at the grasslands? And who was dealing in this trade? Up early the next day. We saw the first illicit ivory stockpiled next to native huts.

I scribbled notes and clicked frame after frame. Our hired natives retreated to the Rover, knowing they did not want to know why we were here and that they did not want to answer questions.

When I said as much to my Maasai driver, he smiled and said, "Africans are born with some sense that you don't have. Knowledge of another world maybe."

What was ivory's mystery? Historically it had been in demand. Hannibal captured Rome on the back of elephants. The Greeks made Athena an ivory throne. A mysterious attractive nuisance that caused the sculptor's life to fall into shambles. Thinking of this curious historical anecdote I wandered deeper into the Selous which is, at animal resting time, one of the most peaceful places in Africa. Larger than the Serengeti it is sprinkled with giraffes, elephants, gnus. Included in the reserve are grasslands, Acacia forests, wetlands, and in each of them is a unique and colorful collection of African mammals, reptiles or birds to be unearthed. The elephants, which used to number in the 100s of thousands, are down to the tens of thousands. Their tusks, which brighten the lives of Asian monarchs and are used by craftsmen for insets in coramandel screens, game boards, even small figurines, have diminished their number. Since elephants and rhinoceroses, whose tusks were the most valuable, were endangered species, poaching is illegal but piles of shucked ivory like those we had seen by the huts, were picked up by rangers and stored in a huge hangar-like building. What good do they do? Rangers do not keep them; outsiders are known to have made connections for the rangers to market the tusks. But what about this poacher, I wonder. I return, ask for names of colleagues, finally ask who I may contact on his behalf. The old poacher widens his eyes until they cover his face.

"You help me?" he says, the sarcasm so bitter I stood back as if slapped.

"You white people who have no babies, take ours and subjugate

us?" He turned to the wall.

When I met up with my driver we went into Arusha to find another poacher who he said might talk. This tall warrior carried only a spear, a leathern shield and a necklace of ivory tusk tips around his neck. His long ears hung to his shoulder, pierced with a piece of wood from the baobab tree. He looked away at first when he saw the cameras, but finally with $200 in his pouch he smiled, leaning on the spear and began his story,

"I have large family, elephants pay well. As a young warrior I killed lion to earn spear, must now pay old fool half my pay to keep it sharp. In another life, the warrior says, I will make spears, more consistent living. Always people killing, always need spears. Black women fertile; black men virile. Make babies. Can't feed. Daughters become prostitutes. Our daughters are sold to pimps to help families eat. My daughters are all over the world. Best lovers in the world, we hear. All our girls send money home. When favorite daughter leave to sell herself, I tell wife, "No more of this. I kill elephants. We eat." He grinned and continued, "Now daughters stay home."

"I no hurt animals like men hurt my daughters. Spear death is efficient death. Animal barely know it. I place spear next to heart, animal die immediate."

But if the animal charges, the poacher has a more clever scheme. He carries two spears: one for the heart, one for the brain. Poachers are more interested in rhinoceroses than elephants this man tells me. They fetch more money. They are rare and the Chinese pay many dollars for them. These poachers, sons of hunters who were white man's animal trackers, have learned to hunt like white men. If they did not learn from the great white hunters, they join up with a wildlife park ranger and offer to count animals for them. Rangers are desperate, sometimes very timid, chosen by the Ministry of Tourism. This ministry is inefficient, under-staffed, filled with an overpaid collection of upper class Tanzanians. I ask the man how he tracks a rhino.

"I climb a tree," he says, "wait for them to come to a grassland and graze, then I follow them for kill."

Three distinct knocks at Neissa's office door announced her dinner. She checked her watch. Exactly eight o'clock. She walked to the terrace off her office where a complete service for one was placed. Neissa's eyes glistened when she surveyed her meal. Each small plate was covered by a silver belltop, although not everything was hot. She smiled at her enticing meal. She had perfected this system of dining with her first house servant. Solitude was her choice of dining companion and she nodded at its pleasant absence as she removed the first belltop. A cold avocado soup was served in a crystal shot glass. As she finished her chicken breast her cell phone rang.

She frowned and didn't answer.

After she finished her flan, she checked the message and telephoned her foreman.

"What do you mean they won't let you in the country," she said in a shrill voice.

"I'll get back to you," she responded. She dialed her connection in Dar Es Salaam and asked in a low snarl, "What's wrong?"

"I know it's contraband but you've had no trouble before. Yes I'll put an additional $20,000 in your account."

Neissa quietly finished her dinner, rang the bell, re-entered her office through the glass terrace doors and went upstairs. She closed and locked her door, then made her phone call. To remain safe and secure she changed maids annually. Neissa would have trouble giving this maid up. She was a particularly good cook.

When she left her mother's house at fourteen, she was fascinated by her grandfather, his skills and his devotion to Africa.

Did she have a skill that Africa might need? She fled across the country, muscular at 16 by the time she reached New England. In Boston, she stowed away on a cargo ship bound for Marseilles. When at last she was found she made herself useful as a cabin boy, she learned how ships worked and that not everything that went through France was strictly legal. She begged the French cabin boy to teach her French, paying him with the last of her saved allowance—$15. By the time she reached Marseilles, she could speak passable French and she had learned from the bartender how to make every drink he knew. She stole away from the ship and made her way to a pub where she used her smattering of French to speak with the American bartender, who was so overwhelmed with drink orders, her stately bearing and passable bartending abilities that he hired her on the spot.

She had found a pension in Marseilles and enlisted a teenager to teach her nearly flawless French, then she wandered back to the dock and boarded a ship for Morocco. She attached herself to an old French couple, the Abencours, and asked if they needed help in their home.

The former French consulate to Morocco eyed the 18-year-old warily and said in English: "Are you certain you can give up 'life, liberty and the pursuit of happiness?' Morocco is a kingdom. Woman are discriminated against in the heavily Muslim populated nation."

"I need employment, then I will find a trade. Since I ran away at fourteen before my younger sibling was born, I have never been missed. The United States has not been home since I was sixteen. My mother, still mourning my father, did not look for me after he was born. I received a recent letter from the family lawyer—how he found me, I don't know—but what remains of the family estate after my mother dies has been left to my brother. I have been doing demanding chores since my early escape from America. France is a great catchall for runaways, once you learn the language and to defer to them. The latter lesson I learned as a teen, the language I learned when I landed and once moderately conversational, I learned to sail, make drinks, scrounge food." She laughed. "I can mix any highball you might imagine. And a few you may never have heard of."

The consulate's wife scrutinized the strong child thinking about all the lonely children in their home country and said, "Of course we'll employ you, until you find a trade. I was alone once myself."

Neissa stayed with the Abencours, worked her way into their lives, asked to be part of their family for several years. She attended high school and received a certificate. Ms. Abencour, childless, was taken with Neissa and under the disapproving eyes of her husband, begged him to adopt her. When they did, Neissa took their name and got a French passport.

Four years after she arrived, Neissa Abencour was ready to move on. She scanned the papers daily for a viable trade and was intrigued by a vague posting about financial genius and ivory tusk trading. Her application was accepted. She thanked the Abencours for their hospitality, promised to visit occasionally and moved into a small flat. She began as a clerk at a firm called Ivory Post and took over the business when tusk trading laws were passed. She bought her secluded Moroccan home on her twenty-first birthday after it became clear she was endangered at port towns in Kenya and Tanzania where her goods were traded. She read of the Abencours' deaths about one year after she left them.

CHAPTER THIRTEEN

Alphonse stared out the double pane safety glass in his Istanbul office. Below him was the 40 foot yacht he used for pleasure and transport—The Madeleine II—rocking slowly in the Marmara Sea at the mouth of the Mediterranean. The presence of the Lehrman boy in Africa troubled him although he knew police investigation was not this young man's field of expertise. Once in love with Stuart's mother, Alphonse had left Tanzania and moved to Kenya when she had refused him. In hindsight, it had been a lucky break. He married an Englishwoman and had one daughter. They had lived in Nairobi until his wife's death. While his father Anton had remained friends with the Lehrman family, he had no further contact with the Atkinson-Lehrman family. When his father was gored, Anton's business affairs were switched to Alphonse's name, which together with his ivory trade set him up for life.

A spineless man, Alphonse never told his daughter that his best friend had killed her mother. Instead he made the man indebted to him and kept him imprisoned in the paperwork of Alphonse's business because of his guilt. He sent her to boarding school and Oxford in London and bought a sailboat. The year his father was gored, his daughter had just broken off with a boyfriend.

When Alphonse encouraged her to quit school and look after the old bastard she was more than happy to leave London.

That was the only time her father visited her at university. He knew she divined the circumstances around her mother's death were contrived and never allowed himself to be close to her. When he went to Africa, he stayed in the Nairobi mansion he had built for his first wife. An underpaid but honest South African colleague ran one end of his business in an office near the Indian Ocean; he handled everything else from Istanbul. His boat and his apartment near the Hagia Sofia were his refuge. He lived on his yacht in the South Seas when it was cold. A native African, he spent the winter chasing warmth. Istanbul was lovely in the summer—25 Celsius or slightly higher. In winter his trade picked up and he moved back to the Nairobi office. During one cold summer he sailed into the warmth of Fiji and met Selina, now his second wife. He considered moving his office to the Pacific Islands. The clever gangs in the community, however, jeopardized his work. The first shipment that went astray brought the Britzes back to the Istanbul and Kenya offices.

He disliked the Nairobi house—as it renewed thoughts of his dead wife—and the Istanbul apartment as it reminded him of work.

He was happiest when sailing. The freedom of the open sea, its intense breeze blowing through his thinning hair and the capable cooking of his young wife made every day at sea an experience he treasured. Having recently checked his email, Alphonse paced outside his office, waiting for an update so he could sail South into equatorial warmth. His wife would remain in Turkey where she had established some African business interests that kept her busy.

Alphonse converted to Islam, enabling him to hire more efficient traders from Turkey and North African countries.

Uncomfortable in the presence of dark-skinned people he spent little time in Central and East Africa. His employees were always fair-skinned wily continental residents or descendants of French colonials. His wife was the fairest of South Sea Islanders.

His principal competitor, of Anglican heritage, worked alone or with Muslim Berbers and other African tribes throughout Africa. While the Indian Ocean was the most direct route to his Asian and African consumers, his tradespeople traversed the Atlantic to reach Turkey via the Mediterranean. In Istanbul he was on the cusp of Western European, African and Arab cultures. At this historic moment, as when the Ottomans ruled, the Arabs seemed to have the upper hand.

A soft knock on the door indicated several sailors had arrived for interviews. They were scheduled to arrive every two hours in pairs for the next four hours. He used as small a team as possible because he trusted no one. Beaten mercilessly as a child with his father's camera bags and walking sticks, he had never raised a finger against his employees. Owing to his coloring and aloof demeanor he commanded their respect. He was so fair that his employees believed him to be god-like. He advised one laggard that his father had received parts of the Christian god into his soul when he was gored. The Christian god did not tolerate idleness so they should beware.

From his first wife he had developed an admiration for the Maasai's strength. Four lived full time at the Nairobi house. Each one was hand-picked by him and he asked them to inform on one another. Tribal loyalty superseded all other loyalties so he never heard of any wrongdoing.

Alphonse ignored the evening call to prayer but walked across the street from his apartment to the Hagia Sofia to study the remains of the Byzantine mosaics, passing Mary holding the baby and the large repaired face of a rather Turkish-looking Christ.

He rarely missed his daughter and past life. Examining the mosaic, he marveled that European bloodlines ran through his veins. His cell phone rang, announcing the arrival of the next several sailors and a shipment for him at the dock. He indicated he would be there at once. He ordered his old Arab secretary to send the sailors to the dock.

His spies had intercepted a shipment of tusks bought by his main competitor. He valued the clever deviousness of the Turks and the absolute honesty of the North Africans. He figured the men who worked for him probably took a slice of his profits by underpaying their traders. Who cared? He had the ivory. He could send in the other shipment. When he left the cell phone area he walked back by the mosaic, winked at Mary and muttered *Inshallah* to the Christ figure.

He phoned his secretary and said, "Tell Xiang Yu a large shipment is coming his way. I need the payment at once. Phone Anton and tell him to prepare for a large shipment and send the exacto knife on my desk to my daughter special delivery. Instruct Anneliese to keep it in her studio."

"Any messages?"

"Only from Xiang Yu who re-iterates his need for ivory which you have fulfilled and your father who would like you to phone. He believes the Lehrman boy in Africa may complicate your shipments."

"When you phone Anton tell him not to worry." Britz rubbed his chin and wondered what he and Xiang would be required to do about George Atkinson's grandson. Would Madeleine be devastated if her son were dead? He rubbed his hands together, thinking he'd give it some thought.

On his way home he stopped by his mistress's house, found

her business slow and her large white girth comforting as he slid effortlessly inside the mammoth woman. He stopped by the Health Club, walked on the treadmill for thirty minutes, showered and went home. His wife had prepared a goulash with a slice of meat for him. She barbequed the meat quickly, then walked to the terrace where Alphonse stood. She embraced him, her head barely reaching his chest, knowing full well his attention was elsewhere. The intercepted boats' cargo was successfully transferred and new cargo loaded onto the empty boat. He chuckled.

"Successful transfer, I guess," his wife said softly.

He nodded. "Stolen goods in exchange for rebel treasures."

She frowned. While she did not fully understand her husband's work and he never spoke of it, she believed it helped a few people but harmed more than it helped. Alphonse had told her once that, "he profited when others lost."

CHAPTER FOURTEEN

Neissa slammed down the phone and shrieked at the maid, "My trading log. At once!"

Struggling under its weight Neissa's diminutive maid carried out a stack of five thick books which, when combined, were as thick as the hard bound OED. Taking the massive tomes, Neissa tied back her shoulder length hair and flipped the worn pages one at a time until she found the text she was seeking. She pushed autodial on her phone and spoke a name and address into the receiver.

Within moments she heard sirens down the street. She walked to the terrace and watched an ambulance and police car screech around the corner to a nearby hospital.

Her phone buzzed about twenty minutes later. "The ship owner is now dead," the text read.

Sorry to have several disloyal employees—the captain and crew—she needed to find more. The informant would keep his job and get a raise. Her first choice, the Maasai Omega who once worked for her grandfather George Atkinson, turned her down after Atkinson's death. As was the Maasai way, he never said why. She offered him three times the salary her grandfather paid, but like all Maasai he was exceedingly loyal. She was afraid there was a connection between his loyalty to George Atkinson and her ongoing problems finding good help. She phoned a Berber friend. Not necessarily the most aggressive of Africans, they were, nonetheless, available and they could take orders. They were also, she remembered as she rubbed a scar on her hand, selfish and family-oriented. One of her cooks who was Berber became pregnant. When Neissa kept the cook over her agreed upon hours the woman's husband came after her with a tiny knife. Skilled in martial arts she had received only the hand wound. In this case, she had won the battle with words when the woman agreed to work overtime for the unborn child's school fees and for the family's food and protection.

She phoned a Berber contact in Fes and asked for a captain and crew recommendation.

After several minutes of silence she said, "Well?" "Yes, my brother is smart but will do nothing illegal…..unless….," her voice trailed off, "You start tomorrow."

She hung up and dialed again. "Dalik, what's the game worth? I'll give your team twice that. Yes, I know about him. I want Erewhon out. Yes, I know your team's loyalty is to MIT and Harvard. How about some loyalty to your country? Yeah, you're Harvard-educated but you owe Erewhon nothing—besides it's a stupid name—means nowhere. You're native Kenyan. Wouldn't you like to bring business to your country?"

"We want the best offer and the best circulation of our technology," Dalik said. "Further, my partners are from all over the world. We're based in Cambridge because we met there. The knowledge we've gained will be useful worldwide. It pleases all of us that we can give back after we've taken so much."

"So then, listen up," Neissa interrupted. "With my firm's backing you and my overseas network can create a marketing team that would be impossible for Erewhon or any other bidder to match. Besides I may work together with Erewhon to get you started. So talk to your partners. I fly to Nairobi for my grandfather's funeral and will be meeting with my brother there. Let me know if you are interested, if not in my exclusive offer or a combined Erewhon— Abencours, Ltd. Team offer. "

Desperate for assistance, Neissa had texted her brother. They would meet after George's funeral in Nairobi, not in Arusha.

She remembered her first meeting with Stuart and wondered if her brother would be of help. Would he help her with or without the Dalik and Madeleine threats? He had seemed reasonable when she met with him. But you only determine a person's metal under pressure. She grimaced, thinking *something my mother would say.*

CHAPTER FIFTEEN

Stuart texted Roz and phoned the concierge at the Hotel Arusha, the former to inform her of his whereabouts and the latter to confirm he had a room.

Roz texted back immediately, "So it's not going too well, eh?"

"It will be better when I get out of here, which is in a few minutes. I have a plan. Seems my sister is desperate to help us. Albeit illegal, we may have an African network in place."

"Let me know. Don't know if it helps us to be mixed up in illegal trading."

Stuart walked into the Hotel Arusha where the balding concierge met him with his usual equanimity. "Nice to have you back, sir. The Atkinsons are Africa's friends."

"Thank you," Stuart said. "I had hoped for a longer respite here but my mother wants me to push on. I'll be here overnight only. I'm off to do my grandfather's memorial in Nairobi. Fortunately, I get to do both the funeral and my own work in Nairobi so it won't be all doom and gloom. Speaking of which, do you play videogames?"

The black man's cheeks brightened and he lifted up an iphone with the latest "Star Wars" game on it. "Yessir, I do...it's a favorite African pastime. Our kids waste homework time on the games so my wife and I try to buy them educational ones with math and geography pointers in them."

Stuart sent this almost verbatim to Dalik and copied Roz. "Atkinson's funeral is at the Sarova Stanley day after tomorrow. Would you remind people if they ask?" he asked the concierge.

The smiling black man nodded. "About the service—yes, sir. It was in the paper, but I'll remind everyone."

Dalik answered his text. "The game is to educate Omega's new kid and my older brother's kids. Our one sister has kids who might like it, but don't tell them their uncle designed it."

Doubting he'd ever meet any of Dalik's nephews he ticked off what else he had to do before going to Nairobi.

His new iphone blasted. "Hi Roz. I told you I'd call you."

"I know, but I thought you would love this delicious news. Agarwal and Chen want to turn your grandfather's house into a clinic for a new malaria vaccine. I've told them we'll find funding to back the vaccine if they pay for the re-building of your grandfather's house."

"Grandpa's house is a hole."

"They know that. They want the location and they don't want to have to tear anything down."

"This is great news and we get the vaccine also?"

"Yeah, now you've got to go find all the deeds for the house so we can turn it over."

"I'll search through the diaries and head to the police station, but will have the police fax them when they are found. In the meanwhile I'll phone my mother and ask her if she has them."

"Text me what you know."

"Hey thanks, Roz. Atkinson would love to know that his house was being used to do something good."

"Doesn't hurt us any either," Roz said.

When Stuart hung up, he set the phone down and tried to figure how to break this to his mother. Using his newest iphone, he dialed her cell and just decided to give no preludes.

"Hey mom, Our MOAB client wants to rebuild Grandpa's house and turn it into a native clinic for testing a new malaria vaccine."

Stuart held the phone away from his ear and smiled when he heard his mother shout, "Hooray!" She paused. "Are you safe?"

"Yes, Mom, I'm still safe. Do you have the deed for the house?"

"I have a legal copy. I'll fax it to Nairobi tomorrow."

"Thanks, I'll call later," Stuart replied.

"Careful, son, you have Neissa, the service and the blue eyed Britzes to deal with. I need you healthy. You ought to come home someday. Your apartment sparkles."

Stuart smiled. "Thanks."

When Omega arrived the next day, Stuart walked to the concierge and said, "What do I owe you?"

"The usual and I'll tot it up on the credit card on file."

"Thanks, hope to see you again soon," Stuart replied.

While Omega loaded Stuart's backpack into the taxi, Stuart glanced at the garden and the lobby. He did not want to leave this place, his grandfather's favorite haunt. Or this town, where his grandfather died. The Nairobi visit was necessary. He was honored to pay tribute to his grandfather but slightly nervous about the prospect of who would be in his audience, if the venue was safe or another open shooting range.

The last African stop, Dar Es Salaam—and the blond people actually terrified him. However, with the figurines at his mother's house, the Britz visit could be illuminating and was now necessary. He needed to learn about the figurines, if the figurines were a warning or actually caused death.

Stuart was glad his mother was in Boston. The entry to his pleasant Brookline apartment flashed through his memory. He longed to go home but would never be happy not knowing why his grandfather had died and why he had sent for him when he knew he was in danger.

"Let's go," Stuart said and crawled into the half-car, hands on the passenger strap as Omega raced through the split lanes of Arusha to what Stuart presumed was Omega's home.

"We get other vehicles. I say good-bye to wife and baby." Omega said and pulled up to a modest home with a daylight basement. Pointing to a tan van of Japanese make, Omega said, "Put your things in the van. I return."

Stuart did not take that as an invitation to follow Omega into the house, so he walked to the van, placed his backpack on the back seat and sat in the passenger's seat. He searched his phone for the quickest route to Nairobi and had found it when Omega returned. Stuart looked around the yard, noticing he had parked his taxi next to a Toyota sedan.

"Why so many vehicles?" he asked.

"I like cars. Wife doesn't like the taxi." Omega paused. "Now relax, I blast through town and head straight to freeway. The countryside is barren between here and Nairobi. New York sister-in-law says highway stores look like strip malls in New Jersey."

Stuart stared at the end to end markets, dress shops and people standing around. New Jersey, Iowa, Middletown anywhere, he thought. "Sure this is the best way to Nairobi?" His phone indicated several direct routes that looked faster.

"Not straightest route, but only paved road. Morem comes from near here and is not on the straight dirt roads, which are filled with holes deeper than this van."

"Morem?"

"African asphalt. That reddish colored road cover is African dirt mixed with water and chemicals. Since it's made close to here, this crooked road is the fastest road to Nairobi. Here my country cousins and the Erak people herd their cows because it's easy walking."

"How long does it take to get to Nairobi?" Stuart asked as Omega swerved to miss five or six cows herded by a man covered with the checked cloth that distinguished the Maasai.

"Five hours by bus; three hours with Omega!"

Stuart grimaced, wondering what guardrail they'd go over, but noticed that cars roared past Omega on both sides of the highway, screeching and careening only to miss the natives and their animals.

The landscape changed very little as they drove. Omega had promised dramatic vistas when they went to Dar Es Salaam but nothing special on this trip. On the trip to the coastal Dar Es Salaam they would pass through the Serengeti and stop to see Africa's famous animals. They would see a few animals between Arusha and Nairobi. But only because it was not tourist season and the animals roamed the countryside at will, unthreatened by cameras or trackers or tourist buses.

Stuart looked forward to any animals Omega might find and settled into his seat with the intent to extract some African history from Omega. "Tell me about the Maasai," Stuart said. "I'm told they are good hunters, they hit game so it dies quickly. My grandfather did not die instantly. It was someone who could not throw a spear or someone who hated him that hit him in the guts."

"That is true," Omega began, "about our tribe, let me give you a few basics.

"Tribal Maasai reveal age and marital status through clothing and walking sticks. A married man wears a red checked cloth. An unmarried man wears both blue checks and red checks. Our women are all in blue. Junior Maasai carry thin sticks; senior warriors carry thick sticks. The village elder carries a thin, stick, with a special carved handle. All handles vary."

"My grandfather had an unusual walking stick with a flat head, shaped like a cobra. It was from a source who was a good friend. Would he have been a Maasai?" Stuart asked. *He had loved that serpentine staff. Where was it?*

"Special elders, sometimes laibon or Maasai doctors had such staffs," Omega explained. "I am glad you not think my people kill your grandfather. He Maasai friend. Besides, Maasai do not miss. They hit moving target in heart. A target like your grandfather he die at once."

Omega rolled up his long-sleeved shirt in the late afternoon warmth. "Maasai are from South Kenya and North Tanzania. We have specific tribal customs and we follow them in village. We modern Maasai wear Western clothes, but go home at holidays to be blessed by our parents. Many of our parents are Christian. I am Christian. We stop at my aunt's village on way to Nairobi. Stop for fifteen minutes. I introduce you to Aunt Lou, the healer. Your grandfather come by here occasionally. Good friends," Omega said smiling. "Too old to connect as lovers."

Stuart grinned, glad his grandfather had a friend to visit. He noticed they were passing all the big buildings, moving out of Arusha to the main road. Outside town was a police checkpoint. Stuart wondered why. This country was not at war. The crisply pressed and white uniformed officer scribbled a ticket for Omega while scolding him in the singsong notes of Swahili. It was, Stuart thought, like being chastised by a teacher who knew you forgot words but would never forget jingles. The white gloved man stopped midway and looked at Stuart's white face.

"Tourist?" he said in English.

Stuart and Omega nodded yes.

The man tore up the ticket.

When they passed through the checkpoint, Stuart asked, "Why checkpoints and why the ticket?"

Omega frowned and hung his head. "Kenya has trouble with foreigners, we have checkpoints. I got the ticket because I not wear seat belt. I should pay it but tourism is big business here. Police did not want you to have bad impression. This is large part of policeman salary. Our system is not corruption-free.

"Now I want you to think less about murders and corruption and admire north Tanzania. We pass the mountains soon. Before we leave Tanzania, we pass giraffes, our national animal, humble like Tanzanians. Soon we drive away from the land of giraffes into grass-filled savannahs, the occasional African animal and enter road lined by Nairobi strip malls."

Stuart zoned out while Omega babbled on and on about trees, flowers and national animals.

Just before the Kenyan border, Omega swung the van onto a tiny dirt road. The abrupt movement startled Stuart into wakefulness and before the van was swallowed by a hole in the road Omega deftly moved the oversized vehicle onto a dusty road.

Why would anyone want a large car in Africa, Stuart thought and asked, "Omega, are we on a detour or is this some fantastic shortcut?"

"We're going to my aunt's village," Omega said, "but first

you look up there."

Stuart followed Omega's finger to a dun colored grassy hillside where a lion posed, sharing its perfect profile. When the cat noticed the car, it looked directly at it, allowing the visitors to witness its perfect majesty. "How nice to see a perfect living specimen," Stuart muttered.

"Maasai live among them," Omega said. "Long ago make peace. They seem to know we need them for manhood test; their females fertile, like ours. Not endangered yet. We know they need us to grow maize for fodder or to provide the occasional taste of human to complete their diet." Balancing the van on the narrow road Omega turned a hard left and hard right avoiding potholes. "No hard feelings about deaths. Mutual respect between species."

Stuart nodded, holding the car strap to stay steady. "No morem out here, I guess," he said.

"Exactly. Now you see why we travel on highway."

Stuart nodded as he bounced on his bony buttocks.

When they pulled into the village, it looked empty. The round dung and straw homes looked very much like dirt beehives. They encircled an open space where Stuart imagined the natives gathered for festivals. "Where is everyone?"

"Women inside cooking; men hunting." He stopped away from the huts and they walked toward one. "We go here," Omega said. "Aunt Lou's place. Husband dead. Even her medicine not stop malaria."

"I'm sorry," Stuart said lamely.

Omega shrugged. "You find cure for this problem, many Africans saved."

"Our researchers are working on it. Set up in Grandpa's house. You could run shop."

"Omega no scientist."

"You do business side. Bring in patients."

"Ah, Omega good business man, Omega good African," he said laughing. He stuck his head inside the entrance of his aunt's hut. "Lululi," he sang and began speaking to his aunt in Kurundi. He nodded at Stuart. "We go in."

After the blazing sun the cool dark hut was welcome. Mud benches had been plastered onto the walls of the hut. Stuart sat on a mud bench and squinted to see. He sat straighter as a foul odor penetrated his nose. The dung within the home was worse than an outhouse. But this was cattle dung, he reminded himself. Cattle eat differently from humans. Their offal would be different.

Omega pointed to Stuart's head, which Stuart compliantly bowed toward the small Maasai woman. Her nearly bald head was covered with grey black balls betraying her age. In the photos of Omega's wife and child, Omega's young wife had curly African hair that was as black and thick as an Asian's hair. Although Stuart imagined Omega's aunt's hair was once like Omega's wife's hair—thick and luxuriant, Aunt Lou's thinning hair was nearly gone. The old woman looked satisfied and mumbled something.

Omega translated, "Healed wound, wants you to have final touch."

The African herbalist mixed dried herbs together with some oil and motioned to Stuart to bow toward her again. She dipped her apron into the bowl and rubbed a small amount into Stuart's head. She poured the remainder into an empty vial, closed it with a stopper like those he had seen at the apothecary booth in the Arusha market. She looked up at him holding two fingers. She turned to Omega and muttered a few instructions. "Put this on twice daily," Omega translated, "for no more than one week."

His stomach finally overpowered by the stench in the dark hut, Stuart pointed to the exit, "Need air. Please thank her and ask her how much."

Omega shouted, "She wants your t-shirt."

"Let me get her a clean one."

"She wants that one."

"Fine," Stuart said, gulping in the fresh air hungrily. Remaining outside he changed his shirt and passed the dirty one to Omega. He stepped inside the curved entry, but avoided the center of the hut. "Thank you Aunt Lou." He turned to Omega. "We need to go. The Nairobi event is day after tomorrow and I need to meet with Grandpa's editor."

Omega said his good byes. They crashed back over the shortcut and were soon on the paved road.

"Head feel better, worse?" Omega asked.

It stung like crazy and flies were circling the wound. "I thought it was healed. This stuff is just annoying."

Omega looked at Stuart's constricted face. "Here's kerchief. Wipe off. She applied too much. One application only. You are correct; your hair has nearly covered the graze. And black eyes are gone. You'll be stunning at the memorial." He paused. "Oh, good news—Aunt Lou give ideas on killer. Says she has seen killer. Skinny, not Maasai. Probably not African."

Omega had been silent for several hours. Stuart re-read his grandfather's stories and drifted to sleep. Omega screeched to a halt and shook Stuart awake. "Maybe we go look?"

A large carcass of an elephant flat on its side blocked the road. Stuart raced to the grey unmoving mound and touched its still warm body. "Omega," he shrieked, "come here." Near the female, whose tits still hung full of milk, was a small baby elephant, both with fractured skulls, sawed off tusks and ivory root removal. Blood dripped from the forehead wounds and tuskless holes. "They look exactly like my grandfather described in his recent article."

Omega had his knife raised but when he saw the carnage he could only shrug. "Only in the flesh. It's not pretty. As your grandfather pointed out, it's an income for Africans not otherwise employed."

"Why take down the animals?"

"Tanzania is poor country. We make progress with small farms and tourism but illegal poaching is quicker. Children must eat and poachers do not want to sell daughters into prostitution or babies into foster homes."

"But why not use the tusks that are naturally shed?"

"Asian artisans not like. Not white enough."

Or easy to carve into, Stuart remembered, from his conversation with Xiang Yu. He walked around the animals, staring at two neat bullet holes side by side in the brains of both mother and child. "Such accuracy. Where do they learn?"

Omega shrugged and said, "Don't know."

"Do they have to kill them?"

"Elephant is a big mean animal. It won't just stand still so poacher can take out tooth."

Stuart moved closer to the cow and her calf. Buzzards circled overhead and a flock of Corey bustards stalked slowly across the grasslands, wings widespread. Grey, awkward birds, they seemed impossibly earthbound, too ungainly to ever leave the ground.

"Scavengers by shape not desire," Omega explained when Stuart pointed to the curious tribe of birds on the march. Not far behind, but watching their feet, jackals ran in circles, licking their chops for the final feast on the elephant's bones.

"New dead," Omega said, automatically crossing himself.

Wooden figures with inset ivory that seem to predict death, coramandel screens, even pure ivory netsukes that held Japanese kimonos together or simply sat on the shelf caused this murder. Stuart shuddered at the thought of meeting a woman with clear blue eyes who profited from elimination of wildlife. How did the sculptress and her family insinuate themselves into George's life and death? Ivory must be the connection. And this was his sister's living?

CHAPTER SIXTEEN

Stuart closed his eyes and before sunset the car came to a screeching halt in front of the gates to a tall white building, the Stanley Hotel. Omega shook Stuart's hand lightly, saying, "Passport please." He handed it to the guard who opened the closed gates and waved them through.

"So this storied hotel—what do you know about it?"

When Stuart reclaimed his passport, Omega began, "The New Stanley Hotel is where hunters came to meet their well-known Great White hunters—Bror von Blixen, made famous by his wife, the writer Isak Dinesen, Frederick Selous who sports a game reserve in his name, R.J. Cunningham, Theodore Roosevelt's guide, Frank Allen, a man everyone called Bunny and who guided your famed author Ernest Hemingway."

"So I've read," Stuart said, who, apart from the short sweet prose poem *The Old Man and the Sea*, hated Hemingway's writing and dramatic life. Having offed himself in Ketchum, Idaho, where Stuart loved to ski, Stuart had heard of him since their early trips from Seattle to Sun Valley. "I'm told he boldly introduced the word *safari*, which means trip, into English as a word that meant killing animals, that you could take home and stuff." Safari trophies, that

George's father shot and that haunted George with their strange stuffed faces and marble eyes, were part of this hotel's history.

"It was a different generation," Omega said, backing carefully into the best parking place in the full lot. "And there, ready to greet you is another legend, the finest concierge in all of Africa."

A green liveried gentleman with golden keys on his lapels approached the car, "Mr. Atkinson. Welcome to the New Stanley. We have been waiting for you to work out the last minute details for Atkinson's memorial."

The black man winked at Stuart and said, "The Atkinson name works wonders around here. There are never enough flowers or enough wine or enough anything, but all the suppliers pulled through for your grandfather."

"Folks liked George? So why is he dead?"
"Maybe he knew too much."

Stuart remembered that the sequel to the story published on the day Atkinson died had just come out, that he had a torn story in his backpack together with diaries of notes for other stories. And a roll of soon to be published stories hidden in his grandfather's safe. Would anyone die at the funeral? His mother had a figurine and if the assassin was still in Africa, his or her reach was unlikely to be aimed at Seattle. Likewise, he hoped the Seattle-Boston move would further confuse the hunter.

When they walked inside the hotel he studied the concierge's uniform—pressed, the keys like military awards on each shoulder. "So tell me about the New Stanley."

"The hotel was home to the beginning of tourism in Kenya and Tanzania. We have kept it going by offering the best service, the nicest rooms and connections throughout the continent for any trip, photographic or hunting."

Stuart looked past the concierge into the lobby where a round green leather bench encircled a globe clock, not unlike the large clock in Grand Central Station. He supposed that this was in the original lobby, but rather than ask he rushed to the circular staircase where the concierge had begun mounting carpeted stairs. New, no doubt, but old looking. They wandered into a darkened room with a bar where art deco-like lamps hung over leather bar stools. The concierge opened draperies across floor to ceiling windows across from the bar and the room flooded with light that bounced off the dust circulating in the air. Small prisms formed on the wall flooding the ancient room with tiny rainbows.

"I thought we'd hold the service here," he said. "This is our oldest remaining room other than a ballroom. We will open the adjacent ballroom, if, as I suppose, all of Africa comes to honor your grandfather. The French doors are always open so that smokers can pollute the outside, not the hotel."

Thinking how few smokers he had noticed in Africa, Stuart said, "Who will smoke here?"

"The whites and wealthy who attend. A few drivers smoke when no one is watching."

"The open doors will be nice to have some clean African air even if no one uses the exit to pollute your blue skies," Stuart said. Intrigued by the space, the scent of cracked leather sofas and mold, Stuart studied the layout, tomorrow's task, the ghastly glow of his grandfather's embalmed face hanging in front of him. "I have only my grandfather's ashes which I believe are in the hotel. Let's put the urn behind the podium. I'd rather feature the living not the dead."

The concierge nodded. "So I had planned and yes the urn is here."

Stuart took a final look for tomorrow's service, then left to wander down the hall outside the ballroom. Like a photograph exhibition in a museum, a string of black and white photos lined the wall. "Who are these people? And why are the photos here?"

The concierge who followed Stuart closely, responded at once. "The photos tell the New Stanley's history. They depict the British and other royals. Built and rebuilt several times, the New Stanley has housed them all. England's Queen Elizabeth was on safari when she learned her father died and that she was Queen. She rushed back here and left in such a hurry she left her hat here. We returned it, of course."

"Of course," Stuart echoed.

When they passed the Hemingway ballroom, the concierge said, "Hemingway stayed here before hunting trips. He actually came back here to write some of his books."

"So where does Ian Smith live?"

"I'm taking you there. He usually rests in the afternoon but should be up now, ready for his cocktail."

They arrived at the top floor near a corner room with a gold placard reading, "Ian Smith, International Herald Tribune, Daily Mail." Like the other silenced poets, writers and celebrities with ballrooms or suites named after them, this newspaperman whose connections spread throughout the world, would be remembered at the New Stanley. Remembering his own profession, he thought, a writer's pay is certainly lousy. Businessmen had no corporate plaques. Only wordsmiths, he guessed, whose product would outlive their creators, perhaps glorify the African nation and defy obsolescence, technology's onus.

The concierge knocked softly on the door.

"Yes?" a gravelly voice murmured from inside.

"Mr. Stuart's here, sir."

The voice harrumphed, chortled, coughed and finally shouted in a clear vibrant tone that the entire hotel could hear,

"Well show him in for Christ's sake. I've been waiting to see if he's still shorter than George."

The concierge winked at Stuart and the entourage—the concierge, Stuart trailed closely by Omega—entered the old man's suite.

Clad in a 1970s polyester suit of rust-brown with thin white stripes through it, the old gentleman exited a circle of cigarette smoke and joined the group in the outer chamber where the air was kept clear and light, owing to the ongoing chugging of an anti-smoke machine that was doubtless as old as the suit.

"I receive visitors here," Ian said, the crow's feet around his eyes prominent as he smiled up at Stuart from his five-foot height. "You did grow up. George said you had." He paused. "Have a seat. Who's your companion?"

"Omega," Omega said. "As Atkinson's former driver and assistant, I met Mr. Stuart with the sad news of George's murder. When he learned his was the task of discovering George's assassin, Stuart hired me as a translator and driver, a 'nouveau' African guide."

"Nouveau?"

"Not the safari type. Stuart came with no camera and knows next to nothing about guns so hunting assassins, not animals, is his game."

"I should add," Stuart interrupted, "I'm a business man, not an investigator or killer of animals or men. After my search of my grandfather's house, meetings with Farouk, police and others, I'm not convinced our prey is out roaming and eating or even hunting on the savannah. Rather, from my preliminary investigations and since Grandpa was murdered at his own house and I was target practice in his studio, we're expecting his murderer to be hiding in plain sight. Any ideas? Oh and I do now own a camera, my grandfather's trusty Leica, which is in Arusha where my grandfather's last photos are being extracted by Farouk."

"All good words. Farouk, a good man. Assassin suggestions? A few. But it's cocktail hour. Would you join me for a drink?"

"I've ordered all the right stuff from the bar," the concierge said.

A discreet knock on the outer door produced a waiter with Stuart's draft IPA, Omega's Tuskers and an orange juice chaser, together with Ian's scotch on the rocks.

"Another tray follows in an hour," the concierge said, backing out of the room. "With that I wish you all good day. Supper menus are on the second drink tray."

Stuart bit his lip to keep from laughing. Omega found a chair in a remote corner, covered his mouth and devolved into giggles.

"To the old man," Stuart said, as they picked up their glasses.

"Best goddam journalist, personal friend and friend of Africa, I've ever known," the editor rasped. "A better man I've yet to meet."

"You're looking at his next incarnation," Omega said, his glass to Stuart.

"I've got some hoops to go through first," Stuart said. "First among them is to ferret out who's after the Atkinsons."

"I have many theories, Stuart. Principal among them is that it was someone not from this region. Perhaps, like your grandfather, not originally from Africa. The answer is in Arusha, which I believe you have scoured or in Dar Es Salaam. The answer, your grandfather sensed incongruity and dishonesty and had no trouble revealing it. "

"Xiang Yu or Britz."

"I didn't say it was Britz. Or Xiang Yu. Both are, however, fiercely competitive. Britz lacked talent. Xiang Yu is very good at what he does. Maybe a combination of Britzes, Xiang Yu and Xiang Yu's buyers."

Stuart nodded and brushed his hands through his hair. "This memorial. Will we find clues here?"

"You said earlier the assassin will likely be hiding in plain sight. Let's assume so."

After his second IPA, Stuart shook a snoring Omega and stood in front of the editor. "Ian, I need to get some rest before this service. I trust you will speak a few words?"

"Yes, son, how is your own speech?"

"In its incipient stages."

"Don't use too many twenty-five cent works like 'incipient.' Some of your audience will barely understand English, much less Ivy League English."

"Thanks. I figured I'd send it up for editing tomorrow." Stuart paused, looking at the stocking-footed white man with an accent he could barely identify and asked, "In a word, Ian, how *did* you get into this business?"

"Never ask a newspaperman to speak 'a word or two.' Most of us count our meals like we count our words, few or many depending on the particular newspaper editor. As to how I got into the business," Ian grinned, "always wanted to be a newspaperman. Grew up in Boston when the *Globe* was a great newspaper and the *New York Times* was the Bible. Went to Harvard back when the locals still called it the 'neighborhood school on Mass Ave.' "

Stuart laughed and took a seat on the arm of one of Ian's wing chairs. The story was unfolding, he thought, so much like his grandfather's that the man's narrative was irresistible. Harvard grads, the three of them—George, Ian, Stuart. Was this why the desperate summons from his grandfather came to him?

Ian sipped at his drink, cleared his throat and continued, "My literature professor had a former student working at the Globe in need of a copy boy so he connected me with him. I worked at the *Globe,* got my writing wings and then transferred to the *Times* when their international office needed a rug rat to go to Kenya to cover the Mau Mau rebellion. I jumped at it and have been here ever since. Became a feature editor for the *Herald Tribune.* Took a sabbatical in what the *Tribune* referred to as my "bush period" and went foraging in the bush like a wild animal. I met your grandfather out there who was on assignment for *National Geographic.* Cajoled him into writing exclusives for me." Ian laughed. "His stories were so good that the *Herald Tribune* reprinted them in all the *Times* across the globe (*New York Times, London Times, Los Angeles Times)* I had a large budget then and could hire him full time. Then the internet became the news net. I had to lay your grandfather off." He paused, sipping at his scotch. "When your father died, I was able to offer Atkinson a full time job with the *Tribune* again, something that I think pleased him. I think he was weary of stateside journalism. It angers me that the job cost him his life."

"Ian, I believe he would have much rather died on his sun-soaked porch in Arusha than on a rain-drenched street of Seattle. Although we all mourn his passing, I think you did him a great favor bringing him back to Africa."

Stuart, tired from road travel and drink, roused Omega who had drifted off to sleep again. "C'mon, Omega. See you tomorrow, Ian. Thanks for everything, especially for filling in some holes in my grandfather's life."

"We'll meet again after the service and compare notes."

On the elevator to the first floor Stuart turned to Omega and said, "I'm famished."

"Let me call wife. I'll meet you on the left side of the outdoor part of the Thorn Café."

The Thorn Café, clearly a new addition to the New Stanley, had an acacia tree, the African tree covered with thorns, growing in the middle of the street side outdoor café. Fenced in, the tree was harmless and the decorative glass walls etched with opaque designs that lined the street kept diners out of the vision of curious passersby and walkers alike. Stuart ordered a glass of wine and stared at the blank tablet before him. What to say, how to explain this man whose belief in Africa, in his only child and her son, was a cornerstone in each of the strong fortresses he and his mother had built around themselves. He scribbled furiously in the silence that surrounded him.

CHAPTER SEVENTEEN

The next day, Stuart was first and alone in the family row of the ballroom where his grandfather's service would be held. But then, he thought, so he would be until Ian or Omega showed up. Golden Keys, the ever-smiling concierge, had set up 15 rows of 30 chairs each. The hunter's bar at the front had a podium in front of it. The floor sparkled, the floor to ceiling velvet curtains were open fully to the bright African daylight. The red earth-colored urn covered with cornflowers that Stuart had chosen for the ashes was behind the podium, on the Great White Hunter's bar.

It was perfect, Stuart thought. *Who would fill these chairs? It was two, the service was at three.* At two-ten, Ian ambled in, cane to one side, concierge on the other, Omega trailing closely behind. Ian joined Stuart.

"Who will come?" Stuart asked the three.

"Not to worry. All of Africa will be here. It is early in African time."

Gradually the seats were full, black and white faces filled the chairs and lined the walls. Children spilled into the aisles.

Stuart saw Neissa in a chair near the window. They eyes met. He nodded in greeting.

At three o'clock, Stuart walked to the podium, cleared his throat and began: "Welcome and thank you for coming. We are here to celebrate George Atkinson, my grandfather and perhaps my first best friend. He taught me to laugh, to not worry about my faults. When he shot himself in the foot carrying a loaded gun after a long ride through the bush and an all-nighter writing a story, he called from the hospital and said, 'Stuart, "I'm still a lousy shot."' We both laughed. I had just finished business school and was about to close my first venture capital deal—a sports sneakers company.

"I called him two months later to see how the foot was.

"'Healed,' he said. 'Can I have some sneakers?'

"No," I told him sadly. "The company failed. No one liked the psychedelic colors of the shoes or the odd checkerboard weave.

"'Now isn't that just like the stupid world,' he said, 'boring, like Seattle's rain.'

"Born and raised in Seattle, Washington, but posted in Africa to write for international journals, George Atkinson left his heart in Africa. It was from him I learned some of the continent's secrets. A favorite was that the African elephant's ears, when widespread in the wind, form the continent itself. Hence its species name *Africa Loxadonta africanus*.

"It was from him I learned respect and admiration for the continent and its people. Colonized, tyrannized; they were kind. Each, like each of us citizens of the world, is filled with a unique and special story, be it of family, friends or simplicity and beauty in life. George Atkinson loved those stories. He wove them into narrative that showed a side of Africa both realistic and terrifying, because it was true. He lost his life telling those stories. It is up to us, his friends and family, to continue to tell them. Enjoy each other, the food, and don't stop talking about George."

A tall blond man and young dark-haired woman

approached him as he stepped outside the open French doors for a breath of fresh air.

"Alphonse Britz," the man said, extending his hand. "Anton Britz, my father," the man continued, "your grandfather's first partner, sent me and my wife as our family representatives. Nice memorial. Good man."

Stuart nodded. "I met your father years ago. You have his blond hair. Thank you, Mr. Britz and, yes, George Atkinson was a good man. Why did I not meet you when I met your father?"

"I was away at school, married soon afterwards and then lost my first wife. Thank you again for the service. I will, no doubt, see you again."

When Stuart stepped back inside and away from Alphonse, he noticed Ian, who was among a mix of black and white faces, waving to him. The editor mouthed, "Come meet some friends."

The flash was bright and quick, well-aimed. Stuart felt the breeze and watched Ian fall. Stuart pushed his way through the spectators, racing to the door and rushed to Ian's body. He was closely followed by the concierge. Omega walked out of a collection of red-robed Africans and joined the two other men. Stuart reached for Ian's arm, found no pulse.

He glanced at the man's colorless face and glanced down to hide his thoughts. He looked aroud for a medic. But then why? The man was dead. A perfect shot through the heart that had since stopped beating. Ian was dead.

How he had hoped to learn more from the man who had known his grandfather most of his working life! And, together with his mother and sister who remained to him, Ian knew more about his favorite relative, his grandfather, than anyone. All the unanswered questions that died with him. Stuart sighed, thinking, the diaries, my mother, they're all I have left. Was this whole

African adventure just a tragedy within a tragedy?

Noticing that the noise of the retreating crowd of guests had ceased, he looked up to see the back doors closed and barred by a pair of red-bereted police with crossed rifles. The room was silent as death. All the guests had reseated themselves. The French doors were closed and guarded by another officer. A fourth soldier took the microphone and ordered them to remain until they had been questioned. Stuart was uneasy. Someone was missing. He searched the sea of faces for Britz and his wife. They were no longer in the crowd. *Of course,* he thought, *they were already outdoors. How easy to just leave. But did that make them guilty of anything? He'd seen no gun or bulge on the man's body. But would he know the bulge of a gun if he saw it?*

Stuart stayed by Ian's body until a mortician came with a velvet body bag. Now he shadowed one of the policemen, listening to their inane questions: Name, papers, relation to Atkinson, relation to Ian Smith. The tedious questioning by the guards produced nothing. A few people wandered over to Stuart and Omega's side.

"Thank you for coming," Stuart reiterated until the last guest left. He sank into a chair, the pallor of Ian's dead face a vision that would not leave. His utter helplessness in the face of a gun from he knew not where reminding him of his frustration at being several thousand miles away when his grandfather was killed. What did Ian and his grandfather know that would get them killed? Why was Ian killed although he revealed nothing? His grandfather was author of stories regarding African corruption. Except that he had allowed the stories to be published; Ian was blameless. George had written the stories. And he might have talked; he clearly knew something. It might have been Britz. His exit was convenient, but the man was also, Stuart had ascertained, an illegal trader in African curios and possibly elephant tusks. Doubtless he sent chips of illegal ivory to his daughter for her sculptures. The fewer encounters Britz had with the law the better, Stuart figured. Was he accompanied by guards with high powered rifles or was Ian's death from a powerful pistol like the one that had grazed Stuart's head?

Stuart looked at the shattered memorial. Plates filled with food covered the chairs. Most of the banquet was untouched. Only then did he notice a sole Maasai who stood in front of the French doors holding a spear and a Maasai shield, not far from where the shot was fired. The balding African winked at Stuart.

Omega was still by his side. Stuart turned to him and said, "Why? Ian was guilty of nothing. Even admitted he was a better editor than writer."

"Is it another clue, perhaps?" Omega asked.

"I beg your pardon?"

"Perhaps the stories are offensive to Africans—black and white....your eulogy brought to mind what they most hated about your grandfather and his editor...their truth-telling abilities. Remember that your grandfather's second story appeared a few days ago. It was another story revealing an ugliness Africa does not like to admit. There are two more stories to appear. Who will they offend? Atkinson left no information that they were to appear in the *Herald Tribune*."

"Perhaps we'll see something of note in tomorrow's *Tribune*, hidden amongst the encominiums bemoaning its most famous editor's death." Stuart paused, then pointed to the Maasai. "Is that your clan, Omega?"

"A cousin. Came to honor your grandfather and is now committed to protecting you."

"So why did you think it was not an African killer?" Stuart asked.

Omega looked down. "The antique spear. No African would use it. No other good reason. So what's next? Do remember both my aunt and Ian think the killer might be from a non-African tribe."

"Let the police do their research. We need to find out if working for the *Herald Tribune* is a crime in Africa. Or if some group doesn't like people doing it."

Omega laughed.

"That Alphonse guy," Stuart said, "the one I was talking with before Ian fell. We need to visit his father, Anton in Dar Es Salaam. I think he may have some connection to the illegal tusk trading and the Chinese name on the wall at my grandfather's house."

"At least Dar is on the Indian Ocean. Water is calming," Omega assured him.

"Dar Es Salaam is across the Indian Ocean from Asia making tusk shipment to China rather easy. Who knows, when the sculptor is not sending out figurines as threats, maybe she sells them to the ivory-loving Chinese?"

The head of the Kenyan guards came over to the pair. Six-five and muscular, he had the arrogance of a perfectly fit soldier.

"Sir," he said, "we will need some information from you at police headquarters. Please come there at once." Looking first at Stuart, then at Omega, he said, "Do we need your sidekick?"

"Omega goes everywhere with me, especially if driving is involved. I don't drive. I notice you didn't learn much from the attendees, and they were questioned here."

"We will follow you there. What is the vehicle?"

Omega gave the officer the license number.

Stuart grimaced and asked, "Why must you follow us?"

"The head of the department wants to see you. We want no diversions. I will arrest you, if need be."

"Where is the concierge?" Stuart asked. How could the finest concierge in all of Africa let paying guests be hauled off to jail?

"At his desk, looking after his job," the policeman replied, "and well-paid, I might add."

Paid off to do nothing, the concierge was of no use to him now. Stuart looked up at Omega who shrugged. "Kenya is known for its corruption. Golden Keys might need some extra money?"

Stuart stood and the pair followed the soldier. Cop, Stuart mentally corrected himself, but in full British army gear or fatigues, these policemen looked like soldiers.

Before they left the room, his sister Neissa approached. "Gentlemen, this is my brother and his colleague. Be gentle. Stuart, meet me in the Café here. We have work to do."

"So you said. It's up to these guys."

The cop nodded at the statuesque woman. "We will be brief. Your brother and colleague will be back within the hour."

Stuart laughed and said to Omega, "Nice she decided to show at the funeral and that she texted me she needs us for something, no?"

Omega shrugged and opened the van door for Stuart.

They followed the cop to police headquarters, a palatial colonial-era building, similar to the one in Arusha. Inside the building, they were led to a room and sat face to face with a muscular man. Further extending his military metaphor, Stuart wondered idly if training for the police force was like training for the marines.

He answered their tedious questions slowly and precisely, almost relieved they were not investigating his grandfather's death. With their infantile logic and pay-off techniques, who knew whether the men they accused for crimes had anything to do with the crime they were accused of committing, but were glad for money to admit to crimes. If the inordinate numbers of wrongly accused men in U.S. prisons were his guide, Stuart thought, Africa's jails were doubtless full of citizens with no connection to their convicting offense.

"Tell us everything you know about Mr. Smith," the officer said.

"Never met him before. Don't know the continent. Whoever is wiping the writer and editor out must think there's more to come. That is highly unlikely," Stuart said.

"Neither Omega nor I know anything. Omega was my grandfather's driver," he continued. "I'm a venture capitalist, not a writer."

"How do we know any of this is true?"

"Omega greeted me with the news of my grandfather's death and worked with him from time to time. You wish to check on this, check with my grandfather's mistress, Omega's aunt. You want to check on me, I'll let you talk with my partner, Rosalind Abel." Thinking her fiery temperament and connections in high places in U.S. government might help him get away from these soldiers, he decided to test her, but would give her a few cautionary words before he had her speak to the cops. "With your permission, I'll dial my partner and she can vouch for me."

"Tell us the name of your company. We will phone," the policeman said.

One of the men checked Erewhon's existence and dialed the listed phone on a staff computer.

"Ms. Abel," the officer said and switched the phone to speaker phone, "this is the Nairobi police. Mr. Ian Smith has been killed. Your partner is a suspect. He says you can vouch for his innocence and he advises you may have information."

"Key—rist! Stuart Lehrman, my partner went over to bury his grandfather. Why would he kill anyone?"

"We know nothing about him," the policeman said.

"Please confirm this is your partner," the policeman said, shoving Stuart near the camera.

"That is my partner, Stuart Atkinson Lehrman and if you don't release him immediately, Harold Abel, undersecretary of African affairs will be in touch with you at once. It will be an international fiasco. He is already doing everything he can to help the government sort out the mess your country is making with its internal rebellion. Why are you not concerning yourself with that? Stuart has already advised that your countries do not worry about journalists. So please focus on your internal affairs and release my partner or Mr. Abel will be in touch with you directly."

The officer shoved Stuart back into his chair next to Omega, turning to the Maasai,

"And so your partner has government connections but you, Stuart?" the policeman asked, "why should I trust you?"

"I've already been a target." Stuart brushed back his hair and showed off the scar from the fall into his grandfather's basement. "I don't expect it's over yet. Omega and I must find the killer before he or she hits me again or kills my mother. Ian had no heirs. Considered us family. Hence the reason he's dead."

"I'll need your cellphone number in case we have more questions." The native, surprised by the Rosalind Abel phone conversation re-phrased his demand. "I'd prefer to confiscate your cellphone but we don't need any state department investigations here."

Yay, Roz, Stuart thought. "We're going to look at animals on our way to Dar Es Salaam where we will meet with another of my grandfather's acquaintances. Oh and do remember that I am meeting with my all-knowing and rather powerful sister Neissa in a few minutes. No phone calls, please. The phone may go directly to voice mail for the next week."

The policemen saluted as they exited.

Stuart nodded. "Good luck with your investigation." Knowing full well that there was very little he could accomplish here to find his grandfather's assassin now that Ian was dead, he was anxious to learn what his sister wanted, then breathe the fresh air of the Serengeti before he went to battle with the Britzes. The animals he would see because they were there. He hoped the brief pause in the park would clear his mind, remind him of the Africans he knew and give the Britzes some time to stew in their juices, making them either more or less likely to trip up and reveal what they knew.

When the two left the police headquarters they clambered into Omega's van and raced back to the hotel. Stuart entered the Thorn café alone. Omega sat outside with the concierge. "I'm nearby."

"White or red wine?" Neissa said brusquely when Stuart sat down at the corner table.

"White."

"Send us your best Nederburg Chardonnay," Neissa said to the waiter, "two glasses."

"Alphonse Britz has been stealing my ivory, Stuart. My team and I are meeting at this hotel in the morning to try to settle things. We will travel together to try and find Britz. Would you and Omega kindly come also? I have a handful of skilled soldiers who will accompany us." She smiled innocently. "I had hoped to meet you in Arusha as a brother, a friend, not a needed member of my army."

Stuart sipped the Chardonnay, "Nice Chardonnay. Yeah, Neissa I'll be there. What is family for? We certainly need to find out who is wiping out grandparent and friend, before the target gets pointed at the rest of us. Britz involved? Omega is a new father we need to leave him out."

"The Britz connection might be indirect, but I understand private investigation is your next new deal. Rumor has it Grandpa's assassin was not an African. Britz will do anything for money—but murder Grandpa, I don't know. That makes headlines."

Omega who had begun a slow stroll toward the table said, "Oh no, you don't—leave me out, that is. My clan, myself—we are charged with protecting the Atkinsons. I'm in."

"There's a new building going up on Grandpa's home site. I need to return tomorrow to determine if the builders have discovered any remaining evidence. I stowed some other stories there and Mom wants me to pick up a few items. Maybe I'll find something useful."

"We could only hope," Neissa said. "Meet me in the lobby at 7 tomorrow morning. We'll settle this Britz matter before noon."

"We'll be there, then I've got to get back to the matter of our grandfather's murder. Ian said the killer was one of our tribe. Was it you?"

"No, but I have some ideas. See you in the morning."

Thinking, those are ominous words, the ones that preceded Ian's death, Stuart watched Neissa walk away and turned to Omega. "Any cousins in the area? We might need some back up for this adventure."

"Stuart," Omega said, "This is a dangerous mission. I'll phone the cousin who came to the funeral determined to protect your family. While I have a large family I don't want us to be the cause of their deaths."

"Your cousin won't die on this mission," Stuart assured Omega. "I just want a tail that no one knows we have. We ask him to stay blocks away from us. Someone who speaks some English would be nice."

Omega grinned. "Like I said, we learn English in school. I ask nearby relative if he wants to join the gang. Promise we keep him safe."

"Promise! He will be way behind us and I hope to keep us safe also."

Omega phoned and left a message.

Several hours later, the concierge rang Stuart's room. "You have a guest."

"We will come down," Stuart replied. He knocked on Omega's door and announced, "We have a visitor."

A Maasai, smaller in stature than Omega but similar in face, waited patiently in a lobby chair. Omega and Stuart approached him. Stuart extended his hand and said, "Stuart Atkinson, grandson of George Atkinson."

"The African took Stuart's hand in both hands and said, "Good man, George. Sorry for his death."

"Thank you for honoring him yesterday by attending his memorial. Today's task is not a difficult mission."

Omega explained what they needed in a native tongue and made certain his cousin understood he was a tail, not on the front line of danger.

The African nodded, "I do."

Stuart looked at both of them. "My sister comes at 7 in the morning; we'll meet here for breakfast at six. I will pay you $100 for the day."

"Good rate. See you in the morning," the African said and turned to go. "Best to your family, Omega."

The next morning when they gathered around the expansive African buffet, Stuart said to both men, "Hungry?"

"A little," the man replied.

"So let's fill our plates and eat," Stuart said. "I'm told my sister has a good cook but one who's not accustomed to cooking for crowds. Take an extra fruit and roll up a sandwich in the event she chooses not to feed us."

"You pay me first," the small man said.

"No, we complete mission first."

Staring hard at Stuart and twisting the keys in his hands, Stuart wondered whether the man would pitch the keys in his face and go home to his family.

"I have a small sensor on your car and can follow it on my phone," Omega said. "We will keep you informed via text."

The man nodded and strode toward the warm food, took a plate and piled it high with meat, fish and poultry. Within moments he walked back to the table, picked up another plate and filled it with an equally large portion of vegetables and fruit. He sat down and began eating.

Stuart took oatmeal, fruit and toast. Omega did likewise. "We will eat well when we return," Stuart said. "Best to stay lean and mean in the presence of my cagey sister."

With that the small Maasai slowed down and eventually left half of his plate.

Just before seven the three finished and walked to the lobby to wait for Neissa.

CHAPTER EIGHTEEN

At precisely seven, Neissa arrived clad in skin tight black waterproof leggings and a white long sleeved bug and waterproof shirt that covered a white chemise, clearly dressed for any weather. Surrounded by eight good-looking and thin black men wearing white pants with black tops, the group looked like a rock group of whom Neissa might be the female lead.

Stuart walked over to the group and glared at his sister. "They're all coming?"

"I never go anywhere without them," Neissa replied in a monotone.

"Meet Omega," Stuart said when the Maasai reached his side. "I never go anywhere without him."

Neissa scowled. "So that's why you wouldn't work for me?"

Omega sighed. "I have a job. I work for Stuart. After your grandfather sent for Stuart, he asked me to look after him."

Stuart's head jerked up. "You never told me this."

"I didn't think it was important," Omega replied.

"He must have known the Atkinsons were all in danger," Stuart remarked.

Omega nodded. "He was working on five articles. The first two have been published." He mouthed, "You have shreds of the third."

"He sent for you?" Neissa said, her color rising. "And you have an unfiled story?"

Stuart shook his head. "I have no idea what I have, Neissa. When I crashed through the levels of Grandpa's house I may have buried the remains of any of his ongoing work."

"You crashed through his house?"

"Neissa, this is your party. And that was then. I'm here looking for Grandpa's assassin. You hired us to help you find Alphonse. I need to get back to my main mission, but in the meanwhile to keep you from slowing me down in my assassin tracking I'd like to help you keep the rest of the Atkinsons alive. So please tell me everything you know about Alphonse so that we're prepared for the best and the worst."

"I know nothing other than what he looks like, which I learned at our grandfather's memorial.

"Nice eulogy, by the way," she interjected, "Britz---- blonde hair is rare on this continent outside of South Africa. His men are fair-skinned, dark-haired Turks or white Africans because he does not like dark skin."

"Britz's heritage is South African, I think? And this far north his hair should make him easy to spot and his racism genetic," Stuart noted.

"I'm not sure about that," Neissa said. "He runs an illegal business and is effective at staying out of sight."

"So I've learned," Stuart said. "Do you know who handles his accounts? Or have you any tangible evidence that he stole your goods?"

"Why?"

"Just curious what we're up against."

Handing him a paper with an internet and street address, Neissa said, "This is all I have on the guy."

"That's great," Stuart said, typing the info to Roz who snapped back with a "How's the evil twin?"

"She's fourteen years older than I am. A few more grey hairs, I'd say," he replied.

"Backatcha, Stu," and almost as an afterthought, "Careful, please. Erewhon needs you."

My god, emotion from Roz? Stuart thought. Scary or good news? His prior and current hunting expedition elicited no emotion. But then much had happened since the Boston celebration. "Hey lady, make certain there is no building on the site until I check one last time for murder clues and retrieve a photo roll."

"Good as done. Let me know when you're back in town."

"Omega and I have one more excursion to make—Dar Es Salaam— after we stop by Grandpa's house. First we're going to this head-on collision between my sister and her competitor."

"Please check in after the Big Event."

"You can count on it," Stuart texted.

The group headed to a safari-type bus that could seat about ten people in three rows.

Omega whistled. "Nice car and just big enough."

One of Neissa's Group of Eight nodded and said, "I don't think the tourism guide will miss it."

Stuart wondered if there were cameras or trophies or guns under the seats. He and Omega took the back seat. Omega texted the van license to his cousin.

Neissa sat in front next to the driver the entire span of the vehicle and seven muscular men between them. Had this tall muscular forty-something ever been a child? Ever even played with those kid toys he found in the trunk? Stuart wondered.

They drove to the border where Neissa and the other Africans went to one window and Stuart to another. He turned to her and asked, "Why don't you have an American passport?"

"I wasn't old enough to have an adult passport when I came over here on a freighter. When I was old enough to acquire one I was living with French people, the Abencours. They adopted me and legally I'm Neissa Abencour, French-American blend."

"Did you never tell anyone your history?"

"No need. Morocco has collected a large number of expats owing to its proximity both to Europe and Russia. White coloring is not uncommon in the capital where I first lived. Many Arabs are light skinned."

"Did you never want to come home?"

"No." Neissa shouted back at him. She turned to the driver. "Let's go."

"Where?" Stuart shouted.

"Britz's Kenya apartment."

"He's not there," Stuart said, re-reading the note from Roz indicating that the man was in Turkey at an entirely different address.

"I know, but there are some goods in his Kenya apartment that might be of use to me."

When they arrived on the quiet Nairobi street and stopped at a large home topped by razor wire, Stuart watched Neissa's soldiers find a crack in the fence and scramble over. They swung the gates wide open so that Neissa, Omega and Stuart could enter.

Omega's cousin texted Stuart. "Am two miles down the road. Let me know if you need me" While Neissa was organizing her men for a search Stuart texted back, "Stand by."

They entered the large marble foyer of a one-time wealthy

businessman's home and headed directly into the ballroom/salon. A dozen wooden boxes were stacked in a neat row and were marked "AK47/Britz-QSZ-92/Xiang Yu."

"Rifles?" Stuart murmured to Omega.

The African nodded.

Stuart texted Roz, "Find out names and nationalities of people who work for Britz and what these weapons are, if you can. This might be my group of assassins."

"Go partner, go," she replied. "I'm on it."

Neissa turned to Omega. "We will need your help to transport these to the van."

Omega scowled. "I work for Stuart, ma'am, and take orders only from him."

Neissa reached into her khaki pockets for a small powerful pistol. "Omega, you're working for me right now or you die and work for no one."

Stuart stepped in front of Omega. "Neissa this was not part of the deal. We are not thieves and Omega will not help you steal."

Omega, who was facing the door, shook his head at Stuart, pointing behind them, then crossed his finger across his lips. "Shhh, don't move."

Stuart turned to Omega, then looked where he was pointing. He caught sight of blonde blue-eyed Alphonse before he yelled.

"Hands up, Neissa!" Alphonse Britz barked. Surrounded by a group of muscular Turks and two cops the tall blond man strode in front of Neissa, a revolver pointed at her neck.

"Alphonse, how nice to see you. I believe you have a boatload of goods that belongs to me. I wonder where I might find it."

Alphonse laughed. "You won't. It's in the bank now. The Asians purchased the whole lot. Great stuff, by the way. Adding to the winter coffers as the tuskers continue to disappear."

Neissa motioned to her men. Alphonse signaled to each of his. Both Neissa and Alphonse moved behind the men. The men shouldered their rifles and, as centuries had taught them, they offered themselves to protect their employers. They fired simultaneously and a group of dead Africans and Turks encircled Alphonse and Neissa.

A blonde woman approached the circle of dead men and put a gun to Neissa's temple. Neissa kickboxed it from her hand. Omega raced behind her and pulled the slender woman's arm behind her back. He shoved her out the front door. "Judgment calls, Atkinson children," the blonde shouted over her shoulder.

Two Nairobi Policeman had entered with Britz. They took the blonde from Omega, cuffed and locked her in their crude car within minutes. The cops returned once the blonde was locked up. They turned to Neissa and pointed their rifles at her. "Face down or dead."

Neissa did not move.

"I repeat," the policeman said, "face down or dead."

"Charges?"

"Breaking and entering."

One of her eight men had not been hit, but had feigned death. He stood and pointed a revolver at the police. "Back off or you're dead." The cops left.

Alphonse moved toward Neissa and killed the native first then pointed his revolver at Neissa. "Get out of my house."

Neissa said nothing, but her hand moving surreptitiously upward pointed a QSZ-92, a powerful Chinese pistol, at Alphonse's gut and fired twice. "Once for my grandfather, twice for his editor. Have a miserable death."

As Alphonse slid, he too, shot Neissa in the gut. "I did not kill Atkinson. The other one yes."

Neissa motioned to Stuart, breathing heavily. "Come here. Let me die among family.

Stuart raised her head. "Thank you for coming to Boston. Thank you for allowing me to meet you when you were well and for trusting me to share your worst hours."

Struggling to speak, Neissa inclined her head and said, "Regarding your mission, I think the possible assassins are connected with Xiang. I know they were not Africans living in Arusha; Maasai and Kurundi loved Grandpa. Maybe Berbers from around North Africa colluded with Xiang and Britz. Berbers are light and dark-skinned have intermixed freely with French and Arabs; Britz liked white faces. Many are Muslim. Look around my house. Maid is Berber. She might be able to help you with their language." Struggling she whispered, "Enjoy your life. Best to Mom."

Adversaries now dead, the two police returned and approached Omega and Stuart. "You'll need to provide eyewitness testimony before leaving this house."

"Fine," Omega said firmly, "then we must return to Tanzania to complete our investigation."

Stuart nodded. "I'll advise Roz and Mom another of our kin is dead. Further, that we have for the moment hit a dead end. It may be a long conversation. My mother had very little sense of the adult Neissa and held the small child image in her memory."

Omega touched his arm softly. "She's a lawyer. Tell her that her daughter brought down one criminal and that the bad man's men shot her in retaliation. She doesn't have to know the gory details. I think she will be pleased that you escaped unharmed. Your sister asked for your help but never kept you out of the line of fire."

"I'll also tell her George's beloved elephants may be safer because several tusk traders are dead." Stuart retreated from the room, stood outside to phone and returned twenty minutes later paler than usual. Facing the cop, he said, "Do you need anything else from me? May I simply arrange for my sister's removal from this place and retire to my hotel?"

"I will need your testimonies before the grand jury before you leave the area."

"Can you convene it soon?" Stuart brusquely observed. "I would like to get away from this brutal place. I know who killed my sister but she is kin and would like to do her memory justice with some silence. I would like to take her body to her home, so would like you to have her cremated, whatever the cost and leave me now." Stuart looked down at the mutilated corpses surrounding his grey-haired but still youthful looking sister. He'd been no brother to her but then, he only met her as an adult. His eyes misted as he thought of the United Front they might have been against parents and the unhappy life she had spent alone. Glancing at Omega's serious face, he thought, I hope the Africans loved her like they loved George.

Turning to the cops he said, "By the way, this mass murder has no outstanding culprits except you people who might have done more to stop it. Be advised that I'm still looking for my grandfather's murderer. Since this misadventure has neatly solved Ian's murder, but not my grandfather's, I will need to be moving on. The trail grows cold. The woman in the car, who is she?"

And, he thought bitterly, does our deposition matter anyway? It was common knowledge that police rounded up people that may or may not have something to do with the crime committed. Moreover, the statements taken from guests following Ian's murder and Britz's absence from the questioning made the effort to find his grandfather's assassin appear more futile. The system was, he had read in the words of a recent murderer, corrupt from the bottom up and criminals, like Britz and Neissa, exploited and even engaged in this corruption.

He turned to Omega. "Can they convict a dead man of murder?"

"It is not a common occurrence in Kenya."

"They can hold a trial *in absentia* in the states," Stuart said. "But in the absence of a written confession I doubt Ian's estate; i.e., the newspaper, will collect anything."

Omega nodded.

"May we leave the country?" Stuart asked.

"No," the officer asserted. "And the woman in the car is Britz's daughter. He wanted her protected."

Stuart raised his eyebrows, thinking daughter? Also evil— part of their bloodline?

"May we record our statement? Another question, what make was my sister's pistol. It looked like a handgun but fired like a rifle and may have been similar to that used on my grandfather and me. You must now let us go. This carnage, I repeat, is a result of police force ineptitude."

The officer asked his photographer to stop shooting photographs of the corpses and to take photographs at all angles of both Stuart and Omega. He turned to Stuart and said, "I will tell my superiors we have mugshots that can be posted internationally if we find you are connected with this crime. I will phone my superior and ask him if you may leave before the grand jury or if you need to be present. The gun. It's Chinese. A QSZ92. I'll mail the slug that killed your sister to the Arusha hotel after we do the autopsy."

"Can it be fired at long-range?" Stuart asked.

The Nairobi cop hung up from his cell and turned to Omega

and Stuart. "Yes, the pistol can be fired with precision at targets both near and far away. You may leave, but I need a complete itinerary of your next week's plans."

Stuart was silent, then began, "We will be at the Arusha Hotel, at my grandfather's house on Atkinson Lane, or in Dar Es Salaam to visit with Alphonse's father. Here are the addresses. For your information, here are photos of how my grandfather's house looks today and another set indicating how it looked the day my grandfather was killed. These are on file at the Arusha police station. I'm certain you can have them sent to you."

"I will take these," the officer said. "You will get new ones."

Stuart sighed, saluted and released his hold on the photographs to the red-bereted man, thinking how quaintly colonial these British East African countries are. "One more thing, officer, there are likely to be bulldozers at my grandfather's house to prepare for a new building."

"Who would build in that place? It's haunted," the cop said, unable to suppress his interest.

"American scientists who want to develop a malaria vaccine. Scientists don't typically believe in ghosts and they like its location."

The cop shook his head. "Americans! Make the recording, then leave this country, before I change my mind."

Stuart and Omega recorded their testimony into the tiny tape recorder, Stuart handed his card to the cop, asked for an email copy of the notes and returned to the van. Once seated he dialed the Arusha policeman who had shown him the body and the murder weapon and who had indicated he would like updates on Stuart's investigation. Stuart recounted the two crimes he and Omega had witnessed, including Britz's confession of Ian's murder. Memories of his meetings with Neissa, still an unknown relative and her seemingly lonely life, crashing down on him, he tried to explain both the murders and the police behavior. Hoping he had made a mysterious duel as clear as he could and his need for new prints of his grandfather's death obvious, he said, "Omega and I are returning to Arusha. Would you have the crashed house photos and the photos of my grandfather dead on his front porch copied out for us?"

"Of course," the man said. "You are doing both Nairobi and Arusha policemen a service by investigating your grandfather's death and supplying any evidence you have to the Nairobi police to help them unravel this awful mass murder."

"I've asked the Nairobi cop for his investigation notes. Will you make certain I get them?"

"Indeed. May I read them?"

"Yes sir," Stuart said.

CHAPTER NINETEEN

When the two of them rolled into Arusha after the murders of Alphonse Britz, his team and Neissa Atkinson and her team, Omega drove straight to the police station where Stuart picked up another collection of photos. "Do you need testimony from Omega and me regarding the Nairobi crime?"

The rotund policeman shook his head. "Nairobi has what it needs. If there are additional questions both they and I know where to find you-- nursing a beer at the Arusha hotel or where to find you when the bulldozers arrive to level and lay turf to rebuild the old man's house."

"You know about this?" Stuart asked.

"A Ms. Rosalind Abel has been in touch with us."

Stuart frowned. "My business partner."

"So she said," the policeman observed.

Photos in hand, the pair drove to the Arusha Hotel where the balding concierge smiled with pleasure. "Mr. Stuart, welcome back. You've avoided poison mangos, rifles and your sister's assassin and accomplices."

"But how do you know all of this?" Stuart asked.

"African drummers have been busy since the Britz-Lehrman

encounter started."

"How does this work?" Stuart asked, uncertain what drums had to do with information gathering.

"Police pass news to nearest drummer. He drums news to next drummer and so on until it reaches Arusha drummers. They bring here for us to distribute to police. I, of course, read everything that police get."

"Of course." Stuart said, amazed in spite of himself at the clever telegraphy.

The hotel concierge handed him a huge package from Morocco that had arrived special delivery from Morocco yesterday. "Your sister's will and testament and some trivial items, I think. There is also what looks like a cheque from a Raj Agarwal in Boston."

Observing the unopened box, Stuart said, "What's your secret? Special glasses?"

"No," the man said flatly. "Neissa's maid is good friend. If Neissa should die, the maid was told to get this stuff to Neissa's brother, Stuart Lehrman before he left Africa, should anything happen to her. Neissa knew you were rebuilding your grandfather's house and that you stayed at this hotel when you were in Arusha. I told the maid to overnight the package so I could pass it on to you if you did stop here after the Neissa-Alphonse show-down was made known to us via the drummers. She packed the box; the letter from Boston had nothing to do with your sister's death. It was sent here while you were gone. Since I was curious if it was important immediately, I steamed it open."

Stuart shook his head, thinking how much he missed the simplicity of Brookline and his Erewhon work. Nobody dying. No one watching his every action. Just the daily drudgery of work. "Thank you for your help."

"Your regular room is ready," the concierge added, "and an IPA, Tuskers and orange juice await you at your usual table." Looking at Stuart's amused face, he said, "Police call ahead to tell me you come here. They want to keep close track of you."

"Nice to be back. Thanks for the room and the preparations." He turned to Omega. "You're excused, good friend. I'll dig through Neissa's stuff, get some sleep, and head back to my grandfather's house. I want to go back to the rubble before the scientists' construction crew arrives. I need to collect some additional items I left at the house. Let's meet up in two days to head to Dar Es Salaam. Regards to your family."

"Thanks, boss."

Stuart nodded, walked to his table and clinked his glass of India Pale Ale to the empty Tuskers.

He untied the crossed strings—one binding the top to bottom surface; the other binding the left to right surface—which fell in a pile across the table. He sipped his IPA, thinking how "Lehrman" like the binding was. He took a deep breath, and opened the box slowly. Would it explode? No, perhaps his sister was finished with killing.

He pulled the paper aside and wrenched the heavily taped box apart. There were two envelopes, one addressed to him, a second addressed to his mother, and a loose key. This all seemed so strangely familiar, but now two, not one, of his kin were dead. With the Monoclonal Antibody (MOAB) physicians arriving in a few days, the circle back to the beginning of this adventure would be complete.

He dialed his mother and took another swig of the IPA. When she answered he spoke quietly, "I'm safe in Arusha and am opening my mail. One was a box special delivery from Neissa with two letters. I wanted you to be on the line when I open mine; I'll send the one addressed to you to Boston. I'm using her phone, hoping it has no echoes. I'll use it until I buy another new phone and a new disposable."

"So as before," his mother said, "I don't call you, you'll phone me?"

"That's it," Stuart said and scanned the contents of his note which was attached to Neissa's will and testament. "My letter contains her will, her house keys and reads as follows: '*If you're reading this, my plans have gone awry. Britz's guards will have been better than mine. I leave you all my goods except for an annual stipend for my maid and butler. The maid is a great cook, if you need one. Do with the house and furniture as you wish; it has no stipulations. Would you see that the second letter gets to our mother? Our grandfather was not killed by me or anyone in my employ. I believe I know who did it and expect you to find that information when you visit my home. Look by a photograph of chained tusks in the den.*'"

"Stuart," his mother shrieked, "Roz phoned me with the horrible news. I've been reconsidering your mission. Perhaps you should come home and please do not feel compelled to investigate Neissa's murder. We know nothing about her."

"Mom," Stuart confessed, "I've met her several times. She sought me out in Brookline, she attended Grandpa's service and she asked for my help. I was, as Roz probably told you, present at her death. I think it is imperative to find out who Grandpa's assassin is and if he is somehow connected to Neissa's death. We will not have a sane or safe moment in the rest of our lives if I don't find out who murdered Grandpa. I watched Neissa die so I know who her killer was but, for all we know, Grandpa's assassin is after both of us."

Madeleine sighed. "I get your point but do not enter Neissa's home without backup."

"I had no such intention. Omega is joining me in a few days.

I cannot leave for Morocco or Dar Es Salaam for several days because he needs to see his wife and daughter. Now that he and his clan are dedicated to seeing me through this adventure alive, trust me, I will be accompanied by Africa's finest."

"Whatever," his mother said, slang uncharacteristic of her speech. She paused. "Stuart, please open that letter addressed to me and read it to me. I cannot wait the week it will take to get here. It may be useful."

Stuart slid his finger into the unsealed letter and held it thoughtfully, wondering what it would tell him about his sister. He read, "*Mom, I am sad I was not the daughter you wanted. I have done well and have considerable property and items which I have left to Stuart. I am sending you my bank number in Switzerland. There is a large sum of money there. Considering it was all gained through desecration of the animals and countryside of your father's Kenya and Tanzania, I trust you will see it gets into the right hands. Perhaps you would like to set up a foundation for African study in George Atkinson's name. I recommend a firm in Boston, not far from Stuart's apartment. The name of the investment firm will arrive from them under separate cover at your Seattle home.*

You will be pleased to know that I met with Grandpa several times before he died. I helped him source a few stories. I do not know who killed him but have some thoughts that I will share with Stuart. Have a good life. Mine has been pleasant. Neissa."

"Stuart," his mother whispered, her voice breaking up, "I think I'll be hanging up now."

"Mom, you could make it in both Grandpa and Neissa's name."

"Thanks, Stuart," Madeleine said weakly. "That's a good idea."

CHAPTER TWENTY

Following a few days of Hotel Arusha and its magical garden, Stuart rang Omega. "Ready for the Serengeti tour?"

Omega laughed. "A break from bouncing the baby would be nice. We leave in the morning. See you at seven. I'll miss the morning scream!"

As they departed the hotel, Omega said, "We're headed South east to Dar Es Salaam. This next excursion will take us through the Serengeti where the animals are in a national park but seem to be free. Serengeti means endless plain.

On the outskirts of Dar Es Salaam, Stuart said, "This is not a visit I relish. A man who may have betrayed my grandfather, father to the man whose son killed my sister and a figurine maker granddaughter who sends predictions of death."

Omega sighed. "We saved this visit for last because we expected it to be the worst. Do you have the address?"

Stuart opened his pack and retrieved a copy of the email that his mother had sent to the hotel that morning, wishing him luck and noting the Britz address. "Do you know Dar Es Salaam?" he asked.

Omega nodded. "Guy lives in the ritziest part of town. Don't know anyone there but everyone knows where it is. Old homes used to be embassies when Dar was Tanzanian capital."

Omega wove through the wide streets of this port city, clearly intended for more traffic than Arusha. Out of the corner of his eye, Stuart caught his first and unforgettable glimpse of the Indian Ocean, an ocean so pale, so green that it looked like a huge swimming pool whose bottom had been painted and repainted until it shone aquamarine. When they came closer to the beach he could see the waves. Yes, it was an ocean. At the waterfront, Omega made an abrupt turn and entered a labyrinth of gated multi-storied mansions, painted white or the soft pastels of Latin towns. The van stopped in front of a locked gate topped by razor wire, behind which stood a three story mansion. Stuart hopped out and searched for a buzzer or a speaker. Nothing.

"So now what?" he said half aloud while his brain whirred. "Omega, we need to ditch the car. Let's park it several streets away. Then walk back. We'll sit over there behind thorn trees and wait."

Omega frowned. "Why are we hiding?"

"My grandfather quit working with this guy. I think Ian might have fired him. He may have orchestrated my grandfather and sister's death. Let's not show ourselves until after we see him."

"What if he does not show himself?"

"Someone will need to come out for mail or to go marketing or for something."

Omega pointed to his temple. "Smart guy. I like this plan. We may live past tomorrow."

They parked around the corner in front of another one of the mansions and went back to the acacia tree where they stationed themselves. Nothing happened for several hours. Then two boys in khakis and blazers with backpacks on their backs approached the gate, parted some vines and pressed on a concealed buzzer.

"Boys?" a woman's voice said from the wall speaker.

"It's us, Mom," the taller boy said. They heard a click and the boys disappeared through a small gate in the high fence. As they passed through in single file Stuart noticed that the boys were similar in stature and girth, brothers maybe, he wondered, and close in age?

"Who? Any idea? The man and his daughter are blond white people."

"Servants?" Omega suggested. "My sister works for someone here. She has young boys. Unlikely she works for Britz, though. Like the rest of us, Ebele was devoted to your grandfather and would only work for Britz if your grandfather asked her to do so. Britz is a devious man and your grandfather may have needed a spy in his household."

"That would explain African servants, which a man like him would normally not have," Stuart affirmed. "He's on the paid circuit for speaking out against colonialism and improved race relations in Africa. We already know his granddaughter worked for her dad. That she also wants the Atkinsons dead.

"Neissa, like my grandfather, hired Africans because she trusted them. The South Africans both fear and loathe them. Remember Alphonse used fair-skinned Turks? I also think he employed white South Africans."

The air drifting up from the ocean was heavy with humidity, mixed perfumes of hydrangea, motor fuel and sizzling meat. Stuart could barely breathe. He pictured the man's awful eyes, the blonde woman's pistol at his sister's head, his grandfather's gored body, the elephant with sawed off horns, Ian's death and wondered at the improbability of this adventure and the disbelief on his friends' faces should he survive this trip and make it back to Boston to describe it.

Straightening his spine he strode to the gate, pulled aside the vine and pressed the button.

A male voice spoke, "Yes?"

"Is this the Britz residence?"

"It is."

"I'm Stuart Lehrman and I responded to a call for help from my grandfather. He is now dead. Anton Britz worked with him in his early career. I'm looking for information. Does Anton Britz live here?"

"Yes. I am Britz. Your mother phoned that you were on your way. I receive no visitors unless my housekeeper and granddaughter are with me. Both are gone. They will be back around five."

"My colleague and I will return then."

"I rarely receive visitors but because your grandfather left some notebooks here, I told Madeleine I would see you to give them to you. But only you."

Omega crossed his index finger over his lips and mouthed, "Not to worry."

Stuart backed away, more uncertain about this man, more determined to return. He rejoined Omega and said, "So show me the town. We have all afternoon." He rubbed his scar thoughtfully. "Curious that he wouldn't see us, no?"

"Sick people are strange," Omega said. "We go to my favorite beach for lunch."

They arrived at the iridescent ocean within minutes. Ships hovered in the open bay for no apparent reason. *Were they in line or was there no port?* Stuart wondered. Then he remembered the dead elephants, their cracked skulls, Alphonse, Neissa and Xiang Yu and his grandfather's poaching story and how illicit ivory made its way across this ocean to Asia. There, he had learned, if the ivory was not already carved, Chinese artisans fashioned the ivory into unusual and invaluable tokens. In resale ivory figures and talismans could be sold at a high price because acquisition of tusks was illegal.

Stuart was not hungry. A gnawing fear in his stomach and the imprint of all the dead bodies he had seen vanquished his appetite. Britz? Why wouldn't he see them? When the cherubic young waitress arrived carrying beers and waters to the men next to them, he ordered a sparkling water. Omega ordered the day's special, fish soup.

Men, women and children floated in black inner tubes near the shore. No colorful whale floats or water wings or even noodles. Just inner tubes. Interesting, Stuart thought, how the black tubes glistened around the black bodies. *He would love to be in that water. The humidity was suffocating.*

Omega's soup arrived, a stunning work of art. No soda for Stuart. The whole fish, tail and eyes glaring at Stuart was swamped in a circle of vegetables with a bowl of broth next to it. Omega laughed and said, "Do it yourself soup." He proceeded to filet the fish with a table knife, leaving a perfect skeleton behind. He sliced the vegetables and dumped them bit by piece into the broth.

"Well done," Stuart said.

"I cook at home. My wife not like to cook."

"I guess I'll go get my Perrier."

"Hang on," Omega said, waving at the waitress who had just arrived with another round of drinks for the men down the table.

"Perrier for the American, please?" Omega winked and whispered. "Waitresses love Americans."

The soda was in his hands in two minutes. Grateful for the cool drink he tipped her too much, bringing a blush to her face. "Thank you."

"See why they love Americans?" Omega said wryly, tipping

his broth bowl to his mouth, slurping like an Asian. Stuart, whose table manners were impeccable, remembered his grandfather telling him that it was rude not to slurp your broth in most parts of the world.

"How are we going to get you inside Britz's house with me?"

Omega swallowed the last drop and held up his finger. "One minute. Fish good, first finish all." he said, exposing some of the pinkish fish flesh on his tongue. He swallowed. "Gate opens I will walk in behind you. Maasai tall but not so tall as Atkinsons. I will hide. I will be around when you need me."

Stuart considered this. "No, if the man is frightened, he'll have servants protecting his grounds. They'll see you. You wait outside. I will press the gate release button when I have entered and will nod if it is safe to enter."

"Just nod, and don't worry about the button. I will climb the fence."

"Didn't you see that razor wire? Why are all these homes gated like prisons?"

"All rich people live in fear," Omega said flatly. He fished in his pockets and produced small scissors with blunt edges. "Remember Alphonse Britz's home? How Neissa's people open door? Omega come prepared—African wire cutters. Not perfect but they work." He looked at the empty plate and checked his watch.

"At least we're learning more about my grandfather's work and Neissa's life and death by visiting the old man."

They returned to the Britz home and Omega parked the van to one side. "You go alone, Stuart. I see you soon." Omega remained in the van while Stuart made his way to the buzzer, which he pressed forcefully.

"Yes," a woman's voice said.

"Ms. Britz?" Stuart asked.

"No, I am Ebele, housekeeper at Britz home and sister to your driver Omega. Ms. Britz was released by Nairobi police yesterday and is also here. I'm a nanny, a cook. Here in Africa I'm part of the family. Your grandfather Atkinson told Anton to hire me and pay me well, that I was not an indentured servant." Lowering her voice, she added, "I was to keep my eyes open for any illegal activities, such as ivory exchange.

"Omega, my brother has always worked for your grandfather and your grandfather made certain our family was treated well." Stuart hoped Omega was near enough to hear these words. He had told Stuart Ebele had a husband and children but he knew very little about her life.

"May I see Mr. Britz, please? I'm unused to talking to boxes, not people."

The buzzer sounded. He pushed upon the tall gate, noticing that Omega slid through and crawled soundlessly to the bushes. *Clever guy*, Stuart thought. Inside the vast compound a tall African woman waited at a white double door and motioned for Stuart to join her. He walked slowly across the bricked driveway, hoping to give Omega time to conceal himself. When he reached the doorway the woman motioned for Stuart to enter the vast marble foyer. "Mr. Lehrman, your grandfather is a hero in our family. First he made Mr. Britz put me on an annual wage and he left a stipend for our family from your grandmother's estate. It paid for my education. Then I sent the money home to my family and husband who was at war. My husband is dead. Britz does not allow me to see my birth family. I still send money to Nbola but do not have his news." Ebele's hooded eyes shimmered slightly. "My salary pays for my boys' schooling. The stipend buys their books."

"Thank you for this complete explanation," Stuart said,

amused that even Ebele, like his grandfather's other acquaintances, felt inclined to explain her connection to George, a subtle assurance that "No, I did not kill George."

He looked at Ebele and said softly, "Why did Omega not know you worked here? Why are you not allowed to see your birth family?"

"I inform no one," Ebele muttered. "It's so stipulated in my contract."

"I should have known. My mother said there was something curious about Dar Es Salaam. That it should remain last on my list of stops."

"Condolences to you and your mother, young Stuart. Your grandfather was good to my people. His work always cast a light over the Africa that had been dimmed by the European colonials. We welcomed his open heart and open mind."

Stuart composed himself, then said, "He was an unusual man. His work, at least what I have read, has given Africa credit for being a place full of gentle tribes striving only to leave poverty behind and to escape global rules for their behavior. Sometimes I have a hard time imagining him anywhere else but here. Certainly Seattle was no home to him."

Ebele laughed. "An original take on a noble man. Perhaps more accurate a tribute than any of us could have paid him." She paused, still smiling. "We all considered him one of us."

Stuart eyes wandered through the foyer. "I had hoped to speak with Anneliese and her father. My grandfather's early stories were written with Anton Britz."

"Mr. Britz has not left this house since he was gored by a rhinoceros on a trip to Zimbawe last year."

A woman with long blonde hair wondered into the room. "Ebele, who is here?"

"Ms. Anneliese Britz, meet Mr. Stuart Lehrman."

The woman's light blue eyes flitted from the matron to Stuart, whom she studied carefully. "So you've met Ebele," The blonde said crisply. "Stuart and I met when my father was shot and I was imprisoned. "

"I was here to find out about my grandfather's death and because we are blood kin I helped her right some wrongs. Remember your father and his men killed my sister before your father died," Stuart said flatly.

"I'll fetch tea," Ebele said in an effort to diffuse the sparks in the air.

Stuart studied Anneliese's face, trying to see the man he had met at Atkinson's funeral, her father Alphonse, and his blurred memory of Anton, the now gored companion of George Atkinson. Terrified by the brutal scene of his sister's death he had barely noticed the woman—saw only her blonde hair. She was not striking in appearance like her father, but shared the same albino paleness and water-blue eyes that made Stuart wonder if they were all ghosts.

Wearing a smock spattered with plaster and paint, bits of teak had managed to find a home in the long hair that was twisted in a tight bun at her neckline.

"I left my Oxford studies when my grandfather was gored and came to Tanzania to be with him. I grew up in this house and my parents lived here and in Nairobi. Upon my return I started sculpting, a task my mother had encouraged but which annoyed my father. When he moved away and married again, I began to sculpt again."

Stuart studied the woman whose parents were so different from his own and wondered that he thought she might be different from the other Britzes simply because she was closer to his age.

Factual, emotionless. Like Alphonse. Where was the joy in this family? On the continent, so far only the Africans, not the colonizers could laugh, he thought, a slight curve to his mouth thinking of Omega clinging to some tree like a fly on a hippo's back.

CHAPTER TWENTY-ONE

"Come join the boys, Mr. Anton, Anneliese and me for tea, Mr. Stuart," Ebele said, "I've made some special treats. Maybe you'll find something pleasant to say to each other between here and the dining room."

The wood foyer, freshly cleaned, shone through the beveled glass that framed the heavy doors. Ebele's boys, who had lingered in the background, walked forward marble tile by marble tile, their black feet speckled with triangles of sunlight. At the parlor entry they each stood unmoving at one side of their mother then stopped at the parlor entry like statues.

"Seems that like all good servants," Stuart said, "there is very little that Ebele does not know. Is she aware you and I have met before?"

Anneliese nodded and said quietly, "Come let's join my friends and family. Perhaps we can find other stories to share."

"Like why my grandfather was murdered and yours still lives? Why you were among those protecting your father when he and my sister killed each other?"

The woman frowned.

"What do you know about my grandfather's death?" Stuart

said.

She ignored his question pointing out artwork in the hallway. "This is the Middle Passage, a photograph my father, a teacher like yours, bought to illustrate the story of slavery and to recapture Turner's painting at the MFA. Have you seen the original?"

"Yes, I've seen the painting," Stuart responded.

At the entrance to the parlor was a photograph of a tall white man with Anneliese's blue eyes and hair, framed by two elephant tusks, chained to the ground.

"Why do you use illegal ivory in your sculptures?" Stuart asked.

Ebele's boys gasped. Ebele rushed them into the parlor and said, "What do you take with your tea, Stuart?"

"Nothing."

"Like all Americans."

Not true, Stuart thought and said, "I would like an answer to my question."

"Later," Ms. Britz said, "after tea."

Tea was a mixed display of Tanzania, England, North and South Africa. There was couscous from Morocco, delicate cakes and crackers from German Tanzania and Dutch South Africa. All were spread on a platter painted with flowers and faces.

"My hand-painted and kiln-fired plate, Ebele's teacakes, and Mr. Britz's crispies and sour cream from Morocco."

Curious, Stuart thought, that Neissa's Morocco was represented here.

Within moments, a once tall, angular man whose thin frame was crumpled into an elfin figure and crushed into his motorized wheelchair, exited a brightly polished brass elevator. Noticing Stuart, he smoothed his wrinkled polo shirt, finger-combed his white hair and said, "Mr. Lehrman?" He pushed himself up and out of the wheelchair and slid into the chair next to his granddaughter. Stuart studied Britz's muscular upper body. Like many wheelchair bound individuals his arms rippled with muscles. Strong enough, Stuart wondered, to wield an ancient spear? But, like his son, motive? Jealousy?

Glad that the boys, aged maybe five and seven, were banging their chairs around, Stuart nodded "yes" and examined the well-furnished room. He noticed a dark lacquered chair inlaid with white chips—ivory again?—and a pink ceramic tile. It was, he thought, another iteration of the Middle Passage with bodies, skulls, chains, carefully re-created using stones and woods of the region. He sighed. "Beautiful chair, the lacquer one. I have some figurines of the same material. Also embedded with illegal ivory. Are they locally made?" Stuart asked.

Anneliese's frown deepened.

How unpleasant this is, Stuart thought.

"Locally made, yes," Britz's deep-throated voice responded. "The chair is an antique, so the ivory is not considered illegal. The colored pieces are from a tile factory in Morocco. Your figures, I couldn't say." The man's deep-throated voice hovered somewhere around Middle C and a collection of intonations connected to the several languages among which he must switch, one for servants, another for his granddaughter.

"Mom had little to tell me about your son. Only you," Stuart said.

"No surprise. Alphonse was devastated when she refused to marry him. Almost as angry as I was when Ian sent me to cover shipyards so your grandfather could write and photograph his best stories of the African continent."

"Condolences on the loss of your son," Stuart said. "I will

not take much of your time. After you and my grandfather quit working together he still saw you. Why?" He paused. "Why did my grandfather stay here when he no longer worked with you?"

"I invited him to stay here whenever he had a nearby story to write. I hoped I could learn something from him by watching him work," Anton said. "Because of my son's illegal trading and my granddaughter's devotion to both her father and me, he knew we were hiding information and he continued to press for it. His servants occasionally brought us gifts and parcels of food."

Stuart studied the two Britz faces, trying to imagine his grandfather with these people. *No wonder his best work was written away from them.* "Did you tell my grandfather about this illegal trading?"

Anton shook his head and looked at Stuart with accusing eyes. "Of course not. When your mother left the continent and married, your grandfather returned to the house he and your grandmother built near Arusha. He never visited us again."

"He was a reclusive man when writing, but I'm certain he had nothing against you two. He rarely visited us and we are kin. I believe it was not only to be near memories of my grandmother and the Arusha home that he returned, but it was Africa itself that was his principal love," Stuart said.

"So it would seem," Anton agreed. "These last two stories we were glad we did not know about. Something Ian encouraged, no doubt."

Stuart shrugged. "I'm sure you heard about Ian. He told me there are several other stories forthcoming in other journals and notes for numerous others buried in the diaries."

"Some of the stories Ian conceived and Atkinson wrote threatened powerful people who they did not want them published. And, yes I know Alphonse retired Ian. He was evening the score for me. But others were after your grandfather. From the looks of you, you may have encountered a few of them. There may now be a price on your head," Anton said.

"Attempts have failed and may continue to fail as my guards include Ebele's brothers, Omega and Dalik and most of the Maasai clan."

"To cover any former connections with either your grandfather, his editor, and bothersome natives, both Alphonse had, and I have, 24-hour security service, recruited from South Africa. You might want to consider it."

"My current group seems to care about my and my mother's safety. That is enough guardianship for me. Besides, I need to move freely about to follow leads, many of which you and others have unwittingly given me."

Stuart reached for one of the cakes. Only the pink and yellow ones remained. Must contain something awful or wonderful, he thought, biting into the yellow one first, pleased with its lemony essence. He hated bananas and had been afraid he would be stuck eating them throughout this Africa trip.

Both Britzes looked grim.

Stuart, amused by their feigned disinterest in his transparent truth, said, "Tell me about the photo of the tall man, and the tusks in the hallway. I'm trying to learn about your granddaughter's ivory connections, her interest in seeing my sister dead, and the meaning of the ivory-studded figurines. Do the figures predict death? My grandfather and mother both received them. My sister received nothing. But then Anneliese was there. I believe my sister knew your granddaughter sells the figurines or sends them to instill fear. That she came to her father's assistance was perhaps in itself a warning to me and my sister?"

Britz closed his eyes and leaned against the back of the chair.

He looked up and murmured, "My son was in the ivory trade and passed along chips or parts he could not sell. My granddaughter has visions none of us can see and which are made tangible in her tiny sculptures that she sends to people we know and sells to Asians at the night market to buy our food. What we know about Alphonse we have learned from Xiang Yu who is a regular visitor here."

Xiang Yu, Stuart thought, a recurring link in the chain. "How appropriate that your granddaughter makes use of her father's ill-got money to sell illegal goods,' Stuart said. "I'm sorry you are so destitute your granddaughter has to support you, but then I would expect your son's death has left you both with a considerable estate."

"As honest as your grandfather. Maybe you're in the wrong trade. You might have been as good an investigator as George," Anton said.

Blushing with embarrassment, but proud that the man should compare him to his grandfather, he corrected, "Thanks but I'm no writer. I'm a financial guy on an investigation and am way out of my comfort zone."

Stuart glanced around the room, his gaze stopping occasionally at an African mask but finally coming to rest on a portrait of a pale white woman, a blue-eyed brunette.

"My mother, age twenty-seven," Anneliese said, "I think my grandfather liked her better than my father did so he kept the portrait when Alphonse moved."

Ebele poured tea, fed the boys quickly and shooed the boys outside. When Ebele stood to follow them, Ms. Britz said, "No, please stay. It is so quiet here."

Rolling her eyes until they were nothing but whites, Ebele muttered a silent prayer, straightened her kanga (wraparound skirt), took a seat and was silent. She was, Stuart thought, a living sculpture. How did one learn to be so still in Africa? Is that how his grandfather was killed? Because he moved when he should have been immobile and the specters thought he was a threatening animal? But he had lived years in this country and would surely "hear" the danger in silence. He was not a noisy unsettled man. Rather, more like Ebele, he was collected, composed, peaceful. Stuart's constant unpredictable motion might explain why he was a target in his grandfather's studio.

Anneliese looked up from her biscuit. "Death is a terrible thing. After years of living in Africa where death occurs with every breath nothing prepares us for personal tragedy. Tragedy is a mask. Tragedy happens to someone else. We heal it and we uncover it. We don't experience it until one of our own dies."

"Was your mother's passing peaceful?" Stuart asked.

"Is any death peaceful?" she said.

Stuart thought of the blood-smeared stoop of his grandfather's Arusha house door and looked away. "I can only imagine my grandfather's passing. You witnessed my sister's death. Why were you involved?"

"South African families bond tightly. Whites have always been different. Apartheid made us hated," she said. "It's almost as if the heavens created apartheid by placing us among people so different from us. We look after our own families and care little about anyone else."

"The scourge of colonialism. Is that why safari hunters, even Maasai, take down animals? To define their dominance?"

"Something your grandfather would say. And perhaps true," Anton affirmed from the secluded shadow in which he hid.

"An implication buried in the most recent article," Stuart said.

"Have you ever seen a dehorned elephant?" Anton asked.

"Several days ago. On our way back from Nairobi."

"You want to know what happened to your grandfather?" Anneliese interrupted, her face reddening.

Stuart nodded. "He summoned me to help him. I arrived too late and am learning that his writing about Africa's problems may have led to his death. And I have determined that your figurines are predictions of death."

"What *do* you know about your grandfather's murder, Stuart?" she replied.

"Only what I read in the papers, which is almost nothing. Additionally, I believe my sister had information about his death in papers which I have not yet secured. I will get them when I go to her house in Morocco."

"Before he was killed, a courier sent us some of George's story drafts and unproduced films. We never touched them."

Anton leaned back in his chair, removed the brakes and turned to his granddaughter, who kissed him lightly on his head. "Will you be staying with us?" he asked Stuart. "Your mother said you were a loner but you are welcome here."

"I have a room in town. Let me collect the papers. I have work to do in Arusha."

"We have the space. Ebele, will you show him to the guest room when you have a chance?" Anton motored to the elevator. "I'm off to rest."

"Sir, before you leave, can you tell me about the photo with the tusks?"

Anton shook his head and squared his shoulders, his weight moving from the center of his body to the top of his head. "That's a very long story."

Ebele took the photograph from the wall and handed it to

Stuart whispering, "One of your grandfather's best."

Having stacked the dishes, Ebele moved to stand before the open window watching her boys kick a handmade soccer ball back and forth, muttering the nonsense words they knew in English and switching back and forth between Swahili and Kurundi; a cloth ball dropping from heel to toe on their imaginary playing field that went the length of the four complex townhouses.

At the far end of the room, Stuart picked up a small wooden sculpture with ivory chips embedded in them and similar in kind to those Anneliese had sent to his grandfather and mother. "These are your sculptures?"

"I made them last year. They are sold outside the continent."

"But with illegal ivory?"

The sculptor studied her sandals and scowled at the painted toes escaping from the well-worn espadrilles. "You heard my grandfather. My father sent me chips from his illegal dealings. Some nations do not mind breaking the ban and will pay well for the figurines."

Stuart set down the wooden animal. "Asian nations, I suppose." He frowned. "I realize the figurines are connected with death. So are you. How and why?"

Anneliese reddened.

"What do you know?" Stuart asked.

"Africa needs your grandfather's activism and his intervention to protect African lives. People like me do not want Africa to change. We colonials benefit from white privilege here. Moreover, Xiang Yu was a good friend to our family. We are strategically located to assist him. He has financed this house, my father's operations and my work."

"But killing people? My mother was born here. She wants to protect the place and is now a U.S. judge. I'm a financial guy and can do nothing, but want to get rid of Africa's colonial trappings. Why target us? I get my grandfather and sister, but U.S. citizens?"

Brakes screeched outside the open windows, bringing Ebele's attention back to her boys. She raced to the door, clapped her hands and the boys ran back into the house. Having heard the screeching tires, Stuart left Anneliese's studio and rejoined the Africans to be certain the boys were safe.

One at a time they wandered into the study, watching the adults warily. "What's wrong?" one boy asked.

"Strangers in the neighborhood," Ebele murmured.

Sensing the tension in the household, Stuart reached into his pack for his ipad and sat next to the boys, "Would you like to play a game?" Anneliese sat on the other side of the two boys. Both watched the children who were studying the device.

"Wow," one said, eyeing the computer.

Stuart opened Dalik and his team's Virtual Safari videogame. "Here, go hunting. This is your land, your animals, a potential product my company will seek to get funded. Let me know if the game is fun." He smiled inwardly, wondering if he should tell them that one of their uncles was a principle designer of the game.

Fifteen minutes later, the younger boy jumped up, dropping the ipad which Stuart caught on its way to the ground. He pumped his fists over his head. "Mama, I won!

Stuart looked deflated but remembered Dalik's comment about having a nephew play the game as a test. "The kid's only six?" Stuart asked, "I'll have to put the geeks to work on the algorithm." He rapidly texted Roz as he spoke both about the young boy's easy win and the designer's relation to the kids. "Time to make it more difficult," he added.

"I need to check on my grandfather," Anneliese said. "Then

I would like more tea, Ebele. Stuart, boys, and Ebele, please go to the formal sitting room. We'll join you in a minute. Do you mind making some more tea? We'll have it in the formal dining room."

Ebele nodded, but frowned. "No supper? More tea in that creepy old room?" she grumbled, "Those floor to ceiling cathedral style windows make us sitting ducks for stray bullets."

Stuart pondered the comment and put his hand to his healed but grizzled scar. He was not anxious to be grazed by more errant bullets.

He studied the large formal room, frowning at the huge cathedral windows where floor to ceiling damask draperies had sashes tied back, the grass median and neighbors' houses in plain view. The room had the unused and dusty smell of the house in north Arusha. The curtains? Weren't they a bit conspicuous? "Shall we close the curtains, Ebele?" he whispered, after Anneliese had gone.

"The Britzes won't have it," she said.

Stuart turned to Ebele, "Maybe you and I could close the curtains, while the old man is resting and his granddaughter is away?"

Worried about the floor to ceiling windows Stuart stared stonily across the median. "I will do it. You and your family are loyal to us; one of your seven brothers is in my employ. I'm chasing another whose product reveals fine programming skills. My grandfather had considerable respect for your family and he also had a silk sofa like that under the windows that were shattered when my head was grazed. I will not be a target again."

Ebele placed her hands together in an Indian Namaste and said, "Thank you for the high compliment to our family. We have been honored to work with yours. The sofas are from a weaver in Morocco and were a gift from Neissa. Your grandfather's was red, not green, striped like ours, wasn't it? We must leave the draperies or I will lose my job." Ebele said. She summoned her sons and seated them side by side on the sofa.

Stuart shrugged, pulled up the internet on the ipad and said, "Have fun."

The boys grinned.

Windows, sofas, shotguns. The pain in his head started up again. The déjà vu was annoying. "You're sure your sons are safe?"

Ebele laughed. "They'll be fine. Come help me with the pastries. And the sofa is by way of the old silk route—wrapped up somehow in that story last week."

"Knots."

"Mm. Ugly children are not sold; they make beautiful rugs and bolts of silk cloth with their tiny hands. Beautiful girls are trafficked as prostitutes."

They walked to the kitchen and Stuart returned to the parlor alone with a fresh lot of pastries and scones Ebele had just baked. Stuart looked up to see Ms. Britz and her grandfather glide out of the elevator like visions in a bad dream. He bit his lip and tried to steady his slightly shaking hands. He pressed hard on the wrist point Omega's Aunt Lou told him alleviated headaches. Britz screeched to a halt precisely by Stuart's side.

Before Stuart could speak a sharp bright light and loud noise of shattering glass reached the hallway. Stuart bounded into the formal parlor, Anneliese close behind him. Britz picked up Atkinson's cobra headed staff from the collection in the corner, placed it across his lap, and motored into the room. Anneliese, having determined only hardware not persons were damaged, turned to the door and ran to her grandfather's side. She took the staff and walked with him to a loveseat next to the two boys. Everyone stood looking at the younger boy holding the frame of the shattered ipad. Between them, a tiny hole in the cathedral window indicated the point of entry. Stuart kneeled, trying to stay clear of the largest bits of glass. Using a scone, he sorted through the broken shards to recover the bullet. When the slug caught his eye he used the scone to push everything away from it and picked it off the floor.

The young man whose face was covered with tears, looked up at Stuart. "I'm sorry."

"Hey, kid," Stuart said, "ipads can be replaced. You cannot be replaced."

Ebele having set the teapots on the hall table raced into the room and swept up both her boys, pulling their faces close to hers. "You are safe, shaken, but safe."

"Who would do this? Just at dusk," Mr. Britz muttered.

"With a shot so precise it could have been striking a sparrow at 100 yards," Stuart added. He studied the staff at Anton's side. "Isn't that my grandfather's staff?"

Britz bristled, "My son bought it from your grandfather."

"But my grandfather willed it to me. Said it came loaded with good luck."

Ebele picked up the staff and handed it to Stuart. "Neither Mr. Britz nor his son knew of that promise, I'm certain." Under her breath, she whispered to Stuart, "I did. It's from Nbola, my father."

"Ebele, only your rebellious cousins and their rebel gang could have made such a shot," Anneliese said, changing the subject, "they have been able to acquire a cache of weapons so sophisticated that no one in Tanzania can come close to them when they are behind the rifles. They're invisible and faster than the bullets they shoot."

"Rifles and pistols they obtained from my sister and your father, Anneliese," Stuart interjected.

Ebele, who was halfway to the tea tray, froze when the front bell rang. "I must look after my children," she said.

Anton moved his wheelchair toward the front door. "We are not cowards, we know most of the rebels. You may all cower in here if you wish; I will answer the door."

"I will join you soon. I must fix my children's hands," Ebele spat out.

Stuart looked puzzled but with his grandfather's familiar staff in hand, he strode confidently behind Anton. He released the latch that the crippled man could not reach and unlocked the door.

Ebele remained in the sitting room, carefully removing glass shards from her boys' hands. She reached behind her for her sewing basket, took out the tweezers and extracted the glass splinters that were deeply embedded. "Sit still," she said, each boy squirming with pain, tears streaming down the younger boy's face.

"Ouch," the elder boy squealed when she pulled out a particularly deep one. When the blood trickled out Ebele wrapped it in the cloth kerchief she wore. By the time she finished both children's hands were wrapped in cloth to stanch the blood flow. The younger boy's face still streamed with tears. His brother took his t-shirt to his brother's face and wiped it. "We must be brave."

"Stay here, I must join the others. Don't leave the room unless I call you." She walked to the door and stood beside Anneliese and Stuart.

When Anton opened the door a tall black man greeted him. "Good evening, sir."

"And to you."

"I'm certain you are aware that Western electronics are frowned upon by both the rebels and the regime, neither of which is complicit with Western powers."

"Which of them do you represent?"

"I cannot say, sir."

"We know the law and obey it," Anton said. "These tools are not ours. We have a visitor."

Ebele passed quickly by the trio and began speaking to the young man in a dialect, unintelligible to the other three.

Observing Stuart's face, Ebele said, "A cousin, from a different branch. Nbola had several brothers."

Listening to her explanation, her fast words, the tall, slender man slumped visibly and addressed her loudly enough to be heard. "I am a soldier. The easiest way to think in the midst of blood, rubble and crossfire is to follow orders." He paused. "How are my young cousins?"

Ebele's fierce expression relaxed. The African's gloomy face lit up as the boys, peering out the door, recognized the man and walked into the foyer.

His face bright, the smile never moving, the man kneeled to the boys' level and took one of each of their bandaged hands. "What's this? Have my cousins been fighting?"

"An ipad broke in the elder boy's hands and when he and his younger brother helped me clean up, both boys cut their hands," Stuart explained.

Anton cleared his throat, pushed up his glasses. "Son of Nyango, nephew of Nbola, please meet Stuart Lehrman, grandson of George Atkinson."

The black man bowed to Stuart and said, "George Atkinson is a hero in this country but he did not support our cause."

Stuart extended a hand which the black man shook and nodded. "My grandfather did not support violence. He believed negotiations could bring down regimes, not internecine slaughter. He once told me that the numerous wars he covered as a foreign correspondent took so many future world citizens' lives that he would never raise a rifle or handgun, neither in offense nor self-defense."

"A true pacifist and a fabulous writer."

Ebele said, "Nyango and Nbola were brothers. This is my cousin."

A wry smile curling his lips, Stuart said, "Thank you for your precise shot. Anything less accurate might have proved fatal to your cousins."

Ebele looped her arm through the crook of her bone-thin cousin. His narrow face stretched and flattened, his almond-shaped dark hooded eyes were a skeletal echo of his healthy nephews' eyes.

Ebele looked at Stuart, "Your grandfather was correct. And this was a mistake. Cousins don't usually shoot their own kin. Nbola, my father did not meet Madeleine before she left the continent. Stuart will meet him and take a place in Nbola's memory along with Stuart's grandfather. Stuart's trusted guardian is my brother and your cousin Omega who brought him to us, then left. We owe George Atkinson our lives and education—his wife's funds sent my husband and cousin overseas to study. I attended school here on Stuart's grandmother's stipend. Why shoot at us, cousin, and especially at George Atkinson's grandson?"

"My grandfather would be sorry to see you and like-minded warriors tearing up the African wilderness," Stuart said abruptly.

"We are guardians, sir. Not destroyers."

"Gun runners and poachers?" Stuart asked. "That's an AK47 brand rifle. Not African made." *AK47s are traded in Europe.* "Was this rifle from Alphonse or my sister Neissa or Xiang Yu?"

"All three individuals sold to us and paid us to run guns through the rest of the continent," the rebel said.

The boys followed the tall Maasai who had shot at them.

"Out of here, boys," Ebele said, "Your cousin has work to

do. In our family, those that make messes are required to clean them up." She passed the young African the Hoover.

Before anyone said anything else, Stuart's Thelonius Monk ringtone broke into the conversation. He flushed scarlet, quickly pressing the silent button on his phone.

"I wanta see," the elder boy screamed. "A phone that sings the blues."

"You all go on," Stuart said. "The boys and I will look at this phone."

The rest of the group migrated to the family parlor where the boys hovered close to Stuart, hoping to see the new toy. "It's my business partner. Private stuff. I'll show you later. What do you two know about the blues?"

"Lots. Dad left us all his recordings. Please let us hear the phone again," the young man pleaded.

Stuart shook his head and said, "I need to return this call. Go join your family."

Stuart called Roz, filled her in on the Britzes and told her he'd call her back soon.

CHAPTER TWENTY-TWO

When they entered the smaller family parlor Anneliese picked up the bellows, lighting up embers from the earlier fire and handed the boys a bundle of kindling. "Feed the fire, please. Let Mr. Stuart work."

By the time Ebele arrived with fresh tea a tiny fire was glowing brightly. Anton was settled back in his chair, a pillow behind his head.

Stuart rejoined the group and said, "Give me a reduced version of your African vision, Mr. Britz. I'm told you turned to teaching after you quit doing journalism and that your son followed you into that career. African continental vision may help me understand why your people believe the continent is worth dying for and why my grandfather returned."

"Africa," Anton began, "is all souls, it is a union of humans that have separated and gone their way. But the land, the people remaining behind, have changed very little."

"Mm," Ebele said nodding. "Our friends and enemies end up killing each other because, like the animals, Africans can find cover in the landscape."

Stuart listened intently, wondering if inaudible and invisible beings, or one of the visible ones standing before him, had shattered part of his world already. *What was it Ian had said? Someone of his own tribe? Someone of light skin? This brittle young South African woman?*

"You will like the safari game, written by Ebele and Omega's brother Dalik. The country's story is written into a tour of Africa that keeps people in their homes and unfolds tribal histories they would never know or care about."

"But animal killing?" Britz replied.

"Africa is, as we've learned yet again today, not a safe place," Anneliese observed quietly.

"And for the unskilled, the non-warrior type, in fact, the pacifist types like myself," Stuart added, "a videogame is a game of wits, one in which a humble human mind tries to outsmart a devious animal mind."

Britz eyed Stuart carefully. "Clearly your grandfather's kin."

"A judge for a mother doesn't hurt either. You grow up watching your mother sort sordid photos of corpses and learn to hate weapons. If my grandfather sought no war, if he sought only to record, why was he a target? His only tool was a Leica and an eye for good stories."

"There you have it. He had words, the most powerful weapon humans have developed."

Stuart raised his eyebrows in question. "So what? Someone speared him taking his life, like this young man murdered the ipad. A lousy toss that made his end miserable, not a careful puncture that killed him immediately. I've seen his wretched corpse, lacerated without thought or interest in accuracy.

"My grandfather was a human who told stories. Yes, words are power. He unveiled Africa's mysterious dark corners in the two we've all read. But why shoot me? Surely, I'm harmless."

"You have the memoir and story pieces he left with us,"

Britz said.

Stuart frowned. "Tell me about the tusks, please. And please tell me, if you have my grandfather's work, why have they not tried to kill you? "

Britz was silent, his brow furrowed. Ebele crossed her fingers over her lips.

Stuart's phone buzzed in his pocket. *Why silence, Ebele?* Stuart thought—*had he lined up the dots and discovered the assassins?*

"I have some overseas phone calls to make. Please excuse me." He moved to the paneled window seat and niche he had just left, closed the curtains around the window seat and dialed his phone.

When Roz picked up, Stuart checked his watch and said, "Talk to you in an hour." Blocking the overlapping concerns wreaking havoc in his consciousness, he dialed home. "How are you, Mom?"

"Fine. And the horrible Britzes?"

"They know more than they'll tell and I believe they will slip up and lead me to the assassin.

"In the six hours I've been here I've learned Britz stole Grandpa's staff; the one with the carved top he had promised me. My ipad got shot by the housekeeper's cousin. She's Omega's sister and Omega did not know she was here because the Britzes made her sign a contract agreeing to tell no one who was her employer. Someone is tracking me like game. I think Omega and I will be heading out of town."

"Good idea," his mother said. "Please phone with an update before you leave their house. This is the best connection we've had. I'm not certain what systems the hotels have."

Ebele's cousin moved toward the table of small figures, which were principally teak with scraps of other materials. Holding each up to the fluorescent light to study them carefully, he said, "In these small figures, you mixed media—ivory, teak, acacia, abalone—material and figures, each with a story of its own, a disunion and non-conformity not present in the self-restricting large figures. Why?"

"I like color, dislike uniformity."

The African picked up several and said, "Please, may I have these? I cannot pay. All rebel money goes to maintain our families."

Chewing her lower lip, Ms. Britz grinned bitterly. "Funny, you should ask."

"Why?"

"Those are illegal, I trade them to Asians, send them to friends when I hear of impending death or trade them to buy our food." Frowning, she said, "Rebels steal from other Africans, like us, to send money to your families. She reddened. "My father desecrated Africa's beauty to feed his family when he lived. He sent me the illegal shavings and required me to work with him when there was a need. I accompanied him when he and Stuart's sister shot each other because of their ivory trade."

The African shook his head, still clutching the figurines. "I protect our country—both animals and regime change, yet you profit from both."

"So," Stuart, who had entered unnoticed, interrupted, "You are killing Africans to save Africans."

The African shrugged. "The regime murdered our family."

"African animals gored my grandfather," Anneliese said. "Stuart's sister and my father killed each other. The world is a cruel place."

The African frowned. "I would like one of these. May I find you food? Kill an animal?"

Anneliese's blue eyes bored holes through the African's

black ones and her voice was icy, "Do not do any more damage to this house. Take a figure and leave us alone."

Standing at the door, Stuart listened silently to the exchange. Unsure whether this man might one day be of use to him Stuart watched, then snapped a cellphone photo of the man's face and profile. "Anneliese, I asked you before how you know of danger that will harm others? Are you connected to the assassins?"

"Look carefully at the faces framed by the tusks in the photo. They were in my father's employ."

The sculptor shrugged and returned to her sketches, She put them on an easel and took out her light brown conte crayon. Stuart glimpsed a narrow pointed knife on her easel tray. He picked it up and asked her, "What do you use this for? Who is your assassin source? Please tell me about your father's employees—now that he and my sister are dead their employees are suspects in my grandfather's death."

Anneliese replied, "I know very little about my father's employees. One of them was kind enough to give me this. It makes the most precise cut into teak and can be used to mold ivory. They are pale-faced Turks and South Africans because my father did not like black Africans. You heard my father say he did not kill your grandfather so why would his employees be suspects?"

"Anneliese, you did not answer all my questions," Stuart interrupted. "Who is your source? The figures have signaled death or destruction in my family's lives and I wonder that you give them away. Why did you send one to my mother? Is her life under threat?"

"Your mother and grandfather's lives were in danger but I am not at liberty to explain. Since my father's death my information source has not re-contacted me," Anneliese explained.

Anton motored into the room.

Leaning on his grandfather's staff, Stuart turned his irritation on the old man. "I think Mr. Britz, it is time you tell me about the staff."

"Why did you have it and did you take anything else from my grandfather's house?" Stuart asked.

Nodding, Anton replied edgily, "Two water buffalo hooves, made into ashtrays, from your great-grandfather's trophy collection. Ebele bring them to him."

"Thank you, Mr. Britz, I am investigating my grandfather's death," Stuart snapped, his patience with this family gone. Stuart analyzed each of the faces in the room, searching their minds, their face shapes and his memory for "Knots" and "Blood and Ivory" in the collection of his grandfather's articles he had read. "It was," Stuart continued, "my grandfather's job to reveal the truths he saw in this continent."

Ebele's cousin frowned and muttered, "There is humanity in Africa's Africa. Your grandfather knew that. So do my father and uncle. We fighters are filled with ego, fighting for a sense of self. Many of us die. Africa will remain. Perhaps your grandfather died because he believed in Africa's goodness and never quit writing about it. His silk road story about exploited children came out the day he died, didn't it?" He paused and continued, "One who exposes the ugly truths of any continent is unlikely to live forever."

"I was thinking about that," Stuart said. "Every investigative piece had an ugly truth in it but every story was written against the background of Africa's beautiful landscape. He wrote only the best of your people, and yet died trying to share this goodness."

Stuart turned to leave. He walked to the window seat. "Your internet server is more efficient than many of the hotels. If you don't mind, I would like to speak with the States before I leave."

"Please," Ebele said. "It's the least we can do."

CHAPTER TWENTY-THREE

Stuart returned to his window seat and found a fuzzy skype connection with Roz.

"Hey Roz, what is the disaster message on my phone?"

"This is damage control, Stu, my man. You're doing a lousy job of taking care of yourself. I want you out of Dar where there seems to be dangers and off to Arusha where you are safe in the Arusha Hotel. I have contacts all around the place and can rescue you again since you are a distinctive six foot two white man....an easily identifiable target. Dar is home to Africans, many as tall as you, who back African trades and tribes who hate Europeans for colonizing them. They've convinced Africans and now prestigious political scientists that NGOs are neo-colonialism and it seems NGOs thrive in Dar and Nairobi. Arusha is currently my new best choice for an Erewhon international outpost. The MOAB doctors want to start work on your grandfather's house and are proposing to fund an Erewhon Arusha outpost. Atari loves the game and developers are playing Erewhon against several Africa-based competitors on this one."

"Dalik's family, which includes my driver Omega, and Ebele, housekeeper at the Britzes, is part of an old Maasai family my grandfather trusted." Stuart added. "Their brother, Dalik is the game designer, told me at the memorial that his marketing manager says Africans love games and will bet against one another during them. He expects Africa to be one of game's largest markets. Additionally, the concierge in Arusha is playing the latest game. However, as I recently texted, it's too easy for Dalik's nephews.

"Since my sister and Britz are dead, there can't be too many other backers in this country. Dalik would like African backers. I think I have a few in mind. Also, I need one ipad and another iphone—I'm taking no chances—express delivery to the Arusha hotel."

"As you suggested we should buy stock in Apple," Roz said. "We're contributing to their profit line. But yes, get the hell out of town. I fear for your life and you're starting to sound like a detective. Don't forget you do have a job."

"I'm not doing nothing," Stuart said. "These outside people, my sister included, were gunrunners to the rebels, selling Balkan made AK47s and Chinese pistols."

"What makes you think so?" Roz asked.

"Didn't you read the box label at Britz's house? The rebel who visited here said he bought guns from Britz, and Neissa. Since both Britz and Neissa are dead, if the trading ring is well-organized it's safe to assume someone else is the gunrunner. Arabs, Berbers and Chinese are all possibilities. My shooter may have been suggesting a Chinese connection with Xiang Yu's name on the wall."

"Ask your state department relative about Chinese and ivory, please."

"I need the information. Since my sister and Britz are dead, this Chinese group seems to be the group of interest," Stuart added.

"If you can get back to me soon, I would be most grateful. At present my and Mom's lives are in the "endangered" category. This is a tricky nation and nothing is certain. Everything takes time.

"And Erewhon, I don't get it. Why Arusha? Dar is a port. Shouldn't we set up the Erewhon outlet here?"

"All we need is an airport. You've discovered Dar's a dangerous place. There are Yemenis, Somalians and a whole ring of terror around the Indian Ocean."

Stuart groaned, rubbing the scar on his head. "Please do remember I got shot in Arusha and my grandfather was killed there. My sister was killed in Nairobi. Maybe we should go to Fes, Tangiers or just about any place but down here." He paused. "Can you get your tech connection to send two ipads c/o Ebele for my virtual safari consultants, aged six and eight? Since Dalik's nephews can second-guess his game I figure we can use them as skilled video game testers. Tell the local Apple store to deliver the ipads in apple crates or the delivery people and the ipads will be pulverized by trigger happy rebels."

"How's the murder investigation? And what are these rebels fighting for?"

"The rebels want a new regime." He tried to compose his face so she didn't hear his grin. "The assassin seems to be a collection of Britzes and other ivory traders. All fingers are pointing at Asia. I'm almost done. I'll be out of here in several more days. Farouk phoned to tell me he has some important information."

"Farouk?"

"The Indian camera guy in Arusha."

"Several days, Stuart? Shall I sublet your office to Ralph?"

"Please tell me you're joking."

Roz laughed. "Of course I'm joking. Bastard just won the new design house on Newbury Street where I was hoping to collect next year's wardrobe as a VC fee. He plastered my email with a lamb in one of their winning designs from last season."

"Send me a picture, please."

When the odd-looking sheep appeared Stuart recognized the creature that Ralph had created. Created by Dalik, the animal had the face of a goat and the wool of an English sheepdog. It was a copy of the wildebeest from the Virtual Safari game.

"That's Dalik's wildebeest. Roz, don't you think you better get the first-run of the Virtual Safari copyrighted so we don't have more problems down the road? I'm allowing every African child and teenager I meet to play it," Stuart said.

"Talk to you in Arusha. Enjoy your second trip through the Serengeti," Roz said. "Zebras, giraffes, cats, you name it. Sorry to put you through this terrible and boring field work."

"Not to speak of my original mission to find my grandfather's assassin and ancillary good times such as being a target myself and watching my sister die," Stuart snapped and closed out the connection. *All of which is somehow seeming to link up with all my Erewhon work. Is that why he sent for me?* He stepped outside the window seat and stretched his back before phoning Seattle.

Ebele, who had been listening outside the curtains, reached for his arm as he returned to the window seat. "Thank you for the ipads. You don't owe us anything. In fact, we broke your equipment."

Stuart said, "How much did you hear?"

The housekeeper blushed. "Only that you need to connect your grandfather's death to gun and ivory traders."

Stuart nodded. "The ipads for your sons are work-related. We'll need your boys to test the game. You'll have to shame your cousin into allowing them to use ipads to make them worth our expense."

"I think he's done with trashing ipads in our house," Ebele said.

"They can work in the cellar."

Softly rubbing his grizzled scar, Stuart said, "Cellars are not perfect. The ipads should arrive sometime tomorrow. I asked Roz to include an iphone for your household. Here's my business card; tell them to try to phone me while I'm still here in Africa."

He pulled her to one side and whispered, "That knife on Ms. Britz's easel. I think the assassin used it on my grandfather. Would you please take it and give it to me as I leave?"

"I'll do what I can. I certainly owe you and Roz. This Roz seems like a good partner. Nice of her to send gifts to my boys."

"Roz is loaded with money. Her fortune is the foundation of the firm, I run the creative side. She loves kids." He stepped back into the window seat. "If you will excuse me I need to make one more phone call on your great wireless system."

Ebele walked away.

To some room where she could hear everything, Stuart thought. He played with the computer until he found a connection that satisfied him then dialed his mother. "Mom, internet access is chancy today and I'm at the Britzes where their internet is better. They listen to my conversations so this will be a short call."

"So where to next?" Madeleine asked.

"Back to Arusha, Farouk has some information. He wants to explain his theory about Grandpa's murder," Stuart said.

"And?"

"I've got to get out of this house to talk with safety."

"But the hotel connection is so fuzzy."

"I know," Stuart said. "But these people are so untrustworthy."

"You met them and we might have clues about the

assassin's group," his mother observed.

He plugged in his earphones with attached microphone, asking, "Can you remember anything about Ebele's people? I'm wondering if there is some curious connection with the assassins at the Arusha home."

"Doubtful. I think her family is protecting you. Remember she is Omega's sister."

"I thought Tanzania's current regime was peaceful."

Stuart grimaced. "Not according to this guy." He continued, "Grandpa hated colonization. Is that why he stayed alone?"

"Your grandfather stayed alone so he could write. As for Tanzania, its political system survives because of corruption, illegal ivory and animal skin trade."

"We'll hope the Indian connection can help you. Shame Ian couldn't tell you all he knows."

"He told me Grandpa's murderer was from our own tribe. I'm wondering about the Chinese and the dead Britz. Puts Ms. Britz in jeopardy and she was at Neissa's death. Anyone else?" He paused. "I think she has the murder weapon."

"Doesn't necessarily implicate her. Find out where she bought it and from whom—Keep in mind that there are numerous whitefaces besides European colonizers."

Stuart nodded. "I guess it's back to the diaries and the new paper. Like you, I think it was a group not a single assassin and proof will be hard to find." he said aloud.

Madeleine coughed and listened carefully to the tone of his voice. "We have stories about prostitutes, guns, child exploitation and poaching. Notes on gangs and other unwritten stories still to appear. What else is there to expose?" His mother paused. "Are you well?"

"Yes, re-reading the articles, trying to understand the

people, the country and its social constructs. Hard to take off my Western mindset and just look at this country as a whole."

His mother was silent for several moments. She sighed and spoke slowly, "Ignore the country. Get your VC contract and find your grandfather's assassin."

"Does seem odd, doesn't it? Now Erewhon needs to bust up the double rings—trafficking and ivory sale."

She paused then said, "Stuart, those Chinese syndicates and Britz's employees, Neissa's Berbers. Watch out for them."

"Neissa," Stuart said frowning, "What did you do to make her so mad?"

His mother sighed. "I'll never know exactly. She once told me and you read in her note that she did not feel that she was the child we had wanted."

Stuart exited the curtains, thinking of the phone conversation and said his good-byes with little affection, even dispassion. There was something filthy in the air of Dar Es Salaam. He did not think it was the ocean. The moldy sick smell of the Britz household, its connection to crime—was enough to move him onward. Ebele escorted him to the front door, handing him a napkin folded many times. "The knife," she mouthed.

"Well done," Stuart whispered.

Omega, who had remained in the bushes until Stuart walked out, now joined him in the darkness. He saluted his sister. "We are gone, Ebele. We will not stay overnight. This is not a safe place. Maybe it's time for you to break your contract. One of Erewhon's clients is setting up a business in Arusha and we'll have an outlet there soon. Want to bring your sons closer to home?"

"Tantalizing," Ebele said, "I'll think about it."

"Agreed, let's get out of this town."

CHAPTER TWENTY-FOUR

When they drove back to Arusha, Omega glanced over at a tree and pulled a hard right off the dirt road.

"Look up," Omega said, "off-road is illegal that's why we're alone out here. Usually I find animals by looking for other safari vehicles. Look up. Enjoy this stealthy animal by yourself." A sleek spotted leopard pranced on her tiptoes across the top branch of an acacia tree, her head swiveling from side to side, seeking, Stuart figured, what she would eat for dinner tonight. Back on the main road, Stuart laughed as Omega screeched to a halt to allow the great migration of zebras, wildebeest and other animals that were crossing the road at a slow pace. *Share the road had many meanings in Africa*, he thought.

Soon the sun had passed from overhead to eye level, identifying the direction they were driving. The silence in the car reminded him of the seriousness of the mission. Frowning, he thought how few substantive clues about his grandfather's assassin or assassins—a bullet shot at Stuart himself, a bullet shot at his sister, several probable weapons, advice that the killer was 'of your own tribe,' but no clues on the identity of the assassin. He must focus on the tangible evidence and the experienced events. Was there an intertwined meaning?

Stuart was grateful for Omega's silence. The Dar Britzes confused him—hospitable but strange. Ms. Britz did whatever her father had asked and sold figures to assassins. Stuart's grandfather wrote his best stories after he and Anton split up. *But was the family's jealousy grounds for murder?* Stuart wondered. And given that the sculptor was small and the father gored, neither could wield a deadly spear. Stuart remembered the mark below the ear on his grandfather's corpse, but whether those cuts sliced his arteries was unclear. Was his grandfather dead before the spear pierced his gut? *Clearly something was amiss at the Britzes. But assassins?* He was not certain.

Stuart looked at the sun to determine their direction. They were headed west, perhaps slightly north. On the outskirts of Arusha he recognized a few stores and that funny meaningless word M-PESA which was how Africans wired money to their loved ones.

At the Arusha hotel, twenty minutes later, Omega led them to the balcony. He ordered Stuart's IPA, a Tuskers for the empty chair and an orange juice for himself.

Stuart looked down at the beautiful grounds feeling as comfortable here as he did in the living room of his Brookline apartment. He glanced at the fan palm tree, thought briefly of Rumila's long hair, and smiled at the colorful flowers that seemed to bloom eternally in the garden. After the beer came, Omega ordered a tray of vegetables and hummus, and was dipping a carrot into the pale yellow paste when Stuart turned back, brow furrowed.

How and why did Britz and his wife disappear at the memorial? Golden Keys had the cops there in moments. What had been their role in this increasingly complex melodrama and what had his sister known? He studied the woven palm tree then turned to Omega. "We need to go to Neissa's house."

"I thought so," Omega said.

"Can you come?"

"You figure out how to make that possible I will go."

"Can your wife and child stay with family for a few days?" Stuart asked.

"I will see wife tonight and make arrangements," Omega said.

Omega paused then continued, "I heard people talking outside the Dar Britzes's house about how stealing boys might divert you from ivory and guns."

Stuart flushed with shame. "I'm sorry for your people's murders and loss of animals but I'm here to find out who killed my grandfather."

Stuart remembered he needed to stop at Farouk's. He showed Omega the iphone text: 'please come to film store,' Farouk's note read. 'Maasai want to see you,' and said, "Can you drop me at Farouk's on your way home? One of your brother's wants to see me. I'll walk back."

Omega nodded and swallowed a carrot slice in one swallow then finished his orange juice. "I'll be ready to leave town in a few days. God knows what this other brother needs. Nbola make too many sons. So you go to Farouk's and find out."

Stuart laughed and climbed back in the van. When Omega stopped at Farouk's he exited and waved, mouthing, "Two days we leave, please?" Stuart approached the counter and winked at Rumila who was waiting on someone else. "Farouk, you summoned me," he said, addressing the camera man.

Farouk pointed to a tall black man with Omega's face who stood by the large Maasai photo. "Son of Nbola," Farouk said, "meet Stuart Atkinson, George's grandson."

The black man nodded. "Hello, Stuart. Condolences regarding your grandfather's death. I bring my father's greetings and an invitation from him to visit at our tribal property. He has some papers Bwana photographer asked him to keep. He would like to pass them along."

"Thank you. I will visit day after tomorrow with my friend Omega."

"Omega, good man. Good brother and good son. Smart. My brother and the man my father sent to look out for Bwana. Now he watch your back."

"How many brothers are you?" Stuart asked.

Laughing, Omega's brother said, "Five or six. I lose count. You met only sister in Dar Es Salaam."

Stuart nodded and said, "I presume Omega knows the way?"

The Maasai nodded. "He home often. Please bring him. He paid Atkinson body guard and he knows the way home."

Stuart walked back from Farouk's with Rumila. "I have work to do," she said as they walked. "Let's have a quick espresso and meet up later."

Stuart noticed that she was clad in her form-fitting blue sari and muttered, "Great." He took her arm and guided her back to the espresso place she had first sent him.

The nice waitress was there; the waitress frowned when she saw Rumila.

"I don't think she likes me," Rumila said.

"No," Stuart said. "She likes me."

"I get it," Rumila said, laughing softly.

"En tout cas," Rumila observed as the woman arrived with a double espresso for Stuart and a perfect crème de lait for Rumila, "don't take everything that Brother Number One says as truth. I think your grandfather had a much closer connection with their father Nbola."

"So I've heard."

Rumila continued, "Clans marveled at Nbola, bearing six sons before a single daughter."

"I guess I'll meet this fine specimen of male soon," Stuart said wryly.

"Don't know," Rumila said, "follow Omega's guidance because your grandfather trusted him and Son One, whose name I don't know."

"Given that he was the first son and the last was Omega, I expect Son One was Alpha."

"I think Nbola is building an elephant sanctuary," Stuart observed.

"Why do you think so? Sanctuaries facilitate poaching. They're dangerous."

Stuart shrugged. "Atkinson is dead, so we know it was a dangerous idea. His letters and pieces of words I have on the pages of the unfiled story. It's my current view, having observed the obliteration of the elephant because of the Chinese demand for ivory carving, that my grandfather died for the damned creature."

Rumila rose, kissed him on both cheeks. "Dinner tonight?"

Stuart blushed and stood to leave. "Eat at your cousin's at eight? We'll finish with my new favorite chardonnay back at the Hotel Arusha."

Rumila nodded and waved.

Stuart wandered back to the hotel wondering about Omega's family and elephants. He found Omega sitting in the lobby. He laughed and said, "Too much noise?"

Omega nodded. "You meet brother today?"

"Native drums again?"

"Phone. Work faster." Omega looked at his watch. "You dawdle? Pretty Indian, no?"

"Yes," Stuart said as they sat at their customary table, where all the drinks were lined up as usual. "Your father wants us to come see him because he has some of my grandfather's items and he wants to show me his work, which he believes Atkinson was writing about. Why didn't you tell me?"

"I didn't know. Family members don't tell youngest son many things. Don't really trust me. Dalik doesn't know either."

"Hey," Stuart interrupted, "don't worry about being young. Younger children are notoriously lucky. I'm the younger of two children and still living. And Dalik is a clever programmer."

Omega coughed "Hadn't heard that. But yes we'll go tomorrow. Now I go bounce baby."

CHAPTER TWENTY-FIVE

Stuart took an IPA off the tray making its way toward him and said, "I'm going to my room."

The bartender looked at him uneasily. "I put two Americans at your usual table who asked for you, along with your IPA and your grandfather's empty Tusker's bottle. This IPA was for Mr. Agarwal."

"How did you know I was in town?"

"Your partner phoned."

Damn that Roz, Stuart thought, *now he'd listen to her whining about a trip over here to cement the deals.* On the way to the table he texted Rumila, who replied, "See you at your cousin's. Eight o'clock?"

"Sounds good," she replied.

Glad to have an excuse to make this business meeting short he made his way to the balcony table. The Indian and Asian researchers stood when they saw him. Agarwal said, "Great table. Super hotel. We always stayed here when I was a boy."

"Is that the attraction to my grandfather's place?" Stuart

asked.

"One of them and remember I do have a research partner whose first choice was not Africa."

Chen nodded. "I wanted to do the Amazon. But Africans need this vaccine and are more welcoming to enterprise than Latin America appeared to be. Plus the ocean is close. There is a major airport in Nairobi. All these were deciding factors."

"Not to speak of your grandfather's reputation among the natives," Dr. Chen continued.

"Not all mothers are happy to bring their babies to be 'guinea pigs,'" Dr. Agarwal added.

"The vaccine has passed Phase II and is ready to go into clinical trials in humans, I take it?" Stuart asked.

"That's why we are here. Our mice data are solid. And mice we have aplenty at the Brigham," Dr. Agarwal said. "African babies rarely. Those we do get have wealthy parents. We need a general population, one that is most likely to be exposed to the virus."

"The house is nothing but a hole at the present time," Stuart said. "You can create your own sterile facility atop my grandfather's haven. I was planning to go out there in two days and would be happy to take you. I have items to pick up there."

"Excellent. We're staying here and can meet you in the lobby for breakfast, say at eight day after tomorrow?

Stuart groaned, but nodded. "No jet lag, I guess."

"Lots of melatonin and used to this overseas travel gig," Dr. Chen said. "In fact, we'll dine in and head right to bed. We're on the old side of the hotel. Raj knew enough to ask for it."

"Don't be surprised by the curious shower curtains."

The Asian laughed. "I've already used my shower and managed to get very little water on the floor. Remember we do work in hospitals so we are accustomed to curious bathing arrangements."

"Great attitude," Stuart said. "I'm off to dinner across town."

"Until two days then," Agarwal said.

CHAPTER TWENTY-SIX

Stuart walked along the now familiar dirt pathway past Arusha's central park. He struggled to remember the side street of Farouk's brother's restaurant. They had gone in through the kitchen. The man's name, he thought, what was it? Ahead he saw a neon sign saying 'Sayed's Place.' Sayed? Sounded right. He walked through the open door, looked toward the back to his grandfather's table and saw Rumila, her long hair down, not braided. Together with the smell of the tantalizing curries emanating from the kitchen, the lovely Indian was a welcome sight.

She stood and walked toward him. "Let's hear about the adventures you described to me in abbreviated form this afternoon."

He nodded as she kissed both cheeks. "As I noted, some good, some bad. I have met my sister again. I have watched her die at the hand of Alphonse Britz, her most serious competitor in the illegal ivory trade, and a principal suspect in the intricate web of my grandfather's murder. He killed George's editor, but said he did not kill George—I believe there is more to the story. As I told you this afternoon," he continued, "I hope to learn how Africans themselves are saving the elephants and will visit the sanctuary tomorrow. I'm told the Chief is parceling out only enough fallen tusks to keep his sanctuary running and to keep the people well-fed. I believe he has some important information about George I have been seeking since early on."

"I am sorry about Neissa but am glad you are learning the origin of the curious tusks that hid the diaries and the curved tusk photos. I picked up one of my grandfather's famous photos of several people standing under tusks. My dying sister said to pick up something like that at her house. Xiang Yu is there and several white people. I'm hoping to get more clarity at her house."

"Is the sanctuary it?"

"Not," Rumila said, "a reason to murder Atkinson, but a link in the chain maybe?"

"I had no idea that all of you, including Omega, and my mother, knew so much about all of their interwoven lives until, bit by piece, you are confirming it to me as I discover what was the root of George's passion myself."

"I believe your grandfather called you because you have new eyes to cast across an old problem that he could not solve."

"Chinese poaching?"

Rumila nodded. "I think so."

"Neissa left me her house and her trading logs revealing the ongoing trade and the intermediaries." He paused. "My grandfather's first writing partner and Alphonse's daughter are devious, unkind people, involved in all these deaths I've witnessed. I have little doubt they are connected to George's death."

"I believe you are on the right track," Rumila agreed. "Now it is time to refresh, before the last journey."

"Exactly. Connect with friends and conduct some business. The research scientists got in last night."

Rumila frowned. "Aren't you tired?"

Stuart stared at the Indian ocean mural over Rumila's head and was silent. When he spoke, his voice was labored, almost hollow in sound. "Mostly, I'm hungry. As for my mental state, I need friends tonight. I need to be reminded what my work is—to help others get started in business. I need to know this world can solve its own problems with the gentle prodding of people like my grandfather, Nbola and his family and all their heirs. Together my mother and I will finish his story when I retrieve the ripped portion and make certain the unpublished stories in the photograph roll are published, then find a willing publisher who will also publish the diaries. Tomorrow I will be Stuart Lehrman, venture capitalist, with the science researchers as I help them set up their clinic in my grandfather's house, hoping to convince them no one will die there. They will do good there."

Watching her uncle approach, Rumila said, "Ready to eat?"

Stuart nodded.

The aging Indian arrived at the table his arms filled with plates of naan and Indian starters. "My dear Stuart and beautiful niece. What a joy to see you again." He turned to Stuart. "You have been busy, young man. Condolences on your sister."

Stuart shrugged. "Such a small town this is!"

"Except for the death of your sister, we hear only good news. Enjoy the food. You've earned sustenance. Neissa was not an African star," the Indian said with a slight frown, "but she was your kin and we all hate to lose them."

Stuart nodded. "I have so few. Any missing ones are noticed."

"Why not make more?" the old man said, winking at his niece.

"Uncle!"

"Let me dine, invigorate myself after my exciting excursion

through Africa, then we'll talk," Stuart said quietly.

The old Indian nodded and set down the food.

Rumila, her face redder than the cayenne in the sauce tray mumbled, "I'm sorry, Stuart. Please forgive a meddling old man."

Stuart looked at her steadily, "Of course, on a few conditions. Walk home with me. Sip some wine in my room and I'll tell you my tales in seclusion."

"Perfect," Rumila said, turning to her uncle who poured them each a glass of champagne. "And take the champagne with you. Stuart says he has a South African Chardonnay on ice for us in his room."

"Of course," her uncle said. "The cook has your dishes prepared."

After the stressful voyage through East Africa Stuart did his best to eat slowly. Five days with native chefs and Ebele's young children left him with a mix of manners. He finished well ahead of Rumila. Dinner complete, he escaped to the men's room and texted the concierge at the Arusha Hotel, "Nederburg Chardonnay on ice to my room, please?"

"Of course. Your clients have retired to their rooms."

Why is it I always think Africans can hear what you are thinking, Stuart thought. *Because of their primordial sense of order and sentience, perhaps?*

He returned to the table where Rumila had finished, and together they walked to the kitchen to say farewell. Once outside the restaurant they took the well-worn path that passed a central park where men and women had gathered to sing once again. A random collection of Swahili words and sounds, Stuart observed that their music, like their gently swaying bodies, blended into the landscape. "Do Africans have funerals?" he asked.

"Tribal routines vary. A Chief may have a ceremony. The

increasing number of African Christians do have ceremonies in churches."

"Sounds like the old way was more in keeping with their general approach to life."

Rumila said. "Why such macabre thoughts?"

"Curious about what will happen to my grandfather's old friends," Stuart said, his gaze far away, wondering where Nbola and his elephant sanctuary were located.

"My father will die in my middle age. Uncle will be gone soon. Papa and I will take him to India with my mother."

"Nbola will have a ceremony?"

"I don't know. Omega might know," Rumila added. "Ask him or ask Nbola himself."

When they arrived at the hotel the concierge winked at Stuart. "All is set."

"I don't think my clients are anywhere near us, but let us keep our voices down until we get to my room. I'm too exhausted to discuss malaria vaccines at the present time."

"Agreed," Rumila said quietly. "Now about that wonderful wine?"

"I'm not certain it will go with your uncle's meal."

"But you like it, no?"

"I do indeed. My sister, who was a wine connoisseur, introduced me to it in Nairobi the day before she died," Stuart confirmed.

"Let's hope we can change the memory and divinity and bring you back safely from your visit to Nbola. I look forward to a taste," Rumila said.

"Perhaps I can play 'extract you from the sari' first to change the course of African memories."

She nodded. "Why not?"

He caught a piece of the cloth and spun her around, looking for an end or a zipper or anything. "Somewhere is the end of this thing." Finding it tucked in at her waist, he grabbed a piece, pulled enough so that he had a good grip, then spun her like a top.

Laughing and breathless, she fell on the bed.

"Not exactly the most graceful way to unclothe," Stuart said, his shirt open and pants in a pile on the floor.

"Ah, but it's not over yet," he continued as he found the zipper to her white undergarment. Her erect breasts now exposed he sucked briefly on each as he kissed her neck passionately and found her femininity. He entered the moist opening with his fingers, retracted them, then entered her. Following the explosion in his ears and her soft hands rubbing his neck, they rested quietly.

Rested, still staring at the ancient textured ceiling, Rumila asked, "About the wine?"

"It's on the table. The concierge and I are old friends," Stuart said reddening.

"So this is your usual technique?"

"I haven't had any women in Africa. And certainly none as tightly wrapped up as you are."

Rumila laughed. "A unique technique, to be sure, but never mind."

Stuart pulled on his t-shirt and poured the wine into a chilled goblet the concierge had left with the chilling wine. Taking the other goblet in hand he handed her a glass and raised his own "To my first sari unwinding and my new favorite Chardonnay!"

"To good memories and our next adventure," Rumila said, sipping gently at the wine. She slipped into her white undergarment to warm up in the air conditioned air. "Thank you for the pleasant evening and wine far better than my uncle's champagne."

She laughed again."Won't he be jealous when I tell him it is your favorite new Chardonnay?"

"Maybe he'll add it to the menu. And, I must say," Stuart continued, "that was the respite I needed before chasing the last clues in this intercontinental race to find George Atkinson's assassin."

"Will you be back?"

Stuart frowned. "I don't know. Our last port of call is Morocco. Sell enough photography equipment to make a trip to the U.S. with your father. I'd love to show you around the Northeast. You might want to consider the U.S. for your graduate studies."

"Might do," Rumila said as she wrapped herself in the blue silk cloth once again. "My father has always wanted to see the country of the 'great white hunters,' and the colony that made a better pass at democracy than did India."

"Not all would agree with you there. But if that's the mythology that is necessary to bring you to the U.S. let's leave it."

"Goodbye, Stuart," Rumila said.

CHAPTER TWENTY-SEVEN

After she left, he phoned Roz and listened to her spin a tale of remarkable information.

"How did you get all this?" Stuart asked.

"The same way you will get the game. We're clever," Roz said.

"Are the researchers okay that I have not found George's assassin yet?"

"Yes, they believe the assassin won't touch Africans."

"Interesting thought. Worthy of note."

He hung up the phone and took out a black lined schoolboy's notebook he bought in Nairobi and wrote it down, piece by piece:

FACTS

1. Ms. Britz and Anton were illegal ivory goods traders to Asian markets. They sold Alphonse's tusks to Chinese. Alphonse connected to Xiang Yu through employees; Neissa dealt directly with Xiang Yu

2. Alphonse had so covered his tracks, his contacts could not be traced. And he was dead.

UNKNOWNS

3.   How small was the bullet in Ian's gut? A pocket revolver?

4.   Why always the gut? Hunger? Or was it even the same person?

5.   The MOAB drug was selling. Yay! But use of his grandfather's house? At least he knew a good Indian family nearby for the MOAB physicians to contact if they needed help.

6.   Assassin might not touch Africans.

Stuart ran his fingers up and down the list trying to think of relevant questions to ask his mother. He dialed her cell. She picked up in an instant. "Where are you?"

"In my hotel," Stuart said. "I have an IPA in hand and a laundry list of questions for you. Ready for the questions?"

He looked at the ceiling, slowed his breath and glanced down his list. "So here are the facts I have so far," he said and enumerated them. "Maisie got shut down. Her stuff was coming from Britz. Would Britz have Grandpa killed?"

"I don't know much about the adult Britz," Madeleine said.

"Does it make sense to you that Neissa or Alphonse's employees might have shot Grandpa since he was going to publish the sanctuary story making it fair game for any trader?"

"That's a good thought; anything Neissa might have said or might have in her home would help you out there. I think Morocco is on the list of African visits."

"It is. There's an important photograph there and good loyal Africans... Got to close an Erewhon deal here in Arusha, meet Nbola, then I'll persuade Omega to take me to Morocco."

"Keep in touch, son. Glad you returned from the Britzes alive."

After he hung up he laid out all the solid information on the Arusha bed. This time he divided it in half. On one side was his grandfather's note summoning him to Africa, his grandfather's house and safe deposit keys and his staff, the photograph of himself with the Africans from his childhood visit, the photograph of the Maasai spear that had gutted his grandfather, the exacto knife that probably killed him. On the other side he laid Neissa's keys, the bullet that killed her, her ashes in a brown paper box. She had asked for no special service or attention upon death, but Stuart had her cremated and would scatter her ashes in the Mediterranean near her home.

He sat in a chair opposite the bed, studying the pieces carefully. *Should he ask Omega if he could leave at once for Morocco?*

He flashed a phone photo of his collection of memorabilia and sent it to Roz asking if she observed any sensibility in any of the puzzling parts.

The Bush Years, he thought, when Ian met his grandfather. What was his grandfather doing? And when did the elephants come into the picture? And Mr. Yu? Neissa's photograph would help but the Britzes who were directly connected to Xiang Yu? Roz had confirmed the Dar Es Salaam Britzes shipped Alphonse's tusks and that Dar was the African 'gateway to Asia.'

He wandered through the back streets of Arusha, hoping to avoid beggars. The African hustler that hovered along the road between Farouk's, the Hitowa coffee shop and the Arusha Hotel clock fell into his stride just past the clock. Stuart smiled inwardly at how omnipresent the man was. "What do the Maasai have to do with the elephants?" Stuart asked him.

"My clan. Some are trackers for poachers. Some poach for money. Chinese pay well. Generally, Maasai and elephants behave like Maasai and lion. We live in harmony."

"I've seen African leopards and lions in Tanzania and will now visit the elephants. Did the African animals ever live in Arusha?" Stuart asked.

"Elephants were everywhere before white man came and killed them and Chinese carvers began to make artworks from them."

"Tell me about the Chinese carvers."

"Use your imagination. Did you visit the Wood Carver's market?"

When Stuart nodded, he thought again of Xiang Yu. "Of course." *Do some tusks cross the Indian Ocean, already carved? Easier to disguise? And was this among the remaining stories in the roll—the one that read "Neissa", the other "Xiang Tong"?*

CHAPTER TWENTY-EIGHT

Stuart rose and showered at five in the morning. He ignored the plastic that served as a shower curtain, shaved and dressed quickly, checked his messages. There was one from Omega. "Nbola can't wait. I see you for breakfast."

Another from Roz. "MOAB wants a conference call when you return. They're ready to start testing. They need a contract"

"I'm meeting them in two days. Off to see the elephants. Please fax the contract to me here."

Stuart was in the lobby at 5:45 and watched the capable hoteliers set up their breakfast display. The repetitiveness of their movements was calming. In the small room the smell of pork, beef and poultry mixed with various eggs and vegetables. Africans did breakfast with gusto, Stuart thought, watching the balcony bartender create an elaborate display of fruit and vegetables into a multi-colored sculpture of food, resembling the African tribal headdresses he saw on the street. Interesting, he thought, few Africans go out of their way to assert their tribal heritage, their ancestry. But they were at home. You're the odd one out, Stuart, he thought.

Omega took the seat next to him, followed his gaze and said, "Penny?"

"Thinking how complete this country is," Stuart responded. "Everyone is what they are."

"You thought different?"

"No, just thinking how isolated Africans would feel if shipped overseas, ripped out of this beautiful place confronted by people not like them." Stuart paused. "I'm beginning to feel how lonely slaves must have felt."

"Is that how you feel?" Omega asked.

Stuart's eyes widened and he shook his head. "I came here by choice."

"Did you?"

"As you said and the policemen confirmed, no one else will find my grandfather's killer," Stuart said. He turned and looked at Omega full in the face. "Let's go see the elephants."

When they left Arusha, Omega pulled onto the major highway to the interior and drove rapidly, looking neither to the right nor the left. Stuart texted Dalik they were going to see Nbola and invited him to join them. He declined saying he was still working on a new variant of the wildebeest. "Fine, we'll catch up on the terrace. Send upgrades to your nephews. They are my test site." Stuart wrote back.

Stuart, who was watching the landscape whiz by, tried to determine where they were, checked his iphone and learned they were somewhere between Arusha and Dar Es Salaam. Expecting to continue at this pace for some distance, he was surprised when Omega pulled the van to the side of the road and said, "We walk from here. Van would not pass through this trail."

Feeling the familiar uncertainty Stuart had felt since arriving at any location of danger, Stuart asked, "What's the likelihood of the van's still being here when we return?"

"Fifty-fifty," Omega said, reddening. "Who's your back up, another of my cousins?"

"How about a brother? They would know where we are. Give me a number." Stuart dialed and began, "Hello, Alpha. George Atkinson's grandson, Stuart here. We met at Farouk's the other day. Omega is driving me to see your father and there are car thieves around this neighborhood. Can you watch Omega's van? We're about fifty kilometres out of Arusha—you know the place—near a stretch mall with maize and beautiful women.

"No you don't have to stay here. Just drive by every day." He remembered the check from the scientists for his grandfather's house. "If you can stop a car-jacking," he continued, "I'll pay you an extra $500. My daily rate is $100. We'll be back in two to three days and will phone immediately upon our return."

"What?"

Stuart ignored his question and said, "Yes, we'll give Nbola your greetings," confident that a son and brother would know the danger they were facing by undertaking this trek.

Omega touched Stuart's sun-burned bare arm, crossed his fingers over his lips and pointed to a spot in the reeds on one edge of the savannah. "Cheetah," he said as the snow white spotted cat stood up to survey the herd of animals in the middle of the grassland. "Rarely show themselves. They're diurnal so hunters or workers are busy when they're hunting."

Stuart, annoyingly anxious to see the world's fastest land animal run, said, "Can't we startle him so he'll race across the plain?"

Omega shook his head, a lop-sided grin on his face. "You tourists! We're on a wildlife refuge. They're endangered and number so few that each ranger has charge of a handful of them."

Stuart removed his long range binoculars from his pants pocket and studied the cat's face. His grandfather, he remembered, had bemoaned the absence of a photograph of this beautiful animal, an odd mixture, Stuart thought, of a snow leopard and a tan leopard. Famous, he knew, for odd markings around the eyes, he could just make out the 'tear stripe,' the stripe running from eye to nostril end. No actual tear drops, just a line suggesting ongoing weeping? Was the cat the creature of most feeling in the heavens' format of African animals? Stuart wished the animal had attended the funerals of his loved ones. Maybe the killings would stop.

Something about this trail and savannah looked oddly familiar, or did all African savannahs look the same? When they reached a hilltop and Stuart saw the narrow trail they must travel he knew he had been here before. "Is it likely my grandfather would have taken me to your father's house?"

"Yes, my father has been trying for years to help Africa and our family. I fear," Omega paused and continued, "that Nbola is not thinking clearly and is now doing Africa harm."

Stuart was breathless when they reached the top of the trail, but he gasped when he looked at the savannah below them. About one hundred old elephants—true tuskers—chomped idly on the fresh grass beneath them. Near them was a small herd of females with young calves suckling or sleeping. He considered how alike all mammals were, alternating between sleep and food. On the other side of the grassland, young boys were throwing spears or firing guns at targets.

"We will take the long way around," Omega said, leading Stuart to a narrow path that spiraled like a hidden staircase into the grasslands below. "Follow me and watch your step."

Stuart did watch his step but was more fascinated by the elephant dung than put off by its foul odor, less stinky by far than the cow dung used on Maasai huts. Decorated with pieces of grass and leaves that the large mammal consumed Stuart reflected on how harmless—how ecologically valuable—this gigantic mammal was. Consuming branches and grasses that grow back they ensured that the cycle of life in the African nations was untainted. Once on the savannah and close to the herd, Stuart was amazed at how comfortable he was near these large mammals. He pointed to a female on its side offering her teats to babies.

"Nice to see a living elephant and her babies," Stuart said.

Omega nodded.

The males stood apart from the female and young animals, but were sniffing the air suspiciously as they caught wind of the humans. "Should we leave?" Stuart asked anxiously.

Omega shook his head. "These large forest animals have not been hunted for years. They do not fear us."

"What about Xiang and his people?"

"My father pays his native boys to climb trees outside the sanctuary and survey the contiguous area. His men are trained to wound the poachers with arrows in whatever arm they carry a weapon. They are essentially better shots than the poachers who train for months to make quick, precise brain shots that will not harm the tusks."

"They are required to study African animal anatomy before they are hired."

Stuart hesitated, then asked, "Who teaches them?"

"Nbola and his brothers."

Stuart grimaced. Thinking of poachers, he remembered the Britzes. "Do the Britzes know of this place?"

"My father has killed several Turks who tried to enter," Omega replied, "So, yes I think Alphonse knew about the sanctuary but, no non-African besides your grandfather has been inside."

Stuart did not think these Maasai were out for his grandfather. They needed his help. *The exacto knife Ms. Britz had on her easel? An Alphonse employee gave it to her, yes? Thank heaven another of Nbola's children, Ebele, had her eyes on this pair.*

Walking through these peaceful beasts, Stuart wondered about his grandfather's prize-winning photo. "Does the female in 'The Charge' still live?"

"No," Omega said. "But her children and grandchildren wander out there. My father kept her through her lifetime out of respect for your grandfather. She is long dead."

Stuart's face brightened at Nbola's thoughtful tribute to his grandfather and asked, "How do they force such peaceful beasts to charge," watching an old tusker scratch his head on the acacia tree. "Threaten their young?"

"Are you kidding?" Omega said, his black face covered with an ear to ear toothy grin. "Too dangerous. Trackers click sticks from a safe distance."

"This is your father's doing?" he asked Omega, the surprise evident in his voice.

Omega nodded. "He thinks he is saving our animals, Africa and teaching African boys to be men."

Stuart stopped. "He's providing poachers with an ongoing income. You knew of this all the time we have been together and you said nothing?"

Omega reddened. "You can believe me or not, but I did not connect what he was doing with the damage it might cause. Your grandfather had drafted a story about the sanctuary and after he showed it to my father, George ripped it in half, asking Nbola to save it for you. You were on your way to Africa and would cover for George should he be murdered. George swore me to secrecy because he thought that by keeping the animals alive he would remain alive. He had no idea who was tracking him but was certain it had to do with Africa's elephants. He suspected but he did not know they would cause his death."

"What he did not know," Stuart added, "I expect, was how to solve the Chinese puzzle."

"Exactly. I think he knew who, just not why and how."

"Your father is in grave danger," Stuart said.

"I know. My brothers and I did not know about all the Chinese connections, their commercial willingness to kill for ivory, until you and I discovered it together. Nor did we know—though I believe your grandfather did—about Alphonse, your sister and the Dar Es Salaam Britzes." The African sighed. "Stuart, remember my brothers and I are 'city Maasai.' We're educated, have jobs and live far from the tribe. I have seen more killing in the two weeks I have spent with you than I have seen in my life. None of us have killed men, only the obligatory lion.

"Little brother Dalik begged off shooting anything to go to college."

"I think my grandfather's connection with your family may help Erewhon clinch the deal with his team. Dalik asked your father for his opinion on my character. Also it appears all other African competitors are dead." Stuart affirmed.

"True enough," Omega claimed.

"Will your father give me the paper?" Stuart asked. "He may not like how my mother and I try to re-write George's story of Nbola's sanctuary."

"Not to worry," Omega said. "The chief is old enough to have killed people and they trust blood lines. He liked your grandfather. Most Maasai are herders. Peaceful people."

"It's uncommon for Maasai to become warrior-like and break international laws."

"Like your father? One who protects elephants?" Stuart asked.

Omega shook his head. "I'm certain he knows about Xiang because he is selling ivory."

"He's selling ivory," Omega repeated coolly. "He needs money to maintain his elephant sanctuary."

"What a twist of logic," Stuart interrupted.

"Isn't it? The ivory was poached by people your sister and Britz hired and who could outsmart the kids or worked under the veil of night, and elephants are mass produced by Africans. Now that Neissa and Britz are dead, someone else will step into their lucrative tusk-trading businesses. Why shouldn't Africans get a piece of the action? My father also sells calves to zoos for people who can't visit Africa."

"We need to talk with your father and get my sisters' trade logs," Stuart muttered. "Then we can connect the ivory, the Britzes, the Chinese and my grandfather's death. Further, we need the other half of that paper because we must find a publisher for my grandfather's story, "The End of Elephants" or "The End of Ivory.""

"Follow me," Omega said sadly. "We will find him."

Wondering at the Maasai's sorrowful face, Stuart said, "I will turn the books and the drawings over to the policemen. They will not imprison an aging warrior trusted by my grandfather. Perhaps they'll even get the government to fund his elephant hideout."

"Let's go get that paper," Omega murmured.

Sneaking one last glance at the peaceful large mammals, Stuart turned and began his ascent up to the village. He turned halfway up, focused his phone and snapped as many photos of the mammoth animals and their young as he could.

An elephant sanctuary, he thought. Run and maintained by

Africans but funded by illegal exports to foreigners. Surely there was no crime in that? Except for killing the elephants. And who owned the elephants? Surely this was the ripped story? Could he help realize all these old mens' dreams by contacting Foundations, African Wildlife Foundation, International Elephant Foundation? Or could he set Roz up with that 'cause.' She'd love one—not since college had they been able to march for or pamphlet for anything other than new start-ups. His sister left him the logs and the Moroccan house—surely, it would bring in enough to buy them a seat on some board. Roz would love it. He texted her the photos and added, "Let's fund this thing."

She responded immediately, "Wow! Wouldn't that be slightly illegal?"

"It's tribal land. I wonder what rangers would think of a sanctuary conceived of and run by Africans themselves to regain stature, feed their children and protect their continent's animals?" Stuart returned.

"An African run African animal sanctuary—I'll get on it! Can I see the elephants some day?"

"Of course, I'm not coming back. Once I close the deal with Dalik I'll set Agarwal and Chen up at my grandfather's house in a few days. Now I'm onto solving a crime. I've assembled most of the clues to substantiate the murder of my grandfather. I need to finish this and return to Boston. You can travel to the elephants when I come back to Boston. In the meanwhile, get some funding so we can make this old man's sanctuary legal."

* * *

As they made their way back up the trail from the elephant savannah, Stuart was as apprehensive as he had been on his way to meet Farouk and Ian, both companions of George. They arrived in the village, a small circle of round wooden huts, each with a thin wisp of smoke emitting from cooking stoves. Smaller but nearly identical to the village where Omega's aunt lived, Stuart was, as before, impressed with the careful use of natural materials.

The circular huts woven of twigs and plastered together with grass and cow dung were small, although well-made.

"Do these sticks fall from trees or do the warriors chop them? "Stuart asked.

"Our people use what nature and animals discard. Only occasionally do warriors have to find twigs for the women to weave the huts. Our women stick large pieces of tree branches to frame the house and take flexible branches to connect them, like they weave their cloth. The combination of dung and urine is the mortar that covers the wooden frame and holds the structure together. Come," Omega said walking across the circle to the largest hut, one that actually had a woven door where most of the rest of the huts were open. The large one was covered with a cloth that was rolled open.

Open door policy, Stuart thought and said aloud, "How are problems solved in the tribe?"

"A Council of Elders comes together which includes my father; they discuss whatever problem is at hand."

"Do we present the problem of the ivory and the question of the story to your father first or must he convene a meeting?"

"He will decide. Wait here. I know you are not fond of African hut's air ventilation. I will bring my father to you."

Stuart stood aside, gratitude shining from his hazel eyes. Africa's sun was at its zenith and while extremely warm, he did not look forward to the sun-drenched scent of the chief's house.

Omega's family emerged within moments. Next to Omega a taller more muscular man wearing the traditional Maasai red cloth stood at his side. A diminutive grey-haired woman in a blue kanga walked behind them. When she reached Omega's side, she looped her arm through his. Covering the short distance from his house to Stuart with two strides, the balding chief stood for a moment then spoke, "Stuart Lehrman, I presume."

"Yes sir," Stuart said, extending his hand to the older man, vaguely mindful that this might be inappropriate, but uncertain how else to greet the famed tribal chief.

The old man took his hand, then dropped it, his gaze steady on Stuart's face. "Welcome."

"I have heard about you from your sons and am attempting to make sense of a split story my grandfather left with you. I have seen your conservation project and understand you may have some papers for me; this split story may have been about your work."

The old man nodded and reached into his waist pouch for a bag. "This part of your grandfather's writings was in my safekeeping as your grandfather did not know when or if he would survive the threats on his life, both for this African story and for other exposés. He warned me there would be trouble but often old men, like your grandfather and me, do not listen to what we do not want to hear. Additionally, he knew his granddaughter was involved in poaching and did not want to precipitate her death."

Stuart frowned. "These traits made my grandfather a careful journalist and loyal family member. That he waited to publish this article was likely to give you more years to make your sanctuary successful." He paused, looking first at Omega and then Nbola. "I am a venture capitalist, working with interesting new companies. My partner loves children, our company and large animals. She is searching the states for funding for this place so that you will not have to trade ivory illegally. When the tusks break off, do with them as you will, but please, in my grandfather's name, accept our help with your cause because I think your family helped him live through all but the last threat on his life. Do not sell elephant tusks to maintain the sanctuary; that is a contradiction in terms. You are killing animals to grow others. Allow them to live out their lives.

"I hope to piece together this last story, and integrate African policy, like yours, and Chinese travesty like Xiang's, into the story. I will have my deceased sister's trading logs that trace the profit in ivory sale to the Chinese. With these sources we can set up trade within this sanctuary to keep the elephants and the ivory business successful. This idyllic place will be a certain stop on future Tanzania safaris."

"Careful, Stuart," Nbola said. "The now-confirmed Chinese scourge operates under the veil of tourism. Many Asians visit the wildlife parks. The syndicates are so well organized that visitors in search of ivory mingle in large crowds, then hire hungry Africans to do the killing. Here," he continued, offering the pouch to Stuart. "The sanctuary story is here."

"Now you go get your sister's trading logs. Your grandfather would not implicate his blood kin. In both their memories you have a story that is amplified with the hard proof of your grandfather's research. Keep those horrible men out of here."

The chief turned on his heel and strode back into the hut. Over his shoulder he said, "Good luck, Stuart Lehrman. We have elephants to tend."

The diminutive woman hugged Omega and followed the chief into the cool hut.

Stuart stared unseeing into their absence until Omega shook his arm. "Time to go to Morocco."

Stuart nodded and followed the African down the curious pathway. He paused and coughed. Omega turned back and looked into the idyllic savannah filled with large grey elephants. A sanctuary worth saving.

As they walked down, Stuart saw narrow paths encircling

the savannah. Omega chose one and the two followed it. Stuart turned to Omega and said, "Who or what makes these trails? Clearly the elephants don't climb in and out."

"Dik-dik," Omega replied, pointing at the small grey antelope racing in front of them.

"Like a dog," Stuart observed, thinking how different in stature these small animals were from the large brown and white Thomsens and red Sable gazelles.

Omega nodded. "Some clients have tried to catch them to take home, but they survive on local berries and grasses and could never live outside our country."

"Except in a zoo," Stuart said. "Think how awful that would be. Here they have all the food they want. Doubtless my grandfather considers this in the sanctuary article."

Arriving at Omega's van they drove west into the setting sun and north into the darkness. Still unclear as to the location of the Maasai camp and sanctuary he looked at the red paved road. He figured the sanctuary was on the road to Dar Es Salaam, making it easy for poachers to ship out ivory. "Are we near Dar or near Arusha?"

"Halfway in between."

"But close enough to the main road to get the ivory to the Ocean where it is shipped to China."

"That's right," Omega answered. "And close enough to ship animals out."

"But why all these boys?"

Omega reddened. "Perhaps to slow the trade? Read your grandfather's story and your sister's logs. You'll see why Africans need and fear ivory trade."

When they drove into the now familiar split highway lined by African shops and young men on motorcycles Stuart breathed easier. "Will you have an orange juice?"

Omega shook his head. "Please tell the concierge where we are going. It is unlikely we'll return to this place. You can fly on to Europe from Tangiers."

CHAPTER TWENTY-NINE

When he returned the concierge said, "Your room has been cleaned but the items scattered on the bed have been left untouched. When you have moved them call me and I will have the maid change the bed."

"Thank you for the attention. How did you know I was in town and do you have any adhesive, known as scotch tape?" he asked.

Looking at Stuart's amused face, he said, "Police call ahead to tell me you come here. Go to your room. We will look for scotch tape. I'll phone you when we find it."

"Thanks for the room and the preparations." He turned to Omega. "See you in two days to head to Tangiers. I need your help tomorrow also if you can spare a few hours."

"Of course. Where are we headed?"

"We need to take the scientists to my grandfather's house first and pick up two Atkinson stories I left there and be certain I've missed no evidence. My mother asked for a few items which I have yet to locate."

Omega nodded and said, "Of course, boss. Back to the screaming kid. See you soon."

Stuart asked the bartender for an IPA and returned to his room. He checked to be certain the tangible clues and list were still intact on the bed then moved them all to the desk. He called the concierge and asked about the tape and asked him to send up a maid.

If only the sanctuary story also provided proof that the assassins were connected to the Britzes. That the knife was brought to his daughter by Alphonse's employees, that they were big enough to gore his grandfather after having sliced a critical head vein and that the Britzes generally speaking had it out for the Atkinsons was becoming more and more evident. This story, he reminded himself, was about African's saving elephants not people murdering Atkinson. With luck, the transparent truth would be, as his dying sister said in his arms and repeated in her will, somewhere in Neissa's house.

The phone rang, and the knock announcing "housekeeping," interrupted his meditation. Dalik asked to meet him in the terrace to hear about the Nbola visit and discuss the videogame.

Perfect timing Stuart thought entering the Arusha balcony where he had asked Dalik to meet him.

The tall Maasai was seated at Stuart's corner table, staring out at the grounds. Stuart made his way over to greet him.

As he approached, the night air mingled with a strong odor of men's cologne. A new YSL that he had considered for himself. Dalik has good taste, but then he'd noticed his tailored suit at the memorial. At least he'd never have trouble finding him. He would always be the best-dressed Maasai in the room. Stuart had looked at Dalik's CV the night before as he considered what to offer him for the game. Stellar recommendations; he had turned his Ph.D. project—a program that ran programs—into a small company.

Seating himself across from the twenty-something, he said,

"Who were the principle investors in your software company?"

Dalik laughed and sunk lower in his seat. "Apple invested. Jobs liked the idea but his board did not, so he invested his own money and I was able to procure a few other backers and keep it private. It's licensed to Apple and a few other companies. My partners and I use the technique in programming."

"It's a program that simplifies mathematical computation?"

"Exactly. We use it to make the gazelles wander across the Serengeti, allow the lion to sunbathe and the leopard to kill."

"Why didn't you sell it? It sounds useful."

"The bidding was too low so we kept it. With the lucrative licenses it provides us with funds to live on while we create crazy projects like the safari."

The white coated waiter hovered around their table. "Gentlemen?"

"The usual IPA," Stuart said.

"I'll take his usual IPA also," Dalik echoed. "And water, please."

After his second sip of beer, Stuart said, "How did you come to know my sister?"

"Neissa?"

"That's the one," Stuart replied.

"Condolences," Dalik said.

Before he answered Stuart said, "Thanks. Were you involved in her illicit trading?"

"You know about that?" Dalik said, his black face flushed.

"Doesn't everyone? And that she was bidding for your game."

Dalik shook his head. "She said she was off the grid."

Stuart scrutinized the Maasai. "She is now since she's dead. You knew my grandfather?"

"Old man Atkinson? Yeah, I knew him," Dalik said, smiling. "He loved Africa. Articles helped Africa help itself. He liked our game. Said it would educate kids about good people and animals in Africa. He employed my brother, helped my sister find a post and helped all of us get into primary and secondary school. Even made certain my sister's employers sent her to university."

"So she told me. The Britzes, though—they seem to be the port of exit. Know anything about that? And Atkinson. Any idea who killed him? His articles exposed the precipice Africa dangles upon. Your family is on that ledge." Stuart said.

"His métier was a good reason to be rid of him. We are a dark continent of extreme goodness and extreme badness, sometimes the forces are at war within territories, within cities."

"Do you know if my grandfather had any African friends he trusted?" Stuart asked.

"Aren't we off task?" Dalik said, laughing. "But yes, my father was his good friend and I think you've met Farouk."

Stuart grinned. "Yes, we're off task but my reasons for being in Africa are both business-related and personal. My grandfather had one daughter, my sixty-year old mother and one grandson. I was duly elected to find his assassin while I wined and dined your crew. Further, it seems the only people looking out for me and perhaps my grandfather is your family from Nbola on down. So why did Atkinson and Ian die and why am I still living?"

"I was in the crowd when he sent for you. Told you my brother worked for him. I told Omega to look out for you. Assassin? Someone who profits from his death? Britz, Xiang Yu, Neissa?"

"Yes we met at the MOAB event in Cambridge. Wasn't that several months ago? These leads are good ones but all but one of them is dead. Who are Atkinson's living African connections?" Stuart asked and paused to sip some beer, thinking of the torn story.

"Have you been to your father's elephant sanctuary?"

"Yes, my father's living and on your team and it was only a month ago that we met in Boston."

"Would a story about the sanctuary cause my grandfather's death?"

Dalik shrugged. "Don't know. Maybe. But it's more likely to cause Nbola's death."

"About the game," Stuart interrupted, "your nephew solved it within fifteen minutes."

"So you said. I told you to look out for my nephews. I sent him version two and he's still stumped. " Dalik smirked. "In version two, we've changed scenes, hidden animals and given the hunter a bad set of nerves. The user has to figure out how to keep his hands steady enough to actually hit an animal. That takes several keystrokes that change depending on how much the man is shaking."

"The shaking hand. That's a good idea," Stuart said, "human frailty. Something young players might not yet understand. One certainly feels it in the presence of the large animals although I've noticed some of the smaller animals are terrified by footsteps. That minuscule deer. What's it called?"

"Dik-dik. We have ours run under the hunter's feet....to trip him now, but because their scent is better than humans the hunter cannot kill him. He's our eternal beast."

Stuart interrupted, "Omega showed me a lion pride. Those lionesses are terrifying. Do they actually hunt in packs?"

"Yes and there is a pack of them in version two. The hunter goes out of his way to avoid them to save his life and his occupation. No one wants a lioness rug," Dalik said.

"The wildebeest?" Stuart said. "Your brother Omega calls him the foolish animal."

"He's comic relief, man," Dalik interrupted. "We put the rifle in his mouth sometimes. His goatee covers it partly." He paused. "Disney made him famous as the Beast in 'Beauty in the Beast.' We tried to demystify him. He looks just like he does in the Serengeti and does not transform into anything but his silly self."

"How do you know this?" Stuart asked. "How does the hunter know which gun to use?"

"We might need to introduce the idea of an arsenal of guns. So that he has to choose."

"Sounds good. Give me a prototype copy tomorrow." Stuart looked down at his phone and saw a recent startling text from one of Ebele's sons. "Oh, Dalik, one of your nephews just texted me, advising me he and his brother have been kidnapped," Stuart said. "He was able to find the location on the phone's GPS. Here are the coordinates and photos. Do you know the place?"

Dalik looked at the iphone photos from the boys and said, "Yes. They're at my father's sanctuary. The latest recruits, I guess. They will be safe with Nbola and the other boys."

"Let's meet for breakfast. I need to deal with my grandfather's story from Nbola first and talk with Roz about your proposed changes."

"Of course, give me a call in the morning. Erewhon looks like our best option since Neissa and Britz annihilated themselves. I'll look forward to your offer."

CHAPTER THIRTY

As they passed the front desk the concierge held up a black holder with clear tape inside in one hand and a white tape for bandaging wounds in the other. "Here's your adhesive, Mr. Lehrman? Which one do you want?"

"That one," Stuart said, pointing to the black holder. "How much? I'm likely to use it all."

"10,000 shillings."

Stuart grimaced at the $10 fee for a half-used roll of tape but handed the man 12,000 shillings and said, "Keep the change," thinking he should be happy the place had any tape at all. He went back to his room, noticing the clean sheets and well-made bed. He looked at the desk where the tangible clues and note lay untouched on his desk and spread the pieces of his grandfather's torn story on the bed. He'd have to tip this maid well. He smoothed a place on the bed and began piecing the fragments together.

The title changed from what he had imagined was 'The End of Ivory' –his half of the ripped sheet was 'The End....' now changed to the 'End of Ivory and the Beginning of Balance.'

Scribbled in his grandfather's squared off half cursive—half printing handwriting were the words: *"International desk: Herald*

Tribune: find out about secluded elephants — angle is Africans maintaining their land." The writing continued, "playground outside Arusha is a good place to begin this story. On the seesaw, a tall white on the ground will have placed a small African on a precarious edge....the tall white is both the original European colonizers and the neo-colonial "Save the Environment" groups, telling Africans how to order their worlds. Seesaw, past and present tense combined describes both the past and immediate nature of this problem..." The notes continued: *"Traders are Neissa and Alphonse....must find way to shield Madeleine...Anton was helping until he was gored by the rhinoceros he was de-tusking...I knew what he was doing and had reported him....who are his helpers? There is a Chinese link....his name is not known....need help...Stuart could help...will send for him."*

Stuart sat back thinking, these were his grandfather's last thoughts, revealing the threat on his life, the story that made him ask Stuart for help. Was it the Chinese link that was invisible to George? Was it Neissa or Britz or a combination of all of them that so mystified George that, as Rumila believed, he sent for Stuart's fresh eyes and analytic mind? Or was it fear? Stuart began to connect his grandfather's facts--the Britz connection — how easy and illegal. Nbola's sanctuary. Was the Chinese connection deadly?

Stuart was exhausted. He needed to talk to his mother, consolidate his thoughts and his acquired facts and the new pages. He picked up the connected notes/story hid them in the suitcase and slipped between the sheets. He was asleep within moments.

ROTFL

CHAPTER THIRTY-ONE

Showered and ready for breakfast he phoned Dalik, "Hungry?"

"Sure. See you in twenty minutes at the buffet?"

Next, Stuart phoned Omega. "Can you be ready to head north tomorrow?"

"I'm ready anytime. Sure you don't want to go now?"

Hearing the screaming baby in the phone noise, Stuart grinned and said, "I'm meeting with Dalik. We need to seal that deal before I head back to Boston. We need to take the Americans to Grandpa's house. Dalik is coming along Come by and join us for breakfast."

"I'll be there," Omega said joyfully.

Stuart went back to his room, filled out the standard Erewhon Term sheet offering ten thousand dollars up front. High, he thought, Roz would be angry. He did have some of Atkinson's house sale money on hand. There would be more when he sold Neissa's home. He'd ask Dalik to program a woman trader in to complicate the game in her memory.

He phoned the front desk and asked, "Will you print a document for me before breakfast?"

"Yes, sir. Bring down your computer." While used to it by now he flinched at the 'sir.'

He sent the document off to Roz with the note, "generous up front is from my grandfather's house sale and dead sister's mansion sale."

The immediate response, "You're crazy wild with our money but since part of it is your inheritance spend it already. How's the other investigation?"

"Almost over," he responded.

"Whodunnit?"

"Answer soon," Stuart wrote, followed by a smiley face.

Stuart walked to the concierge, yawning. He handed Stuart the copied papers.

The man winked, "Busy several nights, I hear."

Stuart blushed. "I will miss having my every action watched," he said. "In case you haven't heard, I've invited the good luck Schwarmas to Boston for a visit. Maybe you can all come together and I can rent a tour bus to show you around."

The man nodded. "I'd like that. I'll start saving my tips. Now you go close that deal."

When Stuart frowned, the concierge continued, "I read all the mail, remember. Maybe I can be useful to you some day?"

"Maybe." Stuart strode toward his customary balcony seat where Dalik was waiting for him, his back to the wall, his eyes flitting between the door and garden. Stuart looked first to the right and the left to see what was blooming then faced Dalik. "Thank you," he said, "for meeting me before dinner."

"No problem," Dalik said. "What's your offer?"

Stuart handed him the paper, saying, "$5 million upfront, my partner has contacted a gaming investor, which would bring our total upfront investment to $10 million. We'd ask for 10 percent post sale valuation on a sale of $20 million, stock options and a seat on the board. I think it's a hot item and we'd love to be a part of its nascence." He paused. "This is all contingent on your making the changes we discussed. I've set your nephews up as game testers so you might want to give your sister a call."

Dalik opened his wide eyes and grinned the ear to ear smile that Stuart had only seen in this Maasai family. While Africans were generally the happiest people he had encountered on this continent, he had not seen Africans other than Dalik , Omega—even Nbola smile so wide he was afraid their temples would throb.

"Let me call my partners," Dalik said. "Our Chinese programmer could be a bit touchy about the smuggling entailed in adding the Neissa portion, but the other African will like it as I do. So, I predict, will the native California math geek. A basic trust-buster type, she will have fun scrambling the environmental issues into an ivory-depletion, save the elephant scheme. I can't wait to reprogram the wildebeest to laugh at the world. We plan to name him Beast. Shall we name the evil trader Beauty to mix the metaphor?"

Stuart smiled. "I was going to suggest that. Can't ask you to name them Neissa and Britz as that is a rather transparent giveaway and perhaps a clue to these brilliant African kids. We're going to have to put out a guide for this game to educate the parents.

"As you predicted, one of our best markets is right here. Your nephews are really good. Even the hotel concierge has a videogame on his phone. The Africans might have seen the Disney movie?"

"We'll see about names. Most Africans don't have money for movies. It might be a giveaway in the U.S. but not here. Besides it won't help to know the animal and trader's names to win the game. I'll phone Ebele," Dalik said.

"In other news," Stuart said, "Erewhon will have other business here with the malaria physicians. Would you like to help them recruit? Of course they'd pay you."

Dalik laughed. "For malaria, they'll have swarms of people. Maybe they'd like a data cruncher?"

"That they might and that you are connected with their own institutions is likely to make you a desirable candidate. Not to speak of the fact that few in Africa have your computer programming skills. I meet with them today before Omega and I leave for Morocco. We have to take them to the site."

Dalik looked up and waved at a man standing in the doorway. "Speak of the devil."

Omega sauntered over to the table. "May I join you?"

"Of course," Stuart said, laughing. "What are you drinking in this momentary pause from the baby?"

"How about a coffee?"

Stuart caught the waiter's eye. "New orange juices and coffees for all of us and a full Tuskers for Omega."

"How's the wee one, Omega?" the waiter asked.

"Noisy except when eating or sleeping and she's awake now." He turned to his brother, "Wait until you make your first million before you have children."

Dalik nodded. "Worry not. My wife is committed to medicine and I like programming. Looks like this game will give me a good start on a savings account for kids if we find time for them. Since the local investors shot each other, Stuart's made me his best offer and given me a whole passel of upgrades to make so I'll shop the game around to determine if this is the best I can do."

Omega shrugged. "Don't burn any bridges. Who better than Stuart, my boss's only grandson to sell it? Besides, the big money backers in Africa-- Neissa and Alphonse are dead. So, Dalik, take it from your slightly older brother, our family has always stood by the Atkinsons. This might be the time to let them stand by you. With all the tragedy it's brought to users will the game sell at all?"

Stuart interrupted. "Of course and thanks for the Erewhon pitch. We ARE about the last ones standing. As for the danger involved? We'll use these facts as marketing tools. People who like videogames are the same crew that think the slots in casinos are rigged so they play the video slots that require their character to run through gunfire. A videogame with guns and one that caused several deaths might intrigue them."

"Drink up, good friend. We meet the researchers in the morning for breakfast. Then we're off to bury my sister and visit her house. Neissa left me her house—the bulk of this generous offer to Dalik's company comes from her estate."

"She did try to buy the game but texted it was leverage she didn't need. You agreed to help her with Britz, no strings attached."

Stuart decided not to think about this until he saw Neissa's home, stepped into her life for a moment. Instead he walked across the square in the direction of Farouk's camera store.

Stuart approached the Indian pair quietly. "Hello, you two," he said, a question in his voice.

"Stuart, Stuart, my man," Farouk said. "Come in please." He grinned. "So you like my cousin's cooking."

"Best Indian food I've had since I left Boston."

"Your meetings?" Rumila asked.

"Successful enough, I think." Stuart looked curiously at Farouk. "I'm trying to secure the contract for a video game I'd love to have you sell here."

Farouk frowned. "I don't sell videogames."

"This one is a virtual safari designed by Africans. It's all moving photographs, pictures of guns, no real ones. The player goes on a safari in a game."

"You win that contract," Farouk said testily, "then we talk."

"Wise man." Stuart paused. "Is the photo finished?"

Farouk nodded and handed it to Stuart. "And about my videogame, it has a great story that might help sales."

"My in-country competitors were Neissa and Britz who shot each other. The videogame designer is one of Nbola's sons, young Dalik."

"Like Nbola's family, from Alpha to Dalik," Farouk said, "Erewhon gets Dalik and team to sign on, I'll sell it as a special thank you for all the Maasai family has done for me."

Stuart took the photo from the Leica sealed in a manila envelope. It confirmed his earlier suspicions. With luck there was rock-hard information at his sister's house. "Farouk, thank you. How much do I owe you?"

"Nothing, Stuart," the old man said with a sly smile on his face. "You come back. You take my Rumila back to that Boston school. Maybe she could do Harvard, not Oxford. Study in a freed colony, not the oppressive motherland."

Stuart laughed. "I think my grandfather wrote in his diaries that you were his best source because if you were not told something directly you would figure out how to ask leading questions that would give you an answer." He turned to Rumila. "Was the interrogation awful?"

Rumila shook her head. "Our cousin gave my father all the information he needed. I did not suffer at all." She dropped her eyes. "Besides, there was nothing to tell."

"So we will meet again?"

Rumila blushed. "I hope so. Now go, be safe and remember you have both Omega's native wits and your own analytic mind."

"Walk back with me, Rumila. I need to stop by Xiang's then

join me at the hotel for an *Orangina* in the gardens."

"Go daughter," Farouk said. "I am rested. The store is in good hands."

"Why are you and your father helping me?" Stuart asked.

"Your grandfather always treated us with respect. Indians, though they are Africa's model merchants, often suffer discrimination. My cousin's wife, for example, is a physician and she works for an international health non-profit because Arusha's largest hospital is filled with African physicians, but does not allow Indians to work there."

Stuart looked up thoughtfully. "Interesting. Reverse discrimination?"

Rumila shrugged. "Here's the market."

Stuart walked into Xiang's shop. He found the carver engaged with a tourist interested in purchase of a carving like 'Noah.' Can you have it finished in two days' time?" Xiang looked around at his full shop and nodded. "We will be done."

When the client had gone, Stuart walked to the carver. He pulled the blurry photo from his pack and pointed at the Asian standing next to a white man. "Did you kill my grandfather?"

Stunned by the directness of the question the carver said, "Yes, with help. Now prove it."

"I have almost all the evidence. Are you coming with me or must I have you arrested?"

"I will not come willingly and I may be difficult to find."

He waved his hand and a man with a pistol approached Stuart. "Now get out,"

Stuart walked slowly toward the Arusha hotel, wondering if a more clear photo was what he needed. He believed his grandfather died of a gunshot wound. He would have to contact the police. Pushing his worries to the back of his mind he joined the dark-haired Rumila on the balcony.

On the balcony, Stuart ordered an *Orangina,* an IPA and the obligatory empty Tuskers for his grandfather. "I need your help," he said. "I need you to look after your father and the Asian and Indian researchers who are rebuilding my grandfather's house. They are also staying in this hotel. Do all this with great care. Whoever is after me knows your family has befriended me. This will put you all in danger. Perhaps you can engage the city Maasai and his family to act as your secret service. Sayed also needs protection. Have you anywhere to go?"

Rumila nodded. "We can go home. No one will find us there."

Thinking of how he had hid his mother at his place in Boston he nodded. "Yes, do that. Please write the address and Indian state. I will have my business partner monitor it once you go." He paused and said, "Maybe wait a few days to leave?"

"Um," Rumila said, her dark eyes hooded, blocking any visible emotion. "Sounds like you have a great business partner. And one who monitors you."

Stuart laughed. "No threat. Great partner, divorced, committed to single status and to her young daughter."

"Delhi is our home. It's in the Punjab province. The region is impossible to penetrate. Here is my sister's address and business. I get lost walking from the market to her office on our rare visits to her home. We will stay with her. My father has not yet seen his new grandchild and is anxious to visit. We'll take my mother's ashes to her homeland."

Rumila stood to leave. "Take care, Stuart Lehrman. I hope we meet again."

CHAPTER THIRTY-TWO

Precisely at 8 in the morning Stuart was seated in a corner seat on the balcony with the tall Dalik and Omega sitting on either side of him waiting for the Asian and Indian researchers.

Before the researchers arrived, Omega turned to his brother, "Will you check in at my house, now and again, Dalik?"

"My pleasure." Dalik replied. "Number crunching gets old. If I recall, your wife's cooking is better than mine."

"But the baby is noisy."

When the researchers arrived, Stuart made the introductions, pointed out Dalik's mathematic gifts and offered his services for the malaria project.

The researchers accepted gladly and followed the three men to Omega's car, which Stuart observed had been cleaned and polished for the occasion. He wondered if Omega drove into some secluded place to wash his several vehicles so he could escape the baby's noise occasionally.

They drove down the narrow Atkinson Lane which Stuart had avoided since the house fell in. When the road ended, he led the researchers to the path. "We get to the house from here. My grandfather liked his seclusion."

"We'll have to widen the trail," the Asian researcher said.

"People know how to get here," Stuart said. "I wouldn't change it too much."

Omega nodded. "If you change it too drastically, you will ruin the home site and the old man's appeal to the natives—his seclusion and honesty."

"We did considerable research on Atkinson," the Indian researcher acknowledged. "*Trust* was the most common adjective fellow writers and subjects in his stories used to describe Atkinson. This 'trust' is part of the reason we proposed the purchase to Rosalind in the first place. Additionally, Atkinson was well-connected to community and tribal leaders."

"Atkinson was the major reason," Dr. Chen said, "I was prepared to do Africa first. We have no similar contact in the Amazon."

"Hiring Dalik will give you an immediate connection to the Maasai family and clan my grandfather knew." Stuart watched Omega, hopping from foot to foot, a nervous habit that usually meant he had something to say. "When I send Omega, Dalik's brother, back from Morocco, I suggest you hire him also. He was my grandfather's driver, has been mine since I arrived. He can ferret people out who have true need of your vaccine. He can persuade anyone to do anything and he is a diplomatic bearer of bad news. He greeted me at the airport with the news of my grandfather's death. He has saved me from near death several times now. Roz, my grandfather and I pay him well so if I send him to you please continue his wages as they are now. You know what Dalik is worth; he's Harvard-MIT educated, he's one of your own."

"Additionally," Omega said, winking at Stuart, "I'll give you your first infant if my wife agrees. Georgina is several weeks' old."

"We have to finish the teens and twenties and analyze the

data from these age groups before we can do infants," Chen said. Watching Omega's face fall, she added. "Soon we can administer the vaccine to African babies. With your permission, we'll use your daughter on a poster to attract more infants. Infants against malaria: Georgina Oweke."

"Really," Omega said, grinning from ear to ear. "Our daughter on a poster."

"What more effective way to get local participation than to use the granddaughter of a well-known local chief?"

The Indian researcher studied both Dalik and Omega's faces, height and weight carefully. "Are you two actually blood kin or just tribal brothers?"

"Good question," Dalik answered. "We have the same father, different mothers but were raised together. Apart from facial features, height and weight among Maasai varies only modestly. Most Maasai are tall like Omega and I are. City Maasai, whose heritage is mixed, do not grow up with the tribe, eat and live differently, and are often smaller."

"Good inside information," the Indian researcher said. "We had already adjusted dosages for men and women but will make certain we weigh everyone to avoid patient harm."

Watching both men's foreheads wrinkle, he added, "Effectiveness of the vaccine is more complete if adjusted for height and weight."

"How long have you been working on this?" Dalik asked.

"We have been working on this vaccine for over five years in patients with malaria and for several years in healthy volunteers. No adverse effects have been noticed if the dosage is correct. Incorrect dosages result in a non-hazardous rash that stops if the drug is stopped. We have permission to be here because the need is dire."

"Indeed," Omega said, "malaria kills one African child each minute. We are not afraid. In fact we are honored you are here!"

The Asian researcher grinned. "Thank you. Did you know that the death per minute statistic is about infants? 70 percent of deaths occur before children reach age five."

"So you will save my little Georgina."

"Our trial is filed both with the FDA and the WTO and we'll be able to work on your daughter soon. The samples can be returned to the USA for free."

"This sounds like news for the drummers, Omega," Stuart interrupted. "Dalik, will you take charge of that? I need your brother for my Moroccan excursion. It will be a short one."

Stuart turned away from the group and walked over to the foundations of his grandfather's home. He lowered himself down the rope ladder the workmen used, saying, "I need one more look around the place."

Omega shook his head and sighed. "Stuart, it's a hole. Not even the stoop with your grandfather's blood is left."

Stuart nodded. "I know, but a piece of me still resides here. Not just blood, but memories and a family history." Easing himself into the pit which laid bare the cement basement floor he waved to the group which split in two, Omega standing above the ladder, his pleasant face wrinkled with consternation while Dalik and the researchers found the architect to understand the clinic plans. Dalik turned to his brother and said, "Why don't you go with him?"

"This is his last visit to the gravesite. He needs to go alone."

The researchers nodded and the Asian added, "There will be a plaque on the clinic memorializing Stuart's grandfather. If we were allowed, we would name it Atkinson Clinic but the money is from WTO and they have stipulations."

The Indian researcher gave a knowing look to the Maasai

brothers. "We're just not telling them about the plaque." Dalik and Omega laughed.

"Grants I know about," Dalik said. "Blood from a stone."

"But there is always the African way," Omega interrupted. "The house is on Atkinson Lane," Omega said, pointing to the white street sign.

Both researchers chuckled. "We hadn't noticed the sign. We will be certain it is left intact."

"You would have a hard time securing permission to change it by the time your patients and medicines arrive," Omega confirmed.

Dalik turned to the researchers. "When DOES the medicine arrive?"

"Three weeks."

"You have very little time to finish this building," Dalik said.

The Asian nodded. "My colleague's Swahili is rusty and mine is non-existent. How would you like to manage our general contractor and any other details before we have data for you to crunch? The grant is generous so we can afford to pay you well."

"Love to," Dalik replied quickly. "I have to stay in town to watch over my niece and sister-in-law while Omega is away. It will be useful to have an income while I'm in town."

"Is this a wife we need to employ?" the Indian said.

"No, Omega's wife has a job. And it sounds like you want to employ him upon his return. My wife is working on her medical degree in Cambridge focused in epidemiology and I'm working full time in IT at MIT and University of Nairobi. We live in Nairobi but I have a rotating fellowship between the Boston and African campuses and am on leave for six months. I can continue data crunching in both Kenya and Boston. Perhaps you will have a job for my wife when she returns?"

"Thanks for supplying continuity and your wife would be useful," Dr. Agarwal said.

While the three studied the plans and discussed futures, Omega paced nervously above the foundation, crossing and uncrossing his intertwined fingers. He was on his fifteenth trip toward the ladder when Stuart's head crested the top of the hole. On his right hand small finger, next to his own red ring, was another identical ring. In his back pocket was a plastic bag filled with dust and a paper roll. Stepping off the ladder, he said, "I hoped to find this."

"Your grandfather's class ring?" Omega announced.

"Yes, he graduated Harvard exactly 60 years before me. It's a classic."

"What is it about you Crimson Kings?" the Asian said and smiled.

"Nice school," Stuart said. "And you'll be working with one of MIT's best, well-known for his data crunching and programming skills. Now Omega and I are out of here. Here's my cell if you need it. Dalik knows more people here than I do. His tribe will be looking over your shoulders to be certain you are safe. I think I heard you say you'd pay him to do both project management and data processing."

"There is also an Indian camera man, a great friend of my grandfather's and a great friend of mine, who will be watching out for you. Dalik, please introduce them to Farouk."

The Indian nodded. "We will need some photo processing and Dalik, I hate numbers. Love dabbling in chemicals but make great use of my grad students. Besides we have a liberal grant from the government."

"Pay him well. He's a professor himself in Nairobi. Erewhon is funding his and his partners' video game," Stuart said. "Omega and I are going to say good-bye to his family then we're off. You are in good hands. Dalik has my cell also and he is staying with Omega's family." He turned to Dalik. "I need the signed paper."

"Thought you'd never ask," Dalik said. "The concierge at the Arusha Hotel has it. Don't forget it on the way out."

Stuart nodded. "Omega will run marketing when he returns. Find some good connections."

Dalik saluted and said, "Already working on it. Our nephews will make good voices of sale also."

"Great idea," Stuart said. "Ask Ebele what we pay them."

"I'll get back to you," Dalik said.

The two hopped into Omega's van, stopped by the hotel where the concierge handed Stuart the signed term sheet and the duo headed out to Omega's house. While Omega said his goodbyes to his family, Stuart pulled the scotch-taped manuscript from his cargo pants briefcase and pulled out a pencil. He traced the lines between the scattered words on his reconstituted text and read:

Britz's gun runners are under the control of Berber group that is gathering forces and could endanger both Africa and Neissa. The North Africans are currently without fear. I have met with several. The first drives a taxi from Casablanca's airport. Name is Rahil, I think. Chinese connection is probably Xiang.

After wife was raped repeatedly by his fellows he took her to the mountains away from the coast.

He told me my daughter was in grave danger. My granddaughter's trade is endangering their lives. They think by assassinating Madeleine and leaving a tusk by her house, they can stop Neissa's slaughter of elephants and trafficking in illegal goods. I know there is no love lost between mother and daughter but Neissa likes her money and her life of luxury. I suspect both like their lives. Perhaps an expose might frighten her. Contact old friend at Morocco Times for Neissa expose. Contact New York Times, Harold B in Africa section for article on Xiang Yu article. Still waiting. Latter is most dangerous. Want it to appear out of Africa first. Will ask H.B. to place it when Stuart comes. I fear they will kill me before I can warn Neissa and Madeleine because I know too much. Stuart is my only hope.

CHAPTER THIRTY-THREE

"Take me to the police station," Stuart instructed. "They have one more piece of evidence I need."

Omega eyed Stuart curiously but turned the van quickly.

In front of the rotund policeman again, Stuart asked pleasantly. "The slug, please, the bullet that killed my grandfather. May I have it?"

The man turned to a file cabinet retrieved Atkinson's file and said there was nothing.

Stuart frowned. "I thought so."

Omega returned with a small back pack and turned north toward Nairobi's Jomo Kenyatta International airport.

"Why Nairobi's airport?" Stuart asked.

"Bigger place. More flights and airlines from Nairobi to Morocco than from Tanzania to Morocco," Omega said. "Check for flights into Casablanca on Royal Air Maroc first," he added, "then start looking around."

"Next one departing is at 3 AM," Stuart said after scrolling through the information. "Now can I sleep?"

"The plastic and the roll?"

"Mom explicitly asked for some red African dirt from the house foundation. The roll? Contained two stories: A copy of a story for the *Moroccan Times,* another for *The New York Times.* I stuffed it back into the hole where I found the diaries—both say unpublished, so I wanted a copy in case these stories didn't get placed. Fortunately the roll survived the crash. Your father's note advises both stories are to be published after I arrive. Can you find the *Moroccan Times* HQ when we get to Tangiers? We'll solve that problem first."

"We'll find the newspaper. As for the airplane, we'll just make it. Hang on to your hat. You can sleep if you don't want to see the last of our animals. You'll be staring at the Atlantic Ocean and Morocco's feral cats for the next few days."

When they raced out of Arusha, Omega swerved to miss a cyclist.

Stuart could feel his lunch moving to his throat. "Must we go this fast?"

"We have many miles to cover."

"Did my sister drive to the funeral?"

Omega shook his head. "Neissa was a rich lady. She had her own plane, her own pilot and was a good pilot herself."

I wonder who she gave that to? Stuart thought. *The pilot, maybe? Or would they find it in the airport full of ivory, guns and other illegal substances?* On the highway, Stuart stretched his long legs and turned to Omega. "Strange that traffic in illegal goods is so profitable."

Stuart picked up the remnants of paper and studied that last bit, wondering if his sister knew George was going to expose her, then drifted off to sleep. When they screeched into the Nairobi airport at midnight, Omega touched his arm and checked his watch.

Just midnight.

"Well-done," Stuart observed. "We still have time to purchase tickets and board the plane."

"If there is room," Omega said when he saw the line at the airline counter.

"Time to flash my passport and sexy name," Stuart said shamelessly. He paused and asked, "Who would fly to Tangiers at this hour?"

"Few Moroccan flights leave from here. This airline has two a day. And remember, we fly to Casablanca first. Many people fly to Casablanca to change planes. The plane will be filled with people going all over the world."

"Two seats to Morocco," Stuart said, flashing his passport.

"George Atkinson's relative?" the agent said.

"Grandson."

"Took this flight many times many times working on a story. Illicit trade or something." The one Neissa mentioned in her note to Madeleine, Stuart thought as the agent continued, "The flight is oversold but I'll see what I can do. You do know it will be over a day before you get to Tangiers." Making the typical two free tickets to anywhere announcement, he found Stuart and Omega seats. "Have a nice flight, sir and condolences regarding your grandfather and sister."

They got in line for security and when Omega said he had relations in Morocco, Stuart said, "Are you related to everyone?"

Crossing his lips with his index finger, Omega whispered, "Save it. We're up next. Anything you say can be held against you."

Safely past the guards and moving along the corridors toward the plane, Stuart took up his cultural heritage questioning again. "Have you family all over this huge continent?"

Omega said, "Africans have big families. They scatter

throughout the continent wherever they can find work. They are obliged to take in family for as long as the family visits whether they come from Capetown, Cairo or New York City."

Stuart groaned. "Quaint custom. No wonder Mom stopped at two children."

"You're not African so our customs don't apply to you. Your grandfather also thought the hospitality requirement was a little stiff."

As the two settled into their first class seats that folded into beds, Stuart said, "Shit. I didn't realize we didn't arrive in the same day. Nice to have the fold out beds. Crazy that it takes a day to fly from mid to North Africa."

When they boarded, the pilot turned on the engine. It made a pleasant whirring sound.

"Trouble," Omega whispered. "In Africa when planes don't start until the passengers are on board, there's no guarantee they have enough petrol to make the designated destination. And about the flight time span, how long does it take to fly from Houston to Vancouver, Canada?"

Stuart laughed. "I get it. Sorry. Not to worry about flight delays, Neissa's maid is African and she's computer savvy. I told her to check for its arrival. The butler is picking us up. Neissa's will says I get her car. Hope you can drive a Toyota. Besides," he went on, "I don't care when we get there. What do you know about Morocco?"

"Toyota, the best kind," Omega responded. "Morocco is beautiful, matched only in elegance by the continental Riviera. The joy of Morocco is that its swimmers will be of many tribes, many colors. When Georgina is older we will all tour the North coast. Wife's sister married a Berber."

"Are you likely to know Neissa's maid's language?" Stuart

asked.

"If she speaks Swahili or English. How's your French?" Omega said. "Like everyone in Morocco, that is probably her second language after her tribal language. I do know a few Berber words but I know no French."

"My French is fair to awful," Stuart replied. "Tried my whole life to learn it but languages are not my gift."

"If she doesn't get your French, speak English, the world's lingua franca." He grinned. "And use your hands for emphasis or inquiry. The French are great with their hands."

The two finally landed in Tangiers where a man frantically waved a sign that said, 'Stuart Lehrman.'Stuart's teeth were chattering from over air conditioning in the airplane. When he returned to the USA, he thought, at least the fresh spring Boston air would be warming. As the déjà vu experience of disembarking in Arusha after someone's death was so overpowering, he comforted himself that apart from Rumila and Omega's family, every African he knew and/or was a relation of his living in Africa was now dead.

He approached the sign, extended his hand and said, "I'm Stuart. This is my friend Omega."

This butler was more anxious for his news than to give him news and greeted Stuart with, "Hello. How did your sister die?"

The moment in time of his sister, her loyalists and Anton and his guards was so frozen in his memory that Stuart could easily recount it.

Omega echoed his words in Swahili and the man nodded, directing his gaze first at Stuart, whose hand he shook and dropped, turned to Omega and said, "Follow me."

The road cut through the middle of the hills, and were covered with olive trees and wine grapes. The look overall reminded him of mid-France or the Napa Valley in California, where the landscape created itself around a river flowing to feed crops. When he saw an inlet enclosed by a high rock wall, he remembered that his sister described some swimming hole. *Was this it?* he wondered. She said the African Atlantic was warmer than the freezing waters of the Pacific near their home. She told him she swam daily. Was this the place? "Ask the man where my sister swam," Stuart said.

"Here," Omega translated.

"Please ask him to stop."

The butler shrugged and pulled the car near the swimming hole and pointed. "Neissa there," he said.

An unknown quantity to him, Stuart tried to understand her thoughts by imagining her here. He stuck his hand in the cool water and tried to imagine his criminal, deceased sister swimming vigorously in this place. No wonder she was strong. Did this bathing expiate her guilt about elephant slaughter, gun trade and other illegal substances? He cleared his throat, glanced across the water imagining he could see Florida and looked forward to finding her soul and her history in her villa. He returned to the car trunk and pulled a bag of ashes from his backpack. He pitched them into the sea, thinking *Swim free and in peace, Neissa.*

"Time to go," Omega said as the butler waved at them.

Once they were reseated the butler looked at Omega. "We stop here." He pulled in front of a large white building. He looked at Omega, explaining that he and Stuart must check in here to be allowed entry into Neissa's house. He told Omega who translated for Stuart, "Show your passport, Neissa's house key and the will. The butler will return in twenty minutes to take us to Neissa's house."

Omega and Stuart entered the building, Stuart unnerved by the familiarity of the police station routine. At least, he thought again, everyone is dead and his mother was safe in Boston. He approached the colonial looking policeman and began in English.

"My sister Neissa Lehrman, also registered as Neissa Abencour here in Morocco, is dead and has willed me her home." Stuart retrieved the short will, Nairobi death certificate and Neissa's housekeys, handing them to the police, together with his passport.

The bereted police listened carefully, examined his passport, then examined his face. "I will escort you there. You have had considerable sorrow since your arrival in Africa. Condolences for the loss of your grandfather." He paused and continued. "Your sister has been here for twenty years but we all knew her illegal activities would eventually lead to her demise. Tell me, how did she die?"

Stuart recounted her death. "Will you remove the police tape around her house? The butler will drive us there when he returns. My friend Omega can navigate the streets once we pick up her Toyota, which, I guess, is also mine, but we have no idea where she lives." He paused. "Where is the butler? He said he would return."

The policeman frowned. "He's probably going around the neighborhood collecting all the mansion's belongings that have been looted so that your sister's house is furnished."

Stuart laughed. "We will give it all to you after I leave. Unless some of it belongs to my mother. We will eventually sell the home so that I can fund my capital ventures. Why is the police tape there anyway?"

The policeman was silent for a few minutes. "We knew she was dead. She had left a photo and description of you as the house's new owner should she die. Since your bona fides meet her filed description, we need only send your fingerprints to Interpol to confirm you are who you say you are."

Stuart shrugged, squared his shoulders and prepared for the

finger printing exercise. "Both hands?"

The policeman nodded. "Many people tamper with fingerprints."

Stuart said. "Surely it would be obvious, the finger had been tampered with."

"It is, but somehow it makes crooks feel better." He sighed. "We have several sets of prints for your sister. Only one for the old man. He was up here several times."

Stuart was intrigued and now reassured. Had he sought to warn Neissa when he was here or only to research his article? It all must be in the house. "So let's hurry and get out there."

"Here comes the response," the officer said. "Yes, you're Stuart Atkinson Lehrman."

"Mm," Stuart said. "Where is the *Moroccan Times* office?"

The police pointed to a hole and an absence on the main street. "It was there. It was blown up two months ago. Your grandfather's story was filed but never published. The editor did salvage the letter press."

Stuart raised his eyebrows, his heart racing. "Did he? Where does he live?"

"Near the American legation." The policeman scribbled something on a sheet of paper and handed them a local tourist map. He marked an "x" in a certain spot. "The legation is a cultural center now. The editor lives near there because his mother was American."

Interesting but not necessarily helpful, Stuart thought, *my mother was African. At least*, he reflected, *he might speak English.* He studied the African's dark eyes. "May we leave now please."

"Yes, the butler has returned and is waiting outdoors."

"Welcome back, gentlemen. I guess the place is legally yours, Mr. Lehrman. I will take you there," the butler observed.

When they drove up to a large house surrounded by a high

wall, a policeman was cutting the tape across a wrought iron gate. The butler stopped the car, then reached inside the gate and pressed a button, quickly retracting his hand. The large black gate slid open slowly and the butler rejoined them. He pressed an overhead button and the three-car garage opened with room only for a small car (in this case, a Toyota) and the butler's huge sedan.

Stuart grinned and said to Omega, "I guess Neissa was less of a car fan than you."

"What I'd give for this garage. Could use a good clean up though."

"Knowing her trade," Stuart said, "I think I'd pay attention to what I moved."

"Sir, "the butler interrupted, "the maid has prepared supper for you both. She is waiting at the front door. If that is all, I will join my wife and family for dinner."

Stuart who was still studying the vast expanse of his sister's Mediterranean villa said, "Oh yes, of course. Thank you for your help. Have you been paid?"

"Your sister left each of us an annual stipend. And I believe there is something in the Will about ground maintenance and personnel."

"There is, I will leave money in the BNP for all of you. Once the house is sold, there should be sufficient funds to cover homes for all Neissa's personnel."

"Of course, sir. Enjoy your meal."

The maid waited at the door for the two men. The butler left them and circled the house to enter through the servants' quarters.

"Gentlemen," the maid said, "Neissa said I should address you in English, as her heritage is American, not Moroccan."

"Thank you," Stuart said. "Omega speaks Swahili but neither of us speaks French, so if English suits you, it would be good for me. And please dispense with the formality. I am called Stuart and Omega goes by that name. I also do not like sirs or madams. Neissa and my parents, a teacher and a lawyer, abhorred the appellations and taught me, at least, not to use them."

"You certainly resemble your sister," the maid said. "Neissa always took her dinner on the terrace facing the Mediterranean and she had only single serving covers. So I have kept your dinners on the stove and will roll them in on our food cart. Are you good to serve yourselves?"

"Of course and thank you."

Omega rubbed his hands with glee when he saw the cart covered with a tureen of warm soup, a cooked and fileted fish for two and a plate of vegetables and fruit. There were dessert plates and two small bowls of pudding.

The maid put several plates, soup bowls and napkins before them and set the rolling cart at Stuart's right hand. She set a long loaf of French bread in the middle of the table and said, "This bread was baked just this morning. There is butter if either of you use it. A special Moroccan wine made only for your sister is in the wine bucket."

"This is a feast. Thank you. We will take the dishes back inside and wash them."

"Oh, no, sir. That is my job."

"I am Stuart, not sir, and I'm a bachelor. I do dishes very well." He paused. "One more thing. Where are Neissa's trading logs?"

"In her office, just inside these doors. By the big computer," the maid responded and left.

After she had gone, Stuart reached across the table and said, "Soup dish please, sir? And would you like some wine?"

Omega handed the bowl to Stuart laughing and scolded,

"Yes to the wine but I must remind you I do not like the appellation, sir!"

"I wonder where we sleep in this mansion," Stuart said, after they had served themselves.

. "Let's find rooms," he added, looking at the seemingly endless, sweeping staircase. "Up there, somewhere, I suppose."

"The woman did like luxury," Omega observed. "My tribe could sleep in this mansion and not touch a bed."

"Maybe they will one day," Stuart said and took the bottle of wine. Slowly they mounted the very large staircase, both uncertain if they were yet entirely safe. They found rooms with double beds facing each other and Stuart pointed to the one on the right.. "That's mine and the one on the left. That's yours. Have some wine and let's go find Neissa's room." They pushed open their respective doors and saw no remnants of personality in either room. They walked down the hallway to a room whose door was slightly ajar. Stuart opened the door revealing a large room with a terrace onto the Mediterranean and a large bed. There were women's pants, skirts and blouses, black and white, respectively in a closet and a vanity on one wall.

Had his sister had a life? Had she known love? Stuart thought. He remembered when she visited him in Boston, she said she had known an American, but he had left her for his homeland. Perhaps she had an African friend. Who knew? Then he remembered the tusk photo. It was there next to her vanity. He removed it and took off its back. Yes, it was a photo like that on the Leica. Turks, Berbers and Chinese Xiang Yu's face was clear, South Africans. The Africans Stuart did not recognize.

Stuart put them side by side and stared at Omega. "How do we find these people?"

"They are Britzes' and Neissa's people and I believe those

who were not killed at the shootout will find us. Look around for a weapon. I only have my knife." Prominently displayed on the vanity was another knife.

"And so we have two."

CHAPTER THIRTY-FOUR

They slept without disturbance until the next morning when the maid knocked at each of their doors at 9 a.m. "Would you like breakfast? Ms. Neissa always had a croissant and coffee. I have put six out, together with fresh fruit and vegetables in her office."

"Thank you. We will be down at once," Stuart said, dressing in yesterday's clothes. He wondered if his sister had a washing machine in this vast palace.

When they arrived at Neissa's office, the maid stood at one side of the sliding doors. She had moved a work table to the center. Breakfast was spread in front of the computer with two plates and napkins next to them.

Stuart looked at the woman and said quietly, "Thank you. Is there a washing machine in the house? And where did the butler leave the keys to the Toyota?"

"Just leave your clothes on your beds and I will use the washing machine. It is in the cellar. The key?" The maid reached into her apron pocket and handed them to him. "He suspected you might want them. This is his day off."

"Don't you get one?" The maid shook her head. "My family lives with me here in the cellar, we enjoy our work. They all help me and I am done quickly with the housework and cooking. Then we do what we wish. Ms. Neissa left us a small car and a healthy stipend. We are grateful for the work."

Stuart nodded. "If you need time off, please take it. I am unused to servants but I want to clean up my sister's affairs before I leave for the states."

"Thank you, Mr. Stuart. I understand."

Stuart retrieved the tourist map from his pocket and asked, "Do you know where this is? I need to meet with the editor of the *Moroccan Times* and I guess he lives near this place."

"That is a dangerous place but you Atkinson-Lehrman's seem to lack fear," she said.

Stuart swallowed a laugh. "I've heard that opinion voiced a few times on this trip but trust me, not all of us lack fear. However, my mother has charged me with a mission and my grandfather was a favorite of mine. So the visit must be made. Perhaps it will give me solid clues to flush out his assassin whom I must identify and convict in a court of law."

She nodded, asked for the map and drew a line from a box she labeled, 'Neissa's house' to a box she labeled 'editor.' The house number is 14 and the editor's name is Maurice."

"French, I guess?" Stuart asked.

"Yes, but his house, although near the former American Legation, is surrounded by Turks from across the Mediterranean." She said, "Be careful. Rumors float that the Turks were involved in your sister's death."

Stuart shrugged, took a bite of his croissant and said, "So Omega, let us eat well and go find them."

"About time," Omega said. "We've had so many false leads and seen so many deaths since your grandfather was taken down in Arusha that I'm looking forward to finishing this quest before

Georgina goes to high school."

Stuart laughed. "Eat up and let us be gone."

When they exited through the front doorway, they noticed the garage was open and the Toyota ready for them. Stuart pressed the button outside the wrought iron gate and they exited Neissa's palace, heading toward the former American Legation. Stuart observed that most of the office and apartment buildings in Tangiers were light in color, like those in New Orleans, also a one-time French possession. They ranged in color from white, to pink, to purple and blue. But curiously many were designed in the boxy Bauhaus style. Its boxiness suited expats but was detested by the Muslims and Africans who liked the rounder look, evident in their mosques or tribal huts.

When they arrived at the white stucco American Legation, Omega turned right and stopped in front of a small Bauhaus style home—square with narrow windows and surrounded by a high fence. A sign on the fence read, *"Moroccan Times"*.

Stuart and Omega exited the car, both sensing trouble. Stuart found the fence buzzer and a voice responded, 'Yes?'"

"I am Stuart Atkinson Lehrman and I have a story George intended for the *Times*. I understand that although your printing office has been destroyed you have saved much of the necessary equipment left to print an edition. Perhaps you can run obituaries for my sister and grandfather and print George Atkinson's unpublished story next to them. A story about your captivity and salvation is also in order."

"Yes," the man said. "I would if I could, but I must be released from those that hold me first."

"Please open the gate," Stuart said.

"Press on the button to your left."

Stuart did as instructed and the gate slid back. A man with

two men at his side stood at the door, their Chinese pistols crossed in front of another small man's chest.

"One for each of us," Stuart whispered.

He and Omega rushed the men as two shots rang from behind them. Their guns falling to the ground, the men released the small Moroccan and one fell dead. The other man whose gun arm was wounded remained close to the editor, his shirt open and revealing the same tattoo Xiang Yu's employees wore in the Arusha studio. Not looking back, Stuart and Omega reached for their knives. Stuart said, "Release the editor then tell me about my grandfather, George Atkinson's murder. Are you the assassin?"

"We are employees of Alphonse Britz, hired to assist the assassin, Xiang Yu murder your grandfather in his Arusha home." He handed him the gun. "Xiang Yu cannot be accused without it. His initials are carved into the handle, but his prints are long gone," the man said. "It is a place to start."

The French editor interjected, "I am an unusually peaceful man. This horror, this captivity happened after Neissa died."

Stuart held up his hand. "Please let these men finish their story. I came to Africa to find my grandfather's assassins. Britz assured me he personally did not kill my grandfather. I am not surprised his employees did. The family is involved in ivory trade which was systemically being revealed through my grandfather's writings. It is unlikely I will find Xiang Yu who masterminded my grandfather's death but at least I have these men."

Turning to the living man, Stuart continued, "I would like to hear the rest of your story."

Stuart turned to the man at his side. "Are you safe, Omega?"

"Oh course, Stuart. A few North Africans cannot hurt me. Besides that was quite a backup team we had."

The butler and maid approached the trio. "Is all well here?"

the small woman said, dangling a firearm at her side. Likewise the butler held a powerful hand gun in his hands. Both raised their weapons and pointed them at the wounded man.

"Don't," Stuart said. "This man is about to confirm his participation in my grandfather's assassination. I have travelled halfway around the world to find this out and Omega and I have traversed the African continent for this very moment. Omega and I have systematically re-constructed my grandfather's route to death by the combined shippers and use of illegal tusks, through a series of African stories some of which have been released and included tribal cultivation of elephants, poachers and prostitutes. The two final stories have yet to appear." He smiled at both of them. "Fine shots, both of you, and eagle eyes."

"There are scopes on the hand guns, Stuart," the maid began, "Neissa taught us to protect ourselves, saying hers was a dangerous trade."

"Thank you for the salvation and thank you, Maurice, for your special edition publishing my grandfather's story. The *Moroccan Times* story is about Neissa's illegal trading and was, I believe, my grandfather's attempt to have her cease the trade, thereby saving her life."

The group gathered round the wounded man. "Xiang Yu shot George Atkinson with a long-range Chinese pistol, like those in your hands," he said pointing to the pistols the maid and butler carried. We removed the bullet with an exacto knife and carved two tusks behind Atkinson's ears to honor our master Xiang. These may have sliced critical arteries. We don't know. However to further confuse the investigators we gutted Atkinson with an ancient Maasai spear in his house. We wiped it clean of blood to further confuse investigators."

"How did you do it without my grandfather's cognizance?"

"We believe he knew we were there and hoped help would arrive before the fatal morning.

"We watched him for several days and learned his routine. We think he knew he would die soon. Every morning he picked up his paper at 7. Together with our master Xiang, we hid in the bush by his front porch the night before and Xiang took him down with a revolver like those of your sister's servants. He bled forcibly but stopped squirming after three minutes. We did not scrape his gut until one hour had passed and his body had ceased convulsing."

"Why did you kill him?"

"We had already destroyed the *Moroccan Times*, because if the story had been published in the *Moroccan Times*, we believed it and another story would be released in the *New York Times* and other major news sources and our employer, Xiang Yu would be arrested. We would no longer have jobs. Since he lost his sources— your sister and Britz and you have appeared to complete Atkinson's murder investigation with all the right answers—Xiang has retreated to Asia and will seek other sources." The man reached into his pocket and handed Stuart a slug that was from the Chinese pistol. "We retrieved this from your grandfather's gut. Again you will note the X Y on the slug."

Stuart picked up his newest cell phone, hoping it had not yet been tapped into but phoned the policeman that had taken his fingerprints. "Please come," he said, "and arrest the one living assassin of George Atkinson. There were two, but one is dead. We are at the *Moroccan Times* editor's house." Stuart studied the Xiang Yu tattoos across the two mens' chests. The living man looked up "We shot your grandfather and wounded you. We did not intend to kill you merely frighten you away."

Stuart glared. "I cannot forgive you or even understand you. I thank you for the slug and I need a village address for Xiang Yu.

You have slaughtered my best friend to save your own neck. George did much good for Africa; your boss raped the continent of valuable goods for his own enrichment. I hope you die in prison. The police and courts will make that determination." The police handcuffed the living man and left with the Moroccans, both living and dead.

Stuart turned to the editor. "You have work to do."

"Before I organize this special issue, let us have tea."

"Tea would be wonderful. With respect to the Xiangya Tong story, according to my grandfather's note, it will be published in the *New York Times* when my sister's story reaches the wire services. Yours was to be released first." Stuart said. "As for the tea. I've heard much of Morocco's mint tea."

The editor winked. "We occasionally spike it with cognac for those of age. Perhaps it's a presentation that would interest you?"

"Sounds wonderful."

The butler and maid shook their heads. "No thank you, sir. While we serve wine we do not drink it."

"Besides," the maid continued, "I must go home and prepare your dinners."

When they walked inside the editor said quietly, "I still can't believe I'm free and am not yet thinking clearly. As we discussed, I should publish your grandfather's story and your sister's obituary."

Stuart pulled out the roll he had retrieved from his grandfather's house remains. "So here's the exposé. It was in a tube that said unpublished but submitted so I did not think it of imminent importance when I first went to the house. As his stories unfolded, I decided I best retrieve it in the event you and the *Times* editor had not received your copies."

The editor sighed with relief. "Thank god there was another copy. I do not have the one your grandfather sent me. It disappeared with all the papers when the *Moroccan Times* was torched."

"So now you have a copy. Fortunately metal letters from a metal press don't burn, Stuart said. "So it will still see the light of day and cause harm to no one because all my family living in Africa is dead. I am leaving Africa tomorrow and my mother is still safe so please wait two days to publish it. Who is H B at the *New York Times*?"

"I will wait. As for H.B, he. is a friend of mine. I will confirm he has an Atkinson story to publish. I will run a single advance copy for you to take to your mother. I will get to work soon," the editor said.

The *Moroccan Times* published its first 'off-site issue' one week later. Before Stuart left for Boston where his mother would meet him at the Boston airport, the maid and butler appeared.

"Best of luck to you, Mr. Stuart and Mr. Omega. We thought you might like this," the butler said, handing Stuart the advance newspaper copy. A handwritten note confirmed the *New York Times* editor had an Atkinson story that was now in print.

"I'm glad you are both here," Stuart said. "Please take whatever you want of my sister's possessions and when I sell the home I will send each of you half the money to purchase your own homes. Feel free to stay here until it is sold."

"Mr. Stuart, Neissa bought us homes in the middle of town. She knew there would be a day when she would not come home," the maid said. "But we will stay here until the home is purchased."

"Thank you for your loyalty." He paused, looking at Omega. "Omega will also be taking the Toyota. He will drive me to the airport then drive home."

"Your drive to Arusha will be a long one, Omega," the butler warned.

"I know. I need a break from the excitement," Omega said. "And I have a screaming infant and discouraged wife waiting for me. It will be a pleasant five days."

Stuart picked up the *Moroccan Times* and began to read his grandfather's life story of Neissa:

The woman hired only Africans—Berber and Maasai. Their interviews were short. She always told them her work and their work was illegal first. If they walked away after that opening she told them "her work was dangerous; did they still want to work for her?" If they remained she proceeded with terms. She could pay them in dirham or drugs. A few took the drugs; others needed the money to feed their families

The boxes were shipped to her from Africans in the South. The stimulants were shipped to her in containers of cloth from across the Mediterranean.

She was generous, often sending the colorful cloth home with her employees whose wives skillfully turned them into clothing for their children and themselves.

The trader kept all the somber cloth for herself and always dressed in black slacks and skirts and white blouses. Her one vanity was her shoes which were of exquisite Italian make. Her maid carefully lined the shoes on double racks and polished them with care each day.

When I first laid eyes on my granddaughter, she was fourteen. At forty-four she resembled my wife, her grandmother.

The Atkinsons have always strived to be Africa's champions. We do not rape Africa's lands or encourage her citizens to engage in illegal maneuvers. This child was an anomaly, perhaps cringing from unseen psychologic pain inflicted at youth? Whether physical or mental, the damage was permanent. It is time to set it right.

Neissa Abencour is my granddaughter, a child of great intelligence and promise. She also trades in illegal ivory and poisons Africans with illegal drugs. She is one of us and must be stopped. I will die soon at the hands of her competition's lackeys. The ivory trade must be stopped. Neissa and her competition, Alphonse Britz must also be stopped. Xiang Yu, or whoever their Chinese enabler is, must also be imprisoned.

If ,when this is published, we are all dead remember us with kindness.

--George Atkinson

"Nice story, Stuart," Omega said, reading over his shoulder. "Good man, George."

"Don't forget to pick up the *Times* when you get home then we'll know it all. How can I ever thank you?" Stuart said, waving as he headed toward his plane.

"Mom and I are doing nothing about Xiang. My grandfather's story is conviction enough. I should imagine Asians will be more careful in future trading. As for you, good friend, when will I see you again?"

"Next year in Boston. We'll all be there! The money you left with Dalik and me will get our families to Dalik's wife's graduation."

Stuart waved as he left his colleague. "Until next year, then." He picked up the latest issue of the *New York Times* and began reading "The Last Posthumous Expose of George Atkinson: 'Tattoos and Ivory.' The story of George Atkinson's Assassination."

TATTOOS AND IVORY: THE XIANGYA CHINESE TONG

The culmination of research on a series of articles about salvation and destruction of the African elephant took me to a shop in Arusha owned and organized by a Chinese man, Xiang Yu who had adapted his name from the Chinese character for elephant. Head of the Xiangya Tong in Arusha, Tanzania, Xiang Yu and his fellow Asian artisans provided answers to the Tribune's last question: what can any of us do to staunch the ivory flow caused by poaching of African Elephant tusks and move

Africans out of poverty without corruption or crime? Xiang Yu agreed to talk with me but required that the story must be held until the Asian-based syndicate he worked for, approved it. He would let me know.

Tong means 'hall or gathering' place in Chinese and are formed where Chinese, who have left the mainland, gather to speak their language, educate their children, perform work and integrate into new country while retaining language and customs. Circulation unearthed one, the Xiangya Tong, that specialized in tusk trading and ivory art in the Arusha market. Illegal tusk trading, featured in the poaching article, suggested these Asian artisans and traders as worthy of an add—on to my African elephant series.

When my driver dropped me off at the market place, he told me to beware. Some Tongs were not just Chinese guilds they were centers of criminal activity. I handed him a copy of their insignia "the Chinese character for elephant framed by tusks." Look for me at the office under this sign should I not return today, I instructed him.

Ivory has been banned from trading and has been illegal since 1989. Nonetheless, it goes on. Chinese power and money have facilitated illegal trade. Skilled in ivory carving, Asians have made use of ivory in decorative pieces, useful pieces since their countries had access to it—first in Malaysia and Burma when the Asian elephants were abundant, but are now an endangered species. Asian elephants are often tuskless and when Chinese and other Asian artisans began to seek alternatives for ivory carving and artwork they turned to their African neighbor.

The elephants of Tanzania, once a source of ivory for the tops of piano keys and the decorative arts, including netsukes, Chinese screens and figurines, are now essential contributors to the country's largest source of income—tourism. Tanzania backed the ivory ban but, like many African countries was embarrassed when elephant monitors found warehouses of tusks—both fresh and stale or old ones, so it allowed the trade to operate mainly to get the tusks out of the country and to feed officers of the State

Department.

Xiang Yu took me to the back of his studio, opened a small door, took me to a nearby warehouse, unlocked the intricate lock and swung open the doors. Once the daylight filtered into the warehouse I saw piles of tusks sorted by size.

I pointed to a small pile separated from the others and said, "Why are these separate?"

"Those are rhino tusks which we ship directly to China, where they are made into medicine which denizens believe cures everything from colds to sterility."

I widened my eyes but said nothing.

When we re-entered the studio Xiang began the story of how this guild had come together. He and the artisans in his studio were sent to work on construction of hotels and leisure facilities but were denied management of them. Xiang says, "The company owners were going to remove us. Having gathered enough skilled artisans to start a studio, I convinced the Chinese managers to give us funding and we would be both their ivory suppliers and their artisans in country. Our Asian-based managers, while clearly breaking the law, formed powerful syndicates and paid us both to acquire ivory, carve it and be an African outlet for Asian commerce."

Having read that Hong Kong based traders facilitated the syndicates, I was not surprised that they were backing the flourishing illegal trade but I was surprised by Xiang Yu's openness. "Why do you do it?" I asked him in his studio, a 40 foot by 40 foot square in a dark alley of the Arusha marketplace. Rubbing his right index finger against his thumb he said, "Money. I have Chinese wife here, small apartment, one child. Most of my colleagues have similar responsibilities. We live near one another in subsidized housing near Chinatown. Celebrate all festivals. Celebrate our world together." He held up a small square and pointed to a hollowed tusk shaped like a boat hull. It had receptacles for ivory poles that would form beams. "This is a sail" He pointed to a man carving what appeared to be circular chopsticks. "Those are ships beams. Once assembled inside boat hull, the piece will be entitled 'Noah' and has been commissioned by one of the syndicate's hotels."

Xiang and his colleagues wore overshirts and loose-fitting garments, similar to the Mao clothing made famous in the United States in the late 1960s. It came from a local hospital and they all faintly resembled medical interns. Heads down and pointed scalpels on their pieces of tusks, they looked, at first glance, to be dark-haired surgical residents, practicing surgery. Each of the men had "xiangya," the Chinese character tattooed on their right wrist. Xiang wore the characters on both wrists and on their chests. Unlike the Tong label, the Chinese character was not framed by tusks.

Why no Elephant tusks?

"That's for non-Chinese speakers. We know that xiangya means elephant."

"Who are your suppliers?" I asked.

"Several sources. Your granddaughter, Anton Britz's son, and your driver's father."

Hearing this modest collection of rogues, I felt complicit in the crime.

"Are you doing this to damage Africa?" I asked, "Or me?"

Xiang Yu eyed me curiously and said, "I'll get back to you. I think you should go now." One of his men, a Chinese pistol in his hand, which I recognized as a small QSZ-92 a semi-automatic pistol as powerful as a rifle, shoved me out of the shop and into the street.

Feeling as much a part of the investigation as the investigator, I raced home to flesh out the notes, emailing Ian we may have "the scoop" of the decade.

###

Stuart's plane landed at Logan. His mother greeted him. He handed her both articles and said "It's over. It's all in here."

END

ABOUT THE AUTHOR

Following completion of her doctoral thesis on the artistic mediation of language in Marcel Proust and critic Walter Benjamin, Anne Hendren began freelance writing and editing for electronics, alternative medicine and arts and literature. Her writings in alternative medicine inspired an interest in various approaches to healing; her work in art and literature ranged from music, ballet and literature critic to advocate for literary arts. She has published a biography of four Idaho women, *Hidden Lives and Unhistoric Acts*, revealing how unknown persons can affect the history of a community.

Curious Tusks is her third work of fiction and is a return to mystery and a foray into the Dark Continent where relationships are shaky and countries are unstable. Protaganist Stuart Lehrman is a venture capitalist determined to make money on early stage investing. His company Erewhon, is successfully doing so until he is called to Africa both to save his photojournalist grandfather and to secure investments from this rich and unspoiled continent.

Project Runaway, her second book, concerns the intrigue in fashion design and focuses on a single designer's desire to come to terms with its complexity. Her first novel, *A Dream of Good and Evil*, addresses sustainable prison architecture and a woman's desire to learn the truth about a friend's murder.

Hendren is currently working on an historical fiction work about the Spanish civilization of the Americas.